IRÈNE NÉMIROVSKY

Dimanche and Other Stories

Irène Némirovsky was born in Kiev in 1903 into a wealthy banking family and immigrated to France during the Russian Revolution. After attending the Sorbonne in Paris, she began to write and swiftly achieved success with *David Golder,* which was followed by more than a dozen other books. Throughout her lifetime she published widely in French newspapers and literary journals. She died in Auschwitz in 1942. More than sixty years later, *Suite Française* was published posthumously for the first time in 2006.

INTERNATIONAL

ALSO BY IRÈNE NÉMIROVSKY

Suite Française

Fire in the Blood

David Golder

The Ball

Snow in Autumn

The Courilof Affair

Dimanche

[AND OTHER STORIES]

Dimanche

[AND OTHER STORIES]

Irène Némirovsky

Translated from the French by Bridget Patterson

VINTAGE INTERNATIONAL
Vintage Books
A Division of Random House, Inc.
New York

Library of Congress Cataloging-in-Publication Data
Némirovsky, Irène, 1903–1942.
Dimanche and other stories / Irène Némirovsky ; translated from the French by Bridget Patterson. —"A Vintage International original."
[Dimanche et autres nouvelles. English]
p. cm.
ISBN 978-0-307-47636-4 (pbk.)
1. Dimanche—Sunday.   2. Les rivages heureux—Those happy shores.
3. Liens du sang—Flesh and blood.   4. Fraternité—Brotherhood.
5. La femme de Don Juan—Don Juan's wife.   6. Le sortilège—The spell.
7. Le spectateur—The spectator.   8. Monsieur Rose—Mr. Rose.
9. La confidente—The confidante.   10. L'inconnu—The unknown soldier.   I. Title.   II. Bridget Patterson.
PQ2627.E4 D5613 2010
843'.912—dc22
2009043711

Book design by Ralph Fowler / ref design

www.vintagebooks.com

Printed in the United States of America
10 9 8 7 6 5 4 3 2 1

CONTENTS

Dimanche

[AND OTHER STORIES]

Dimanche

[SUNDAY]

IN RUE LAS CASES IT WAS AS QUIET AS DURING THE height of summer, and every open window was screened by a yellow blind. The fine weather had returned: it was the first Sunday of spring, a warm and restless day that took people out of their houses and out of the city. The sky glowed with a gentle radiance. The birds in Place Sainte-Clotilde chirped lazily, while the raucous screeching of cars leaving for the country echoed in the peaceful streets. The only cloud in the sky was a delicately curled white shell that floated upward for a moment, then melted into the ether. People raised their heads with surprise and anticipation; they sniffed the air and smiled.

Agnes half-closed the shutters: the sun was hot and the roses would open too quickly and die. Nanette ran in and stood hopping from one foot to the other.

3

"May I go out, Mama? It's such nice weather."

Mass was almost over. The children were already coming down the street in their bright sleeveless dresses, holding their prayer books in their white-gloved hands and clustering around a little girl who had just taken her first communion. Her round cheeks were pink and shining under her veil. A procession of bare legs, all pink and gold, as downy as the skin of a peach, sparkled in the sunshine. The bells were still ringing, slowly and sadly as if to say, "Off you go, good people, we are sorry not to be able to keep you any longer. We have sheltered you for as long as we could, but now we have to give you back to the world and to your everyday lives. Time to go. Mass is over."

The bells fell silent. The smell of hot bread filled the street, wafting up from the open bakery; you could see the freshly washed floor gleaming and the narrow mirrors on the walls glinting faintly in the shadows. Then everyone had gone home.

Agnes said, "Nanette, go and see if Papa is ready, and tell Nadine that lunch is on the table."

Guillaume came in, radiating the scent of lavender water and good cigars, which always made Agnes feel slightly nauseated. He seemed even more high-spirited, healthy, and plump than usual.

As soon as they had sat down, he announced, "I'll be going out after lunch. When you've been suffocating in Paris all week, it's the least . . . Are you really not tempted?"

"I don't want to leave the little one."

Nanette was sitting opposite him, and Guillaume smiled at her and tweaked her hair. The previous night she had had a temperature, but it had been so slight that her fresh complexion showed no sign of pallor.

"She's not really ill. She has a good appetite."

"Oh, I'm not worried, thank God," said Agnes. "I'll let her go out until four o'clock. Where are you going?"

Guillaume's face visibly clouded over. "I . . . oh, I don't know yet . . . You always want to organize things in advance . . . Somewhere around Fontainebleau or Chartres, I'll see, wherever I end up. So? Will you come with me?"

"I'd love to see the look on his face if I agreed," thought Agnes. The set smile on her lips annoyed her husband. But she answered, as she always did, "I've got things to do at home."

She thought, "Who is it this time?"

Guillaume's mistresses: her jealousy, her anxiety, the sleepless nights, were now in the long-distant past. He was tall and overweight, going bald, his whole body solidly balanced, his head firmly planted on a thick, strong neck. He was forty-five, the age at which men are at their most powerful, dominant, and self-confident, the blood coursing thickly through their veins. When he laughed he thrust his jaw forward to reveal a row of nearly perfect white teeth.

"Which one of them told him, 'You look like a wolf

or a wild animal when you smile'?" wondered Agnes. "He must have been incredibly flattered. He never used to laugh like that."

She remembered how he used to weep in her arms every time a love affair ended, gulping as if he were trying to inhale his tears. Poor Guillaume . . .

"Well, I . . ." said Nadine.

She started each sentence like that. It was impossible to detect a single word or a single idea in anything she thought or said that did not relate to herself, her clothes, her friends, the ladders in her stockings, her pocket money, her own pleasure. She was . . . triumphant. Her skin had the pale, velvety brightness of jasmine and of camellias, and you could see the blood beating just beneath the surface: it rose girlishly in her cheeks, swelling her lips so that it looked as though a pink, heady wine was about to gush from them. Her green eyes sparkled.

"She's twenty," thought Agnes, trying, as so often, to keep her eyes closed and not to be wounded by her daughter's almost overwhelming beauty, the peals of laughter, the egoism, the fervor, the diamondlike hardness. "She's twenty years old; it's not her fault . . . Life will tame her, soften her, make her grow up."

"Mama, can I take your red scarf? I won't lose it. And, Mama, may I come back late?"

"And where are you going?"

"Mama, you know perfectly well! To Chantal Aumont's house in Saint-Cloud. Arlette is coming to fetch me. Can I come home late? After eight o'clock, anyway? You won't be angry? Then I won't have to go through Saint-Cloud at seven o'clock on a Sunday evening."

"She's quite right," said Guillaume.

Lunch was nearly over. Mariette was serving the meal quickly. Sunday . . . As soon as the washing-up was done, she, too, would be going out.

They ate orange-flavored crêpes; Agnes had helped Mariette make the batter.

"Delicious," said Guillaume appreciatively.

The clattering of dishes could be heard through the open windows: it was only a faint sound from the dark ground-floor flat where two spinsters lived in the gloom, but it was louder and livelier in the house across the way, where there was a table laid for twelve with the place settings gleaming on the neat folds of the damask tablecloth and a basket of white roses for a first communion decorating the center.

"I'm going to get ready, Mama. I don't want any coffee."

Guillaume swallowed his quickly and silently. Mariette began to clear the table.

"What a hurry they're in," thought Agnes, as her thin, skillful hands deftly folded Nanette's napkin. "Only I . . ."

She was the only one for whom this wonderful Sunday held no attraction.

"I never imagined she'd become so stay-at-home and

dull," thought Guillaume as he looked at her. He took a deep inward breath and, proudly conscious of the sense of vigor that surged through his body, felt his chest expand with the fine weather. "I'm in rather good shape, holding up surprisingly well," he thought, as his mind turned to all the reasons (the political crisis, money worries, the taxes he owed, Germaine—who cramped his style, devil take her) why he could justifiably feel as miserable and depressed as anyone else. But on the contrary! "I've always been the same. A ray of sunshine, the prospect of a Sunday away from Paris, a nice bottle of wine, freedom, a pretty woman at my side—and I'm twenty again! I'm alive," he congratulated himself, looking at his wife with veiled hostility; her cold beauty and the tense, mocking line of her lips irritated him. He said aloud, "Of course, I'll telephone you if I spend the night in Chartres. In any case, I'll be back tomorrow morning, and I'll drop in at home before I go to the office."

Agnes thought, with a strange, weary detachment, "One day, after a lavish lunch, just as he's kissing the woman he's with, the car he's driving will crash into a tree. I'll get a phone call from Senlis or Auxerre. Will you suffer?" she demanded curiously of the mute, invisible image of herself waiting in the shadows. But the image, silent and indifferent, did not reply, and the powerful silhouette of Guillaume came between it and her.

"See you soon, darling."

"See you soon, dear."

Then Guillaume was gone.

"Shall I lay tea in the parlor, madame?" asked Mariette.

"No, I'll do it. You can go as soon as you've tidied the kitchen."

"Thank you, madame," said the girl, blushing fiercely as if she were near a blazing fire. "Thank you, madame," she repeated, with a dreamy expression that made Agnes shrug her shoulders mockingly.

Agnes stroked Nanette's smooth, black hair, as the little girl first hid in the folds of her dress and then poked her head out giggling.

"We'll be perfectly happy, just the two of us, sweetheart."

Meanwhile, in her room, Nadine was quickly changing her clothes, powdering her neck, her bare arms, and the curve of her breast where, unseen in the car, Rémi had placed his dry, passionate lips, caressing her with quick, burning kisses. Half past two . . . Arlette still had not arrived. "With Arlette here, Mama won't suspect anything." The rendezvous was at three. "To think that Mama doesn't notice anything. And she was young once . . ." she thought, trying in vain to imagine her mother's youth, her engagement and her early married life.

"She must always have been like this. Everything

calm, orderly, wearing those white lawn collars. 'Guillaume, don't spoil my roses.' Whereas I . . ."

She shivered, gently biting her lips as she looked at herself in the mirror. Nothing gave her more pleasure than her body, her eyes, her face, and the shape of her young, white neck as straight as a column. "It's wonderful to be twenty," she thought fervently. "Do all young women feel as I do, do they relish their happiness, their energy, the fire in their blood? Do they feel these things as fiercely and deeply as I do? For a woman, being twenty in 1934 is . . . is incredible," she told herself.

She summoned up disjointed memories of nights on a campsite, coming back at dawn in Rémi's car (and there were her parents thinking she was on an innocent trip with her friends on the Île Saint-Louis, watching the sun rise over the Seine), skiing, swimming, the pure air and cold water on her body, Rémi digging his nails into her neck, gently pulling back her short hair. "And my parents are blind to it all! I suppose in their day . . . I can imagine my mother at my age, at her first ball, her eyes modestly lowered. Rémi . . . I'm in love," she told her reflection, smiling into the mirror. "But I must be careful of him—he's so good-looking and so sure of himself. He's been spoiled by women, by flattery. He must like making people suffer. But then, we'll see who'll be the strongest," she muttered, as she nervously clenched her fists, feeling her love pounding in her heart, making her long to take part in this game of cruelty and passion.

She laughed out loud. And her laugh rang out so clearly and arrogantly in the silence that she stopped to listen, as if enchanted by the beauty of a rare and perfect musical instrument.

"There are times when I think I'm in love with myself more than anything else," she thought, as she put on her green necklace, every bead of which glimmered and reflected the sun. Her smooth, firm skin had the brilliant glow of young animals, flowers, or a blossom in May, a glossiness that was fleeting but completely perfect. "I shall never be as beautiful again."

She sprayed perfume on her face and shoulders, deliberately wasting it; today anything sparkling and extravagant suited her! "I'd love a bright red dress and gypsy jewelry." She thought of her mother's tender, weary voice: "Moderation in all things, Nadine!"

"The old!" she thought contemptuously.

In the street Arlette's car had stopped outside the house. Nadine grabbed her bag and, cramming her beret on her head as she ran, shouted "Good-bye, Mama," and disappeared.

"I WANT YOU to have a little rest on the settee, Nanette. You slept so badly last night. I'll sit next to you and do some work," said Agnes. "Then you can go out with mademoiselle."

Nanette rolled her pink smock in her fingers for a

while, rubbed her face against the cushions as she turned over and over, yawned, and went to sleep. She was five and, like Agnes, had the pale, fresh complexion of someone fair-haired, yet had black hair and dark eyes.

Agnes sat down quietly next to her. The house was sleeping silently. Outside, the smell of coffee hung in the air. The room was flooded with a soft, warm, yellow light. Agnes heard Mariette carefully close the kitchen door and walk through the flat; she listened to her footsteps fading away down the back stairs. She sighed: a strange, melancholy happiness and a delicious feeling of peace overcame her. Silence fell over the empty rooms, and she knew that nobody would disturb her until evening; not a single footstep, nor any unknown voice would find its way into the house, her refuge. The street was empty and quiet. There was only an invisible woman playing the piano, hidden behind her closed shutters. Then all was quiet. At that very moment Mariette, clutching her Sunday imitation pigskin bag in her large, bare hands, was hurrying to the station where her lover was waiting for her, and Guillaume, in the woods at Compiègne, was saying to the fat, blonde woman sitting next to him, "It's easy to blame me, I'm not really a bad husband, but my wife . . ." Nadine was in Arlette's little green car, driving past the gates of the Luxembourg gardens. The chestnut trees were in flower. Children ran around in little sleeveless knitted tops. Arlette was thinking bitterly that nobody was waiting for her; nobody loved her. Her friends put up with her because of her precious green car and, behind their horn-rimmed glasses, her round eyes made mothers trust her. Lucky Nadine!

A sharp wind was blowing; the water from the fountains sprayed out sideways, covering passersby with spray. The saplings in Place Sainte-Clotilde swayed gently.

"It's so peaceful," thought Agnes.

She smiled; neither her husband nor her elder daughter had ever seen this rare, slow, confident smile on her lips.

She got up and quietly went to change the water for the roses; carefully she cut their stems; they were gradually coming into flower, although their petals seemed to be opening reluctantly, fearfully, as if with some kind of divine modesty.

"How lovely it is here," she thought.

Her house was a refuge, a warm enclosed shell sealed against the noise outside. When, in the wintry dusk, she walked along the Rue Las Cases, an island of shadows, and saw the stone sculpture of the smiling woman above the door, that sweet, familiar face decorated with narrow, carved ribbons, she felt oddly relaxed and peaceful, floating in waves of happiness and calm. Her house . . . how she loved the delicious silence, the slight, furtive creaking of the furniture, the delicate inlaid tables shining palely in the gloom. She sat down; although she normally held herself so erect, now she curled up in an armchair.

"Guillaume says I like objects more than human beings . . . That may be true."

Objects enfolded her in a gentle, wordless spell. The copper and tortoiseshell clock ticked slowly and peacefully in the silence.

The familiar musical clinking of a silver cup gleaming in the shadows responded to her every movement, her every sigh, as if it were her friend.

"Where do we find happiness? We pursue it, search for it, kill ourselves trying to find it, and all the time it's just here," she said to herself. "It comes just when we've stopped expecting anything, stopped hoping, stopped being afraid. Of course, there is the children's health . . ." and she bent automatically to kiss Nanette's forehead. "Fresh as a flower, thank God. It would be such a relief not to hope for anything anymore. How I've changed," she thought, remembering the past, her insane love for Guillaume, that little hidden square in Passy where she used to wait for him on spring evenings. She thought of his family, her hateful mother-in-law, the noise his sisters made in their miserable, gloomy parlor. "Ah, I can never have enough silence!" She smiled, whispering as if the Agnes of an earlier time were sitting next to her, listening incredulously, her dark plaits framing her pale young face. "Yes, aren't you surprised? I've changed, haven't I?"

She shook her head. In her memory every day in the past was rainy and sad, every effort was in vain, and every word that was uttered was either cruel or full of lies.

"Ah, how can one regret being in love? But, luckily, Nadine is not like me. Today's young girls are so cold, so unemotional. Nadine is a child, but even later on she'll never love or suffer as I did. So much the better, thank God, so much the better. And by the look of things Nanette will be like her sister."

She smiled: it was strange to think that these smooth, chubby, pink cheeks and unformed features would turn into a woman's face. She put out a hand to stroke the fine black hair. "These are the only moments when my soul is at peace," she thought, remembering a childhood friend who used to say, "My soul is at peace," as she half-closed her eyes and lit a cigarette. But Agnes did not smoke. And it was not that she liked to dream, more that she preferred to sit and occupy herself with some humdrum but specific task: she would sew or knit, stifle her thoughts, and force herself to stay calm and silent as she tidied books away or, one at a time, carefully washed and dried the Bohemian glassware, the tall, thin antique glasses with gold rims that they used for champagne. "Yes, at twenty happiness seemed different to me, rather terrible and overwhelming, yet one's desires become easier to achieve once they have largely run their course," she thought, as she picked up her sewing basket, with its piece of needlework, some silk thread, her thimble, and her little gold scissors. "What more does a woman need who is not in love with love?"

"LET ME OUT HERE, Arlette, will you?" Nadine asked. It was three o'clock. "I'll walk for a bit," she said to herself. "I don't want to get there first."

Arlette did as she asked. Nadine jumped out of the car.

"Thank you, *chérie*."

Arlette drove off. Nadine walked up the Rue de l'Odéon, forcing herself to slow down and suppress the excitement spreading through her body. "I like being out in the street," she thought, happily looking around at everything. "I'm stifled at home. They can't understand that I'm young, I'm twenty years old, I can't stop myself singing, dancing, laughing, shouting. It's because I'm full of joy." The breeze, fanning her legs through the thin material of her dress, was delicious. She felt light, ethereal, floating: and just then it seemed to her that nothing could tether her to the ground. "There are times when I could easily fly away," she thought, buoyed up with hope. The world was so beautiful, so kind! The glare of the midday sun had softened and was turning into a pale, gentle glow; on every street corner women were holding out bunches of daffodils, offering them for sale to passersby. Families were happily sitting outside the cafés, drinking fruit juice as they clustered around a little girl fresh from communion, her cheeks flushed, her eyes shining. Soldiers strolled slowly along, blocking the pavement, walking beside women dressed in black with large, red, bare hands. "Beautiful," said a boy walking past, blowing a kiss to Nadine as he eyed her. She laughed.

Sometimes love itself, even the image of Rémi, disappeared. There remained simply a feeling of exultation and a feverish, piercing happiness, both of which were almost agonizingly unbearable.

"Love? Does Rémi love me?" she asked herself suddenly, as she reached the little bistro where he was due to meet her. "What do I feel? We're mostly just friends, but what good is that? Friendship and trust are all right for old people. Even tenderness is not for us. Love, well, that's something else." She remembered the sharp pain that tender words and kisses sometimes seemed to conceal. She went inside.

The café was empty. The sun was shining. A clock on the wall ticked. The small inside room where she sat down smelled of wine and the dank air from the cellar.

He was not there. She felt her heart tighten slowly in her chest. "I know it's quarter past three, but surely he would have waited for me?"

She ordered a drink.

Each time the door opened, each time a man's shadow appeared, her heart beat faster and she was filled with happiness; each time it was a stranger who came in, gave her a distracted look, and went to sit down in the shadows. She clasped and unclasped her hands nervously under the table.

"But where can he be? Why doesn't he come?"

Then she lowered her head and continued to wait.

Inexorably, the clock struck every quarter of an hour. Staring at its hands, she waited without moving a muscle, as if complete silence, complete stillness, would somehow slow the passing of time. Three thirty. Three forty-five. That was nothing, one side or the other of the half hour made little difference, even when it was three forty, but if you said, "twenty to four, quarter to four," then you were lost, everything was ruined, gone forever. He wasn't coming, he was laughing at her! Who was he with at that very moment? To whom was he saying, "That Nadine Padouan? I've really got her!" She felt sharp, bitter little tears prick her eyes. No, no, not that! Four o'clock. Her lips were trembling. She opened her bag and blew on her powder puff, the powder enveloping her in a stifling, perfumed cloud; as she looked in the little mirror she noticed that her face was quivering and distorted as if underwater. "No, I'm not going to cry," she thought, savagely clenching her teeth together. With shaking hands she took out her lipstick and outlined her lips, then powdered the satin-smooth, bluish hollow under her eyes where, one day, the first wrinkle would appear. "Why has he done this? Did he just want a kiss one evening, is that all?" For a moment she felt despairing and worthless. All the painful memories that are part of even a happy and secure childhood flooded into her mind: the undeserved slap her father had given her when she was twelve; the unfair teacher; those little English girls who, so long ago, had laughed at her and said, "We won't play with you. We don't play with kids."

"It hurts. I never knew it could hurt so much."

She gave up watching the clock but stayed where she was, quite still. Where could she go? She felt safe here and comfortable. How many other women had waited, swallowing their tears as she did, unthinkingly stroking the old imitation leather banquette, warm and soft as an animal's coat? Then, all at once, she felt proud and strong again. What did any of it matter? "I'm in agony, I'm unhappy." Oh, what fine new words these were: love, unhappiness, desire. She rolled them silently on her lips.

"I want him to love me. I'm young and beautiful. He will love me, and if he doesn't, others will," she muttered as she nervously clenched her hands, her nails as shining and sharp as claws.

Five o'clock . . . The dim little room suddenly shone like a furnace. The sun had moved around. It lit up the golden liqueur in her glass and the telephone booth opposite her.

"A phone call?" she thought feverishly. "Maybe he's ill?"

"Oh, come on," she said, with a furious shrug. She

had spoken out loud; she shivered. "What's the matter with me?" She imagined him lying bleeding, dead in the road; he drove like a madman . . .

"Supposing I telephoned? No!" she murmured, acknowledging for the first time how weak and downcast she felt.

At the same time, deep down, a mysterious voice seemed to be whispering: "Look. Listen. Remember. You'll never forget today. You'll grow old. But at the instant of your death you'll see that door opening, banging in the sunshine. You'll hear the clock chiming the quarters and the noise in the street."

She stood up and went into the telephone booth, which smelled of dust and chalk; the walls were covered with scribbles. She looked for a long time at a drawing of a woman in the corner. At last she dialed Jasmin 10-32.

"Hello," said a woman's voice, a voice she did not recognize.

"Is this Monsieur Rémi Alquier's apartment?" she asked, and she was struck by the sound of her words: her voice shook.

"Yes, who is it?"

Nadine said nothing; she could clearly hear a soft, lazy laugh and a voice calling out, "Rémi, there's a young girl asking for you . . . What? Monsieur Alquier isn't in, mademoiselle."

Slowly, Nadine hung up and went outside. It was six

o'clock, and the brightness of the May sunshine had faded; a sad, pale dusk had taken over. The smell of plants and freshly watered flowers rose from the Luxembourg gardens. Nadine walked aimlessly down one street, then down another. She whistled quietly as she walked. The first lights were coming on in the houses, and although the streets were not yet dark, the first gas lamps were being lit: their flickering light shone through her tears.

IN RUE LAS CASES Agnes had put Nanette to bed; half-asleep, she was still talking quietly to herself, shyly confiding in her toys and the shadows in the room. As soon as she heard Agnes, however, she cautiously stopped.

"Already," Agnes thought.

She went into the parlor. She walked across it without turning on the lights and leaned by the window. It was getting dark. She sighed. The spring day concealed a latent bitterness that seemed to emerge as evening came, just as sweet-smelling peaches can leave a sour taste in the mouth. Where was Guillaume? "He probably won't come back tonight. So much the better," she said to herself, as she thought of her cool, empty bed. She touched the cold window. How many times had she waited like this for Guillaume? Evening after evening, listening to the clock ticking in the silence and the creaking of the lift as it slowly went up, up, past her door, and then back down. Evening after evening, at first in despair, then with resignation, then with a heavy and deadly indifference. And now? Sadly, she shrugged her shoulders.

The street was empty, and a bluish mist seemed to float over everything, as if a fine shower of ash had begun to fall gently from the overcast sky. The golden star of a streetlamp lit up the shadows, and the towers of Sainte-Clotilde looked as if they were retreating and melting into the distance. A little car full of flowers, returning from the country, went past; there was just enough light to see bunches of daffodils tied onto the headlights. Concierges sat outside on their wicker chairs, hands folded loosely in their laps, not talking. Shutters were being closed at every window, and only the faint pink light of a lamp could be glimpsed through the slats.

"In the old days," remembered Agnes, "when I was Nadine's age, I was already spending long hours waiting in vain for Guillaume." She shut her eyes, trying to see him as he had been then, or at least how he had seemed to her then. Had he been so handsome? So charming? My God, he had certainly been thinner than he was now, his face leaner and more expressive, with a beautiful mouth. His kisses . . . she let out a sad, bitter little laugh.

"How I loved him . . . the idiot I was . . . stupid

idiot . . . He didn't say anything loving to me. He just used to kiss me, kiss me until my heart melted with sweetness and pain. For eighteen months he never once said, 'I love you,' or 'I want to marry you' . . . I always had to be there, at his feet. 'At my disposal,' he would say. And, fool that I was, I found pleasure in it. I was at that age when even defeat is intoxicating. And I would think, 'He will love me. I will be his wife. If I give him enough devotion and love, he will love me.' "

All of a sudden she had an extraordinarily precise vision of a spring evening long ago. But not a fine, mild one like this evening; it was one of those rainy, cold Parisian springs when heavy, icy showers started at dawn, streaming through the leafy trees. The chestnut trees now in blossom, the long day and the warm air seemed like a cruel joke. She was sitting on a bench in an empty square, waiting for him; the soaking box hedges gave off a bitter smell; the raindrops falling on the pond slowly, sadly marked the minutes drifting inexorably by. Cold tears ran down her cheeks. He wasn't coming. A woman had sat down next to her and looked at her without speaking, hunching her back against the rain and tightly pinching her lips together, as if thinking, "Here's another one."

She bowed her head a little, resting it on her arms as she used to do in the old days. A deep sadness overcame her.

"What is the matter with me? I am happy really; I

feel very calm and peaceful. What's the good of remembering things? It will only make me resentful and so pointlessly angry, my God!"

And a picture came into her mind of her riding in a taxi along the dark, wet avenues of the Bois de Boulogne; it was as if she could once again taste and smell the pure, cold air coming in through the open window, as Guillaume gently and cruelly felt her naked breast, as if he were squeezing the juice from a fruit. All those quarrels, reconciliations, bitter tears, lies, bad behavior, and then that rush of sweet happiness when he touched her hand, laughing, as he said, "Are you angry? I like making you suffer a bit."

"That's all gone, it will never happen again," she said aloud despairingly. And all at once, she was aware of tears pouring down her face. "I want to suffer again."

"To suffer, to despair, to long for someone! I have no one in the world left to wait for! I'm old. I hate this house," she thought feverishly, "and this peace and calm! But what about the children? Oh yes, the illusion of motherhood is the strongest and yet the most futile. Of course I love them; they're all I have in the world. But that's not enough. I want to rediscover those lost years, the suffering of the past. But at my age love would be unpleasant. I'd like to be twenty! Lucky Nadine! She's in Saint-Cloud, probably playing golf! She doesn't have to worry about love! Lucky Nadine!"

She started. She had not heard the door open, nor

Nadine's footsteps on the carpet. Wiping her eyes, she said abruptly, "Don't put the light on."

Without replying, Nadine came to sit next to her. It was dark now. Neither of them looked at each other. After a while Agnes asked: "Did you have a nice time, sweetheart?"

"Yes, thank you, Mama," said Nadine.

"What time is it?"

"Almost seven, I think."

"You've come back earlier than you thought," Agnes said absentmindedly.

Nadine did not answer, wordlessly tinkling the thin gold bracelets on her bare arms.

"How quiet she is," Agnes thought, slightly surprised. She said aloud, "What is it, sweetheart? Are you tired?"

"A bit."

"You must go to bed early. Now go and wash, we're going to eat in five minutes. Don't make a noise in the hall. Nanette is asleep."

As she spoke the telephone started ringing. Nadine suddenly looked up. Mariette appeared. "It's for Miss Nadine."

Nadine left the room, her heart pounding, conscious of her mother's eyes on her. She silently closed the door of the little office where the telephone was kept.

"Nadine? It's me, Rémi . . . Oh, we are angry, are we? Look, forgive me . . . don't be horrid . . . well, I'm saying

sorry! There, there," he said, as if coaxing a restive animal. "Be kind to me, my sweet . . . What could I do? She
was an old flame, I was being charitable. Ah, Nadine,
you can't think the sweet nothings you give me are
enough? Do you? Well, do you?" he repeated, and she
heard the sweet, voluptuous sound of his laugh through
his tightly closed lips. "You must forgive me. It's true I
don't dislike kissing you when you're cross, when your
green eyes are blazing. I can see them now. They're
smoldering, aren't they? How about tomorrow? Do you
want to meet tomorrow at the same time? What? I
swear I won't stand you up . . . What? You're not free?
What a joke! Tomorrow? Same place, same time. I've
said, I swear . . . Tomorrow?" he said again.

Nadine said, "Tomorrow."

He laughed. "There's a good girl," he said in English.
"Good little girlie. Bye-bye."

NADINE RAN into the parlor. Her mother had not
moved.

"What are you doing, Mama?" she cried, and her
voice, her burst of laughter, made Agnes feel bitter and
troubled, almost envious. "It's dark in here!"

She put all the lights on. Her eyes, still wet with tears,
were sparkling; a dark flush had spread over her cheeks.
Humming to herself, she went up to the mirror and
tidied her hair, smiling at her face, which was now
alight with happiness, and at her quivering, parted lips.

"Well, you're happy all of a sudden," Agnes said. She tried to laugh, but only a sad, grating little sound escaped her. She thought, "I've been blind! The girl's in love! Ah, she has too much freedom, I'm too weak, that's what worries me." But she recognized the bitterness, the suffering in her heart. She greeted it like an old friend. "My God, I'm jealous!"

"Who was that on the telephone? You know perfectly well that your father doesn't like telephone calls from people we don't know, or these mysterious meetings."

"I don't understand what you mean, Mama," Nadine said, as she looked at her mother with bright, innocent eyes that made it impossible to read the secret thoughts within them: Mother, the eternal enemy, pathetic in her old age, understanding nothing, seeing nothing, withdrawing into her shell, her only aim to stop youth from being alive! "I really don't understand. It was only that the tennis match which should have happened on Saturday has been postponed until tomorrow. That's all."

"That's all, is it!" Agnes said, and she was struck by how dry and harsh her own voice sounded.

She looked at Nadine. "I'm mad. It must have been my remembering the past. She's still only a child." For a moment she had a vision of a young girl with long black hair sitting in a desolate square in the mist and rain; she looked at her sadly and then banished her forever from her mind.

Gently she touched Nadine's arm.

"Come along," she said.

Nadine stifled a sardonic laugh. "Will I be as . . . gullible, when I'm her age? And as placid? Lucky Mother," she thought with gentle scorn. "It must be wonderful to be so naive and to have such an untroubled heart."

Les rivages heureux

[T H O S E   H A P P Y   S H O R E S]

A YOUNG GIRL IN A BALL GOWN WALKED PAST: HER
back was thin and golden, and her fair hair was clipped
behind her ears with diamond slides. Above her long,
elegant neck her face was cold, sharp, and mocking; her
cheeks were flushed from dancing. Mme. Boehmer
smiled with melancholy delight as she looked at her
daughter and thought, yet again, "How beautiful she
is . . . so tall . . . her dress is charming."

She moved aside to allow some couples to linger
under the bunch of mistletoe decorated with blue ribbons that hung over the entrance. She sighed. She was
old. New Year's Eve, with its music, dancing, and young
voices, disturbed and depressed her. Her tired, blotchy
face betrayed exhaustion and her disillusion with life,
tempered by grudging relief that the year had brought

neither death nor serious illness. She looked coldly at her daughter's friends through her tortoiseshell-rimmed opera glasses. "What bad taste . . . all that makeup . . . and wearing jewelry that's far too grown-up for them. Christiane is so different!"

Christiane, surrounded by her friends, was about to leave. Her mother gestured to her to wait. But the girl was glancing around her with the hard, triumphant look of a young woman who views the world as a mirror in which she sees only her own image, made lovelier by the interest or desire of a man; in Christiane's eyes Mme. Boehmer, standing among the other mothers, was simply a pale, calm shadow, surrounded by other shadows.

Nevertheless, Mme. Boehmer touched her on the arm.

"Are you going home, sweetheart?"

"No, Mama, we're finishing the evening at Marie-Claude's."

Mme. Boehmer gave a faint sigh.

"Oh? It's two o'clock in the morning, Cri-Cri . . ."

"I know," Christiane said impatiently. She added in a mocking tone, "I'm not seven anymore, Mama, darling," and she bent to kiss her mother's head with a bird-like peck.

Her friends treated Mme. Boehmer with the teasing condescension due to her age, her position as a mother, and her reputation as a simple soul, a good sort; although this was tempered by envious respect, for the glory of Boehmer Sewing Machines was reflected on the dull, breathless old woman in her plain black dress. One of the girls thought to herself, as she took Christiane's arm, "The rich old bag!"

Smiling, she asked, "Cri-Cri, are you going to meet Gerald? Do you want me to leave with you so your mother doesn't notice anything?"

Christiane shrugged her beautiful shoulders, still gilded from the sunny beach at the Lido. "What a silly idea! I've got mother well trained, you know. Anyway, my parents know I'm engaged to Jerry and I'm twenty-two, after all."

It was snowing outside. The trees in the Champ de Mars were hardly visible, dissolving into a white, icy mist, and every streetlight shone rosily through a halo of frost. Christiane started her car and drove off. She had rolled down the window; the wind blew snowflakes onto her hair and they melted into big, cold, heavy drops. She passed a group of men wearing pink paper hats. "How unspeakably vulgar these public holidays are," Christiane thought. "This time next year, Gerald and I will be in Saint Moritz."

She would often plan six months ahead, saying in her cold, sharp young voice, "In September, I'll be doing this; in March it'll be that. In June I'll be at the Cowes Regatta, then Cannes for the summer." Mme. Boehmer would murmur, "As long as everything goes to plan between now and then, Cri-Cri. Nothing is certain in this life, my poor child." But Christiane would reply, "Your generation didn't know how to want things, Mama. You just have to know what you want." In English, she would add, "Make up your mind and stick to it. That's all."

She crossed the Seine; a very faint lilac light appeared in the east. It was late. Gerald was waiting for her in the little bar in the Rue du Mont Thabor; they often met in this discreet and, at certain times, deserted spot.

As she approached their meeting place, her heart pounded against her ribs as usual. When she thought about him, she sometimes muttered hesitantly to herself, "Love?" This was said in the same way that you might tentatively mouth the name of a passerby you think you have recognized. Gerald had been putting off the official announcement of their engagement for two years. For the first year he had cleverly given their relationship a tinge of anguish and uncertainty that both pleased and annoyed her—and added a secret stab of pain to her passion for him.

She knew he was not ready to break off a long-standing affair. She accepted the situation with the clear-sightedness of her age, the clear-sightedness that some people mistakenly think is blindness, but it is only the young who can treat life and love like a game, because they have never been defeated or had to face cold reality.

Gerald, Jerry, Gérard Dubouquet was a young man

of twenty-five with green eyes, a long nose that tended to twitch like a fox, and fair hair. He was private secretary to Minister Laclos, whose wife was Gerald's loving and jealous mistress. When Christiane spoke to Marie-Claude, her best friend and confidante, she would always say, "He doesn't love her, you know, but he can't leave her. It's just physical, do you understand, darling?"

She could allow anything, forgive everything, if it was a matter of sex, of the weakness of the flesh. She had only a sketchy and incomplete understanding of love and would say rationally and calmly, "I'm not going to cause any problems, thank you very much. I'm not a little innocent; I know what I'm getting myself into." She had a naive, exaggerated understanding of physical desire, rather like a child who, given her mother's jewelry to play with, handles it with exaggerated yet touching respect, not realizing that the pearls she has been given are fake.

In Marie-Claude's little sitting room, or in Christiane's studio, they would talk about sex, about the trap of physical desire, about life "as it is, not as our mothers saw it, poor women." They would shake their young heads knowingly, even though it was still children's blood that flowed beneath the smooth skin of their faces. Gerald, meanwhile, could not bring himself to leave his mistress, who bored him, because he was afraid of making an enemy of her since she might turn the all-powerful Laclos against him. For Gerald was at the age in which a man's desire oscillates between ambition and money, and—as if he were a butterfly fluttering from one flower to another—he sometimes landed on the influential mistress, sometimes on the wealthy young girl, without being able to control his erratic flight. In any case, he thought so much about himself, and still felt so young and healthy, that he was loath to commit himself too soon, fearing that he might miss out on a greater happiness, and a larger dowry, that could be waiting for him just around the corner. He procrastinated, like a trader who is not sure what his goods are worth but prefers to wait rather than risk selling at too low a price.

"I'm in love," Christiane thought, glancing distractedly at the dark and deserted Place de la Concorde.

"I've never loved anyone before Gerald," she said aloud, as she thought back to her life between the ages of sixteen and twenty-two, so short and inconsequential in other people's eyes but so long and full in her own. She smiled as she thought about Gerald's kisses, and a slight blush softened her cold face, briefly restoring to her the wild, shy gracefulness of adolescence.

"It's wonderful, being in love . . ."

At the same time, something older and more mature within her—for we all have several beings of different ages coexisting peacefully within us, from the child we were once to the old person we will become—that bit of her that was already old and wise recognized how her love would survive once she had lost her instinct to defend her wounded pride. She already loved qualities in Gerald that would only improve with age: his intelligence, the adaptability of his ambition, his cunning, and his tenacity. "He has a brilliant future," she told herself, seeing herself as a minister's wife, the prime minister's wife, bringing her influence to bear on matters of state, of war and peace.

"Things would be a bit better organized than they are now," she thought, clinking her bracelets together.

She parked the car. The little bar with yellow walls was thickly shrouded with cigarette smoke. Gerald was not there. The bartender stood up and handed Christiane a note; she read a few apologetic words: "Impossible for me to get to you until four o'clock. Wait for me if you can. I have something of the utmost importance to tell you." Christiane frowned, then slowly tore it up. "How can I go home so early? They think I'm at Marie-Claude's." She thought irritably about her mother. "It's such a bore, lying. Parents are such a nuisance, making difficulties and complications."

She sat down, looked at the men around her, then, with an expression of cold disdain, at one of the women she always referred to as "bar tarts." There was one sitting opposite Christiane, morosely contemplating her empty glass. She was alone. Men would pat her lightly on the shoulder as they went past, casually asking, "All right, Ginette?" She would smile deferentially and reply in an exhausted, husky voice, "I'm very well . . . How are you?"

She was still pretty although faded; her figure was as trim as a young girl's, and her gestures were shy and diffident. Her eyes were pale and vacant, with dilated pupils; her mouth was fixed in a sad, unchanging little smile. She was wearing a black dress whose creases revealed the greenish tint of dye, and a shabby black hat, which she had tried to liven up by sticking a feather into the threadbare ribbon that adorned it.

Whenever the door opened and a man appeared she would look at him with an expression of mingled fear and hope, tilting her head to one side, conscious that in the old days this movement had been seductive, its timid charm contrasting with the makeup caking her face. But the years had passed, and this did not work its attraction anymore. A man came into the bar and did not even glance at her. She fell back heavily onto her stool and, pretending not to care, cleared her throat with a quiet, sensual, tired "hmm"—half-cough, half-sigh— and said to the bartender in her hoarse little voice, "Just my luck!"

The door opened again. She sat up, putting a sparkle in her eyes and renewing her smile, trying to give it the lively and submissive air that men liked, which made them say to their friends, "Now there's a woman who looks nice and jolly." For she knew from experience that

the opposite judgment—"That girl looks like a miserable wet blanket"—was the sort of brief, cruel condemnation that could affect the whole of one's life.

But he did not take any notice of her either. She lowered her head wearily, and her thoughts turned deject-
edly to death and to sleeping peacefully forever. Yet
from time to time someone would sit with her for a
minute and buy her a drink before going away. An
enormous, drunken Englishman came up to her, looked
at her through his large, opaque eyes, coarsely pinched
her thigh, and disappeared like the others.

"What a lout," she thought resignedly. "But some
days are like that . . ."

Even so, her eyes filled with tears of disappointment.
They were so aloof, so indifferent, these men on whom
she depended for money and for each night's supper,
although each of them offered the possibility of security,
happiness, wealth, affection.

She thought, "That one over there looks nice. He's
old . . ."

Briefly she imagined the old man (without any heirs)
becoming fond of her, the dresses she would have made,
the traveling she could do. In her mind she saw herself
relieved of all her worries, made more beautiful by happiness, meeting someone young and handsome with
whom she would cheat on the wheezing old man in the
far corner, who at that moment gave her an unfriendly
glance before obsequiously going up to a pretty girl

with platinum blonde hair who was sucking her drink through a straw and looking around condescendingly with the superficial sparkle of youth.

Ginette turned away, gazing once again at the door. A man she knew came in. Pinning her last hope on him, imagining that his face was inflamed with desire when in fact it was lit up by the fleeting, intense flush of alcohol, she said to herself, "He's not bad, he's got a nice mouth, I'd be prepared to do anything for him."

But after a few meaningless, polite words, he left her to go and join his friends. Too deeply discouraged to be surprised or irritated she thought, "Of course, how stupid of me. I should have remembered, someone did tell me he doesn't like women."

Now when she noticed a man, she was only going through the motions, as she pulled her dress up a little and slowly stroked her stockings, smoothing them with a lazy, sensuous expression, for she knew that she had good legs and that on New Year's Eve a man might be too drunk to notice her face. But nobody stopped. That night every single person seemed cold or unfeeling or else already supplied with women who were younger and more beautiful than she. Ginette lowered her head and closed her eyes, despair flooding through her.

The bar was gradually emptying. It was three o'clock. Eventually only she and Christiane were left. With a weary gesture she brushed away the wisps of hair falling over her eyes and stared at Christiane.

"Some people have all the luck. She's got lovely skin, that girl. But she looks so pleased with herself! They're so stupid, young girls. She's got a good figure. I looked as good as her once," she thought, as she remembered what her body used to be like and how Maurice used to stroke her lovely curved hips. It was hard, having to return to this way of life after a ten-year relationship, almost a marriage.

"Maurice is dead," she whispered mournfully, in a daze. "There's no one who cares about me. I'm alone in the world. It's all a bit of a—joke." She sighed, unable to find any other word to express her despair.

She had forgotten about Christiane, but then looked at her again with a mixture of admiration, hostility, and contempt. How arrogant the girl was, how calm and self-confident! Christiane took a cigarette, tapped the end on the gold case lying on the bar, then held it out toward the bartender and accepted the lit match that he extended deferentially; she thanked him with a vague nod of the head and the bare outline of a smile, as if conferring a great favor on a subordinate, allowing him to hope for some reward.

"What a bitch," Ginette said to herself, "but her boyfriend has stood her up and she's waiting like other women do. So there is a god after all."

Almost unconsciously, however, driven by her usual habit of begging for a drink or a cigarette, she stretched her hand out toward the open case, muttering politely:

"May I, do you mind?"

"Of course," said Christiane. She hesitated; she had never spoken to a woman of this sort before. But curiously intrigued and flattered by the timid way the woman looked at her face and her pearls, Christiane decided to put her at ease. "I can talk to anyone, to a country girl, to old Mme. Donamont, to Laclos . . . It's a special talent," she thought with satisfaction, the corner of her mouth twitching in a proud little smile.

She said out loud, "Not many people around, are there?" She added, "How's business?"

Embarrassed by her question, Ginette turned her head and addressed it to the bartender. He answered, "It's the crisis, and anyway this is a slack time. Those men have finished their drinks and gone to have supper. But there'll be others along soon."

"Yes, and they'll doubtless be just as charming," said Ginette with a shrug. "Did you see the Englishman? He didn't even say good evening to me and I see the fat drunkard every night . . . I don't know what's the matter with men this year. It's as if they're always afraid of being robbed. It must be the crisis making them like that. Although we don't ask anything of them, do we, just a bit of ordinary courtesy."

Silence fell again. Christiane mechanically poured herself more champagne. Her cheeks were blazing. Smiling, Ginette said, "Does you good, doesn't it?"

"Yes. Do you have the time? It must be late."

"No. It's three o'clock, but of course it seems longer when you're waiting."

Tenderly Ginette fingered the necklace of false pearls around her neck, and then said with an anxious smile, "It's a long time, nearly two years, since I first saw you come in here with your . . . friend."

She hesitated over the word, but gave Christiane a timid, reassuring smile, as if to say, "I know I'm speaking to a woman of the world, don't worry, the word 'friend' doesn't mean 'lover' (but you're free to do what you want, I'm not going to pass judgment on you), although of course I realize he's your fiancé."

"And I've often seen you," Christiane said, knowing that Ginette would feel flattered. "I remember I even said to my . . . friend, 'That woman's pretty.' "

Beneath her makeup, which was beginning to run, Ginette blushed faintly, murmuring doubtfully but gratefully, "Oh! Mademoiselle!"

After a moment's thought she added in a low voice, "You're so kind!"

"Would you like something to drink?" Christiane asked. Without waiting for a reply, she pointed at her glass and said to the bartender, "The same for mademoiselle—I'm so sorry, should I say mademoiselle or madame? I don't know."

"Oh, you can call me Ginette. Don't be embarrassed, I'm used to it."

She swallowed a mouthful of champagne and, looking at Christiane with wide, glittering eyes, murmured, "You're nice, and intelligent, one can see that. You know about life."

"Thank God, yes I do," Christiane replied with a smile.

"That's unusual, at your age. And your friend, too, he looks intelligent, and you can tell he loves you! Ah, it's obvious how much he adores you," Ginette said, trying to return the compliment and to please this lovely young girl, who was treating her like an equal, like a friend.

"Just as if I were part of her world," she thought with gratitude.

"It's beautiful, youth." She sighed, as she looked admiringly at Christiane's sparkling eyes, teeth, and jewelry. "But it goes so quickly. Although if you've got real affection in your life, you don't notice you're getting old. When you've had it, as I have, and then you lose it, it's hard. It's nights like this give you the blues," she added vaguely.

"Yes, they do," said Christiane.

"But at your age, how can you know what it's like to have the blues?" the woman said, shrugging her shoulders. "However, that's as it should be, when you're pretty, rich, and young . . . but there are moments, you know . . ."

She stopped, forcing a laugh. "I don't know what's the matter with me," she went on, looking nervously at the bartender, "I'm very cheerful by nature; anyone will tell you that; it's just there are some days you don't feel so bright."

She realized that the bartender was dozing on his chair; reassured, she continued, "When you've had a man's affection, you don't have the strength to live alone. I'm always telling myself, 'No need to worry, Maurice will tell me what to do.' And then I remember he's not here anymore. But I'm boring you, mademoiselle, it's very nice of you to listen to me."

"Of course you're not," Christiane said.

She looked at her with detachment, as if she were a strange animal. Ginette, however, was experiencing the sweet satisfaction of having someone to talk to, of feeling that there was at least one human being in the world who would listen to her and understand her better than the bartender or Captain Alfred ever could. She felt her pain melting away and her depression lifting as she spoke.

"He, Maurice, was my friend . . . a friend I lived with for ten years . . . no need for the priest or the mayor. But he died of a stupid throat cancer that killed him in a few months. These things only happen to me," she muttered, trying to smile as she thought of Maurice's once plump face, his cheeks yellow and hollowed out as if being eaten from within by his illness. "He used to say, 'Don't worry, Ginette! I'll leave my money to you, not to my slut of a sister.' But as his illness became worse, he could only think about himself. When they get close to death, people don't worry much about those they'll be leaving behind. It's as if they're jealous of them, that they think it's enough just to be alive, and their resentment makes them think, 'Oh well, let them manage as best they can. Their gratitude isn't going to bring me back to this earth.' Of course, when Maurice died, his sister took everything, even the furniture."

As she remembered her bed, made of lemon wood and decorated with shining dark bronze angels, cool and smooth to the touch, she felt downcast and her eyes filled with tears. She stretched out her hand feverishly.

"You'll give me one more cigarette, won't you? Let's not talk about all that anymore. Tell me about yourself. It does one good to see people who are happy and who love each other. He's good-looking, your friend. Love is wonderful, you'll see. Of course, there are things you don't know about yet, a young girl like you, but you'll be a fast learner, as they say. Ah! You have nothing to worry about."

"I know everything there is to know," Christiane said, taking a peculiar and rather perverse delight in proving herself to be as mature and worldly-wise as this old sinner. She decided that Ginette had no idea who she was and would probably never find out her name.

"In any case, I'm not obsessed about virginity," she thought contemptuously.

She flicked the ash from her cigarette and said, "I

believe you have to find out beforehand if you're physically suited. After all, that's the most important thing about love, isn't it?"

"It certainly is! Ah, you're not stupid, are you? And of course, in one way you're right, that's why we were created and put on this earth. But in the long run, that's not what keeps you together. What I miss most is . . . affection," she said, having searched for a more intimate, gentle word to express what she felt. "I can assure you, I'm not looking for a boy who's good-looking, although of course I'd prefer that," she said, her mouth tightening in a little smile, while her eyes stayed fixed and sad. "If I could find a man who was kind, even if he was old, who would let me have a small monthly allowance and give me friendship, trust, and affection . . . but it's difficult to find someone like that. They're all the same: 'Hello, good evening, lie down over there.' And they're mean as well, and rude. When you've known someone who respected you, who introduced you to his friends, who called you his wife. His wife, imagine that," she said, slowly shaking her head. "That tells you all you need to know . . . And then from one day to the next, nothing, alone in the world, alone like a dog. Well, we'll have to hope things will improve. I'm not asking for the moon; after all, I'm over forty. I know I don't look it, that I look young, but inside," she said, gesturing vaguely at her heart beating beneath the waist-length string of false pearls, "inside I feel the years, and they haven't been easy at all . . . You're starting life in the right way, mademoiselle."

"Yes," said Christiane mechanically.

She was overwhelmed by sadness and hardly listened to the woman, just nodded vaguely in agreement; she was looking at the time. Nearly four o'clock . . . She couldn't help thinking, "If he really loved me, if he felt affection for me, like the woman says, he'd be here, he wouldn't have left me alone tonight in this bar . . . And what is it he has to tell me that's so important? I'm scared." For the first time in her life she felt a tremor of fear about the unknown. It felt as if an icy hand were slowly crushing her heart. "You look for love and all you get are boys who want to sleep with you or who only want your dowry."

Like a changing stage set, life seemed to unfold in front of her, revealing dark and terrible depths.

"I've drunk too much champagne. My head feels fuzzy and this woman is annoying me. What she's saying has nothing to do with me." And she looked at Ginette in the way that, from the shore, one might notice a man struggling in the water but decide to ignore him because he's too far away and his cries too faint and he looks more like a grotesque doll than a human being.

Ginette was still talking, but she was now so tired and so drunk that she had forgotten Christiane was there; her audience was herself and her memories.

She clutched her gloves in her hand and said, ". . . He woke me up. He was calling out, 'Ginette, I don't feel well. I'm cold.' I brought him a hot water bottle as quickly as I could, but he got irritable. He wasn't ever very patient. He said, 'For God's sake, hurry up, you stupid girl. Can't you see I'm going?' Then he heaved a great sigh and said, 'Leave it, my poor girl.' I sat on the bed and he went on, 'I would have liked at least to leave you the furniture but it didn't work out.' He sat up, kissed me, and lay back down. After that he didn't know me anymore, he called me Jeanne—that was the name of the woman who had left him. Then he died."

A tear rolled down her cheek; she looked at Christiane. "Your life must be so exciting and happy."

Christiane shrugged. Actually, at four in the morning and given the circumstances, life was not that exciting. There were many things that did not bear examining too closely. Gerald, for example. But she put that out of her mind with a shake of her head and a frown, hastily pouring herself another glass of champagne and drinking it. No, the life of a young woman, even one as happy and fulfilled as she, was not much fun. There was always that uncertainty, that anxiety, that search for happiness, for the man who would make you happy . . . Later, once you were married, you could either be happy or unhappy, but at least you were calm, you were settled, you knew where you were. Christiane's life was secret and difficult . . . There were so many things a young girl agreed to "so as not to look like a silly goose," "to be the same as the others," "because she doesn't have any silly prejudices," "because you have to experience everything," "because real life is fantastic," "because boys like that . . ." You weren't quite yet a woman, nor were you still a girl; you were eager yet exhausted.

The door opened and Gerald appeared. Christiane started, as if waking from a dream.

"Here's your friend," said Ginette. Tactfully she moved her chair back, but Christiane had already stopped seeing her; in her eyes she was now part of the decor.

"Jerry, at last!" she exclaimed.

He spoke hurriedly, in a low voice. "Listen, I've been with Laclos. I'm exhausted. I've been at his house since nine o'clock yesterday evening. Things are serious. He's allowed himself to get involved in something nasty. Bartender, a whiskey—Black Label."

He was silent for a moment, then went on, "Have you heard about the sugar scandal? Yes, of course you have. . . . Well, just imagine, the man who personified austerity in my eyes, who couldn't find enough words with which to condemn the least dishonesty or impropriety in political life, imagine, this man is in the thick of it! It's a scandal, he'll be called in front of the House, might even be arrested, who knows . . . Oh, I'd had my doubts for ages, but I didn't think he'd be stupid enough to get caught! He's got himself into a hole . . . It's a sim-

ple matter for me! I must choose between him and
Beralde, his opponent. Laclos won't recover; this business will break him. He's admitted some terrible things
to me. But if I dissociate myself from him, I'll immediately be entitled to Beralde's gratitude. What do you
think? Of course it will have to be done subtly and carefully. I'm talking to you," he said, looking at her with
cold eyes in which there was just a glimmer of real feeling. "Do you understand what I'm saying? I'm talking
to you now as if you were already what I hope you will
be in a few weeks' time, my wife . . ."

"And what about . . . her?" Christiane asked. This
was how they referred to Gérard's mistress.

"Her? Oh, it's over, of course! Laclos won't wait for
the police to nab him; he will leave and she will go with
him."

"You don't think she might leave him for you?"

Gérard shrugged.

"She probably doesn't have a penny . . ."

He wiped his brow slowly. In spite of everything, he
was sad about Martine Laclos and, as he was still very
young, now that the night's excitement had subsided he
felt weary and shaken and had a sudden urge to cry. But
he pulled himself together. He was pleased to have
made a decision at last. Christiane was an intelligent
girl, and they would make an effective couple. Boehmer
Sewing Machines had suffered comparatively little in
the crisis. He imagined Christiane lying in his arms,

attentive, concerned, perhaps slightly disappointed, the shape of her lovely body . . . Suddenly he felt desire and he murmured in a low voice, "So we're engaged, darling . . ."

As she left, Christiane, remembering Ginette, looked around for her and instinctively held out her hand for her to shake. Ginette gave a start, got up, and gave an awkward little curtsy, as if laughing at herself. Then, looking affectionately at the girl, she asked quietly, "Happy?"

"Everything is working out just as I wanted," Christiane said, her usual frosty arrogance returning.

But Ginette murmured humbly, "I'm very happy for you. Allow me to wish you a Happy New Year . . . and thank you."

"Oh, nonsense!" Christiane said with a shrug, but the sad voice and grateful manner had touched her; suppressing a smile, she thought, "Poor woman . . . Well, here I am starting the year with a Good Deed, like when I was a girl guide . . ."

She said, "Happy New Year to you, too, Ginette."

Ginette's cheeks flushed slightly and her heart beat faster. These good wishes at the beginning of the New Year, and the beautiful young woman's smile, would surely ward off bad luck.

She half-closed her eyes, as if memorizing Christiane's voice and words, then said, "Thank you, mademoiselle. Will I . . . will I see you again?"

"Probably."

Ginette gave a muffled sigh.

"I'd like that . . . It would make me happy . . . Happy New Year and good night."

After Christiane left, Ginette's luck turned at once: it was as if those good wishes had an immediate effect, like roses that are in full bloom when they are delivered from the florist and instantly start spreading their delicious if fleeting scent. The door opened and a group of men came in. They were drunk, merry and happy, as fifty-year-old men are who have abandoned the provinces, and their wives, for the night. They invited Ginette to supper in a Montmartre brasserie, and toward morning one of them, a factory owner from Roubaix with smooth red cheeks and a shiny, bald head circled by a crown of gray hair, took her back to his room. It was lunchtime when they parted. The streets were bright under a cold, pink wintry sun, and families were on their way to a formal New Year's Day lunch with a grandmother or an aunt. The parents walked arm in arm, the better-off women wearing a fox fur, the others carrying a new bag or gloves; the children walked in front, dressed in their Sunday best with white fur-lined jackets and leggings, each holding a little bunch of mistletoe or holly in one hand and clutching a new toy in the other.

Ginette strolled along happily, buoyed up with exhilaration and hope. She thought the factory owner from

Roubaix had liked her; she felt the calm pride and self-satisfaction of a good worker at the end of the day. She remembered his words: "When I come again next month, I'll get in touch. We didn't have a bad time together, did we? I'll give you more next time and we'll eat in a little bistro I know, where the patron does his own cooking. I hope you enjoy good food."

"Who knows," thought Ginette. "Some love affairs do start like this. He seemed a bit stingy, as men are when you first meet them. But he liked me. I look good today, and I know it doesn't take much, just the least glimmer of hope. One can change so quickly."

She opened her bag, and through a light cloud of perfumed powder looked smilingly at her parted lips and shining eyes reflected in the little mirror.

"It was that girl yesterday who brought me luck," she said to herself, happily picturing Christiane's face to herself. "If it hadn't been for her . . . I was at the end of my tether . . ."

She crossed the Seine. As she glanced down at the water, she realized with surprise that she walked past this spot four times a day but had never had the courage to plunge into the dark, swirling water. The pale yellow sun was now disappearing behind a mass of clouds. She thought about her unhappiness the day before and how she had walked aimlessly through the cold, empty streets, thinking about the inevitable approach of the night when she would end up on one of those benches in the freezing darkness, alone, lost, useless, doomed. But that young thing had listened to her, had said sweetly, "Happy New Year, Ginette," so genuinely, and had stretched out her hand, as if to a friend. She gave a hoarse little sigh.

"My God, the things one can survive! It's only when it's over that you're surprised you had the strength to get through it. That girl . . . I knew she felt for me. The way she said, 'Yes, yes, I understand.' Ah, I'd like to be able to do something for her, but what? At that age, one does such silly things . . . If there had been someone around when I was young to teach me about life, I wouldn't have ended up like this. Life . . . that's something I know about. I've seen a few things. I could advise her, stop her from making mistakes, prevent years of unhappiness, who knows? She's rich, of course, and only twenty. Twenty," she thought sentimentally, with just a touch of bitterness. "As the song goes, 'I'd like to be that age once more, and know what I know now.' "

And she imagined Christiane, a few years on, coming to visit her in secret, treating her as a mentor and confi-dante. She would never breathe a word to anyone about the visits. She would listen to her, suggest what she should do. She would say, "No my child, don't do that. This man you're telling me about, this friend of your husband's, I don't trust him. You must believe me, my child, I know about life, I could be your mother."

"Yes, I could have been her mother," she sighed,

thinking sadly about the passing of the years. But she imagined herself handing on love letters, or arranging meetings, always being discreet, reliable, and loyal. She thought how wonderful it would be if there were someone in the world who needed her, whom she could help, who might owe her, yes, might owe Ginette, the worn-out old tart, her happiness.

She hummed to herself as she climbed the stairs of the Hotel de Berne and went into her dark, stuffy room; then she stretched out on her bed and fell peacefully asleep.

At that very moment the first white engagement bouquets were beginning to arrive at Christiane's home. Boehmer was nervously rubbing his pale, dry hands together as he waited for the wealthy old aunt whom Gérard had asked to make the formal request for Christiane's hand. Mme. Boehmer, her heavy features flushed with heat, emotion, and indigestion, was wiping her eyes with a tear-stained handkerchief as she talked to her sister Hortense Vallier, of the Vallier de l'Orne family.

"She told us this morning. Not a word to me, or her father . . . 'I've decided . . . Gérard and I . . . I'll do this, I'll do that . . .' Parents are apparently only useful to pay the bills. Well, we'll see if they'll be happier and cleverer than us. Poor child, I hope she'll be happy."

"There, there, calm down, Laure," Mme. Vallier said, her thoughts turning to the gift she would have to buy. "Laure can't expect me to go mad. Now's not the time for it, not with what Georges and Jacqueline cost me!"

Meanwhile, Christiane was telephoning her friends. "Tonight I'm going to celebrate the end of my single life. The official engagement party will be next week, but this evening I'm inviting a few friends around: Chantal, Dominique, Marie-Solange, Jérôme, Marie-Pierre, Jean-Luc. We'll go dancing."

Happiness and pride shone in her face; yet it had a harsh, sardonic expression only partly disguised by her smooth skin and youth. Her cold, mocking eyes, her stiffly held head, the slightly contemptuous pursing of her thin lips, all hinted at the woman she would become in the 1940s, the woman who would say, "The president has sounded out my husband, but I believe . . ." and "It all depends on England," and "Now is the time to forget one's personal preoccupations and think only of the party!" and "Gérard, you must talk to the minister . . ."

It was late, almost midnight, when a group of young women in ball gowns, holding party streamers, arrived at the little bar on the Rue du Mont Thabor. One of them was waving a stick decorated with ribbons and tiny bells, laughing as she said in her shrill and childish voice, "So this is where you've been meeting for the last two years, Cri-Cri and Jerry, and no one knew about it? Where did you find such a wonderful place? You're amazing, you know. Listen, I'm going to take it over, I shall inherit it!" Some young men came in, Gérard among them.

Ginette was sitting in her usual place. The morning's lightheartedness had long since gone, and her face and shoulders sagged. Nobody looked at her. Nobody said a word to her. The bar had the sordid, grimy look of the morning after; the little flags decorating the bottles of whiskey drooped sadly, and some of the mistletoe berries had fallen on the floor, where they were crushed under people's heels. The bartender had taken Ginette to one side. He was a kind if weak man, but he believed the first of January to be an important date in the calendar for its potential moral uplift. It was the day when you could write off the previous year's mistakes, get rid of bad payers, reclaim what was owed to you, and feel the stronger and better for it. He had therefore made it clear to Ginette that she would need to settle her debts. As he thought about his wife and children, who could end up on the streets because of his generosity, he steeled himself with an interior monologue of self-evident truth: "It's all well and good, but I mustn't be an easy touch; if I fall ill tomorrow I'd like to know who'd give me credit?" Aloud he said, "And another thing, after tonight it's over, my girl, okay? You'll have to find somewhere else. The customers feel the same way as I do; they've had enough of being cadged off."

Ginette did not move but went on waiting, hoping fervently that Christiane would arrive.

When she saw her come in, she stood up with a smile. Christiane frowned. "Oh no, I do hope she's not going to come and annoy us!"

Just for a second, however, she hesitated, wondering if it might not be rather good fun and very "modern" to introduce her friends to the woman and invite her to join them for a drink.

"No, I don't think so. She's too obvious, she's not amusing, and those stories about her and her Maurice are a bore . . ." she thought.

At the age of fifteen, when she had found out how much she would be worth, she had learned how to look at people she did not want to acknowledge, how to look straight through them as if they were made of glass, with a cold, fixed stare as if she were looking for something just behind them; how to raise her eyebrows and allow a small, thin, icy smile to play on her lips.

She looked intently at an increasingly pale Ginette, conveying by her attitude, her silence, and her condescension that she was trying really hard to think of this unknown woman's name, that she remembered having seen her somewhere before and exchanging a few meaningless words with her, but that she could not say exactly when or where that might have been; then she turned away.

Ginette remained quite still and alone with her drink, her shoulders hunched. A world that was blissfully lighthearted and happy glittered right next to her but was inaccessible, as if it were enclosed in a transparent bubble. It shone and sparkled, gleaming before her very eyes, but it was not for her. Nothing would be, for her, ever again . . . She listened to the happy young voices ringing out, "Hey, Marie-Claude, Marie-Solange, Dominique, over here!" With a fresh and insolent laugh, a childish voice declared, "They're as ugly as anything, those tarts! And you pay for them! That's what you prefer to us, you idiots!"

A pink-skinned, blonde girl, with clear, sparkling eyes, exclaimed rapturously, "What a night! The amount we've drunk! Look, I bet I've got circles under my eyes, haven't I?"

They were safely on those happy shores, never buffeted by storms, where only a light, perfumed breeze would blow. Ginette looked at them, as, from an old boat being tossed on the waves, one might watch the elegant, proud shapes of palm trees and hills disappearing on the horizon. These were islands in paradise where she could never set foot. A bitter mist of tears rose into her eyes. She tightened her hands so fiercely around her glass that it broke; dazed, she looked numbly at the splinters of glass and the blood on her dress.

One of the girls laughed loudly; another started the gramophone, which covered up their cruel, high-pitched voices.

Reproachfully, the bartender said, "Out of it already?"

Ginette slowly got to her feet, then slowly wound the faded old blue scarf around her neck and tied it under her chin; the scarf had replaced the fur collar, long since sold. She opened the door, silently slipped out, and disappeared into the cold night.

Liens du sang

[FLESH AND BLOOD]

[I]

ANNA DEMESTRE STOOD ON TIPTOE TO KISS HER
sons: she was an old woman, short and thickset. She
tried hard to look lighthearted and happy, but her tired
eyes barely lit up under their pale, round lids; only the
corners of her mouth lifted in a smile, then her plump
face, now creased by old age, relapsed into its usual
sullen expression.

"I was beginning to worry," she said to her sons nervously, timidly. When her daughters-in-law came in,
she said in a sharp, plaintive tone, especially for their
benefit, "I was worried. It's eight o'clock . . ."

She led the way into the cold, cramped parlor, where
the uncomfortable armchairs waited in a circle facing

the empty fireplace. Albert and Augustin shrank back imperceptibly from the arms she held out to them.

The brothers were not at all alike, yet oddly similar. Albert was a heavy-jowled, bald, pink-skinned man in his fifties, with unhappy eyes. Augustin was shorter and thinner, graying at the temples; his pleasant features were beginning to coarsen, and his sensitive, faraway expression at times made him look like a sleeping cat.

Their mother asked both of them in turn, "How are you? Is everything all right, my son?"

They responded, loudly and heartily, in the falsely animated voices they used only for talking to her.

"Of course, Mama!" replied Albert. "I'm very well! What about you? Filthy weather, isn't it?"

Augustin, trying to wipe the thin, cold, abstracted smile off his face, rubbed his hands together cheerfully. "Am I well? I should think so! Never better!"

Then they fell silent, looking at her affectionately, although without seeing her, without noticing that her face was yellower this evening than on recent evenings. They were good sons. For a long time now they had only told her pieces of good news, but these were rare: usually they could not think of anything very much to say to her.

"Here's Alain," said Mme. Demestre, recognizing the sound of her youngest son's footsteps outside the door.

Alain came into the room. He and Augustin were alike, although Alain was taller and thinner. His hard, sharp face wore a taciturn, ironic expression, but it still showed some sort of spark, something long since extinguished in Augustin.

The brothers shook hands, muttering a halfhearted "How are things?"

They stood for a moment in front of the fireplace, silently avoiding one another's eyes. Then they drew up the armchairs, sighing as they sat down. Their wives were still tidying their hair in the hall. As soon as they came in, all three men stood up as one and went to join them.

When they spoke to their wives, their voices immediately took on their usual low, muffled, irritable tone, and their faces, undisguised, lost their mask of cheerfulness and calm. A sort of complicity isolated each couple. When Alain, who was not a good husband, said to his wife, "Couldn't you have explained to that idiot Angèle that the letter was urgent?" he revealed a glimpse into a part of his life about which his mother knew nothing, full of worries and hopes she did not understand and never would.

As she sat in their midst, the mother glanced from one to the other. Her eyes were piercing, but pale with age, gleaming mistily like water in a pond. Nothing irritated her daughters-in-law more than those greenish eyes examining their faces and following their every movement, while her expression remained sullen and lifeless and her heavy, pale eyelids, finely creased like those of some night bird, scarcely flickered.

During these Sunday gatherings the daughters-in-law always sat together on the same sofa. Two of them, Claire and Alix—the wives of the two younger brothers—were sisters. With Alix were her two daughters, Martine and Bernadette: perfect china dolls, blonde, pale-skinned, and with straight hair; two bare little necks rose above identical collars, embroidered by Alix.

Anna Demestre noticed the little girls' collars. She beckoned them toward her and sighed as she felt the gathered cotton linen.

"Are these the collars you embroidered, Alix? They're beautiful," she said with an effort, although one could see from her intent expression that she was eagerly looking for a fault in the workmanship. "They're too tight, you poor little things," she said with ill-disguised triumph as she slipped a finger underneath the collars. "You're suffocating . . ."

She was happy now, and looked for her glasses so that she could admire the delicate embroidery. "It's wonderful, Alix. Your work is as delicate as a fairy's."

Claire and Alix exchanged looks. It was always like this: when their mother-in-law was invited to dine at one of their houses, when they had carefully cooked one of her favorite dishes, she would immediately look suspicious and disappointed. Even if she thought it was excellent, and said so, she recovered her serenity and her appetite only after declaring, "There's too much cream, my dear," or "It's very good pastry, but too heavy."

She made less of an effort to be kind to Albert's wife Sabine, a chubby, faded blonde, in spite of the fact that she was the most placid of creatures, and the easiest to live with. The granddaughter of a famous surgeon, she was rich as well: Albert had inherited a substantial fortune from his wife's family, while Claire and Alix had been married without a dowry.

The three daughters-in-law huddled together on the old sofa; the effort they made not to yawn was making their eyes water. They contemplated with distaste the furniture and the walls of the icy little parlor. The front rooms overlooked the Rue Victorien Sardou, the quietest, grayest, and ugliest street in the area, while the windows at the back opened on to the grounds of the Sainte Perrine home for the elderly, at this time of day and this time of year a desolate chasm of wind, rain, and shadows.

Occasionally the three brothers punctuated the silence with cold, terse comments. It was always like this. They met every Sunday at their mother's house, but for the rest of the time each led his own life, with his own worries and his own circle of friends, utterly different from the lives, the concerns, and the relationships of his brothers. Prosperous Albert; Augustin, who had a reputation for seeing things only through his wife's eyes; Alain, permanently withdrawn in his gloomy thoughts. They sometimes looked at one another as if astonished to be in the same room together, speaking so familiarly. Sometimes (this evening especially, thought Anna Demestre) they seemed barely able to tolerate one another. Were they enemies? Certainly not: it was more that they were strangers who had nothing left in common, apart from their names and a few physical characteristics. When they spoke to one another, or even to their mother, about one of the others, saying "that oaf Albert," or "that pig Alain," their tone of voice was the same, not because of any ill feeling but because of their long-standing brotherly habit of complaining about one another!

"Mama, he did that to me . . . he's taken my things, Mama . . ."

"Mariette is late," said Claire.

Mariette was the sister of Albert, Augustin, and Alain. Still a pretty woman, she was beginning to show her age: she was one of those delicate blondes who, on reaching forty, appear to wither overnight, like a corsage of flowers worn to a party. She had led a chaotic and unhappy life. Once, to her brothers, she had been "our Mariette, our little Mariette," but now she was "good old Mariette, poor Mariette." She had stupidly married a much older man, and even more stupidly divorced him. She had been ravishing; wherever she went, love followed. Her life had been too dazzling, begun too early, and although she had apparently been destined for happiness, everything had ended disastrously, nobody quite knew why. Now, alone and childless, she was getting old and was dependent on her brothers, who passed her from one to the other like an awkward parcel.

She arrived just as they were sitting down in the dining room. The mother looked at her with unusual perception. "Poor Mariette, she used to be so pretty . . ."

She didn't see her sons getting older and plumper, losing their hair, their looks, and their youth; whereas, perhaps as a result of some sort of feminine insight, only in Mariette did she see the devastating effects of age.

They began to eat.

The old white porcelain lamp had been converted to electricity and its circle of lightbulbs shed a harsh glow over the tablecloth. The velvet chairs, the thick carpets, the soft, padded place mats, the maid who silently came in to put the dishes on the sideboard without making the slightest noise or without even clinking the cutlery, at first all this seemed very agreeable to the Demestre family. It made them feel calmer. They exchanged a few pleasantries, and, as they tasted the soup, exclaimed cordially, "Oh, Mama, what a delicious consommé!"

But the meal was long and heavy. Soon they began to flag, worn down by the silence and the effort of smiling all the time, of carefully avoiding any subject that might worry or upset their mother. She, however, was well aware that there was something unsaid between them, a quarrel in the offing. She tried to reassure herself: they never quarreled. They had nothing in common; they lived separate lives. Nevertheless . . . she looked at them. How quiet Alain was. "Alain's tragic expression," his brothers called it irritably. A little twitch, a sigh, or a clumsy remark, which in anyone else would make them smile or pass unnoticed, drove them to an irrational, blind, almost violent fury if they saw or heard it in one another. So Augustin's vague smile, Alain's dark moods, and Albert's clumsiness were at the root of all their grievances, all their resentment and suppressed anger.

"The children didn't come?" Mariette asked Albert.

"No. They had other invitations. No matter how stupid their friends are, they're all worth more to them than their father," said Albert with a heavy heart, as he thought about Jean-Noël and Josée, so remote, so indifferent, who considered his only value to be in how much money he could give them. "They're so cold, so hardhearted," he thought, as he compared himself to them.

Augustin thought, "The only reason Albert comes here is to be able to say to his children, 'I don't put anything above family. You know I could find something more interesting to do than go to Grandmother's for dinner on a Sunday, but I consider it a sacred duty.' "

Albert was looking for insurance against the future. Now that he was middle-aged, by performing his filial duty he was doing his best to buy for himself the certainty of growing old surrounded by his own flesh and blood, and by young people's voices, which would block out the sound of approaching death.

"Why has Mariette come? Oh, to touch Mama for fifty francs, I suppose! And Alain . . ."

Augustin thought about Alain's crazy plan, his dream; he and Albert were united, for once, fighting as strongly as they could. Alain had announced to his brothers that he had been offered a share in a rubber plantation in the Malayan archipelago. He was hoping to borrow the money for his journey and his initial expenses from them, and hoping to abandon Alix and the girls to their care, since he had only what little money he earned.

"Very convenient," thought Augustin angrily. In any case, it wasn't just about money: his leaving was really a devious way of abandoning Alix. And Alix and his own wife were sisters. "Alain's always been a swine: he's always had a special knack for persuading his brothers to get him out of hot water."

Meanwhile, Albert was asking Alain, "What do you think of English shares at the moment?"

Albert was the unluckiest of men. Since he had inherited his wife's money, he had been involved in every possible financial disaster. Alain always said that the English had decided to devalue the pound in 1931 purely because Albert had overcautiously converted part of his fortune into sterling.

Alain did not reply, so Albert repeated the question. Alain seemed to wake from a dream.

"What do I think of . . . ? I have no idea, old man."

"You must have an opinion, don't you?"

"No."

"But you're in a better position than most, aren't you?"

"Why? Do you think I'm a member of the court of the Bank of England?"

"Well, a banker who takes an interest in his work . . ."

"Actually I'm a banker who doesn't take an interest in his work."

"Come on, you must be aware of what people around you are saying? I've got money to invest . . . Alain, my dear little brother, for God's sake, come down out of your ivory tower and be so good as to give me some sensible advice: should I sell my English shares?"

"No."

"Ah! Why?"

"Just a feeling."

"Do you think I'm going to trust your feelings?"

"Sell, then."

"Ah," said Albert, taking notice. "But why?"

"My dear man, what do you want me to say? Nobody knows a thing. Don't try to be cleverer than other people: that's how you've always lost your money."

"Do you think so? Supposing I sold?"

"Oh! Listen," muttered Alain, "sell, buy, do what you want, get them framed, but stop talking about them."

"He's charming, your Alain," said Albert bitterly, turning toward their mother, his flabby face creasing into a sulky pout.

"What are you saying? I can't hear you. What are you talking about? I don't understand," the old woman said in distress.

Her hearing had remained particularly acute, but when she did not like the topic of conversation she immediately stopped listening to it. Each sharp word the brothers threw at one another made her heart ache. She sympathized with each of them in turn. Poor Albert! He didn't deserve the animosity his brothers showed him. They saw only the tactlessness of someone rich, and the selfishness. Yet he wasn't a bad man. Only she understood his touching good nature and the excessive caution that led him into such terrible disasters; his fortune put a barrier between him and his brothers. Neither Augustin nor Alain was rich, but they did not get along either, although they had once been so close, such good friends. Ah, these children just did not like one another, although in her heart, in her memories of the past, they were linked so closely together. Each in turn had been her favorite, and she had been passionately involved in their worries and their moods. Clumsily she spent her life trying to make them closer to one another, trying to wipe out the misunderstandings and rivalries between them. "Clumsily, and in vain . . ." she thought sadly and bitterly.

Her daughters-in-law were irritated by her continual efforts to bring her sons together, by her never seeing them on their own, and by the way she was always pleading with them, "Alain, please don't speak like that to Albert, he is the eldest . . ." or "Albert, why don't you ask Augustin and Claire to your house, they love you so much." Albert would then invite Augustin, who would be horribly bored; neither dared refuse, "so as not to upset Mama," and invariably it would end with arguments and cutting remarks. She knew that, but what else could she do? All she had at her disposal were the traditional phrases of motherhood: "Be quiet . . . Kiss and make up . . . Go and play together . . ."

"It's all their wives' fault!" she thought with veiled hostility. She cast a quick look at Claire and Alix as they sat facing her. They were both extremely pretty, with thick black hair that they had always refused to cut and pale complexions free of makeup. Even that upset her: she sensed that if Claire and Alix did not use makeup, it was less through personal taste than as a criticism of Mariette's rouged cheeks. The mother sometimes saw arrogance in the pallor of their faces and thought their lips seemed bloodless, colorless. She usually managed to stifle her natural dislike out of a genuine effort to be kind, to love them as much as her own children, but this evening she felt tired, ill, and sad—overcome by bitterness and anger. It was all their fault: if her sons arrived late, if they were ill, if they were unhappy, she knew, she was sure, that it was all due to these outsiders.

Quietly she said, "Eat . . . You're not eating!"

But her own food remained almost untouched.

"Are you ill, Mama?" asked Claire.

Her daughters-in-law took a particular, rather cruel, pleasure in seeming to defer to her and to appear loving. As young married women they had been so worried about incurring her displeasure (not that she had been tyrannical or wicked, poor woman; they had just been trying to humor the men they loved), that they still vaguely resented her for it. Now they knew, or thought they knew, that their husbands belonged to them alone; they had eroded the bond between the sons and their mother so cleverly and effectively, so worn it down, that it hardly existed any longer. Now they could afford to be generous. They could say, "Darling, think about your poor mother," or "Alain, have you written to your mother?" But within the affectionately tolerant way they looked at her, there remained a repressed animosity and a longing for revenge.

Little Bernadette was stroking her father's hand, as he distractedly fingered his sleeve. In a low voice, Alix said to her sister, "Poor child, it's pathetic the way she adores Alain. And she gets nothing back," she added, as she watched Alain pull his hand away.

"Pathetic," Alain repeated, raising his eyebrows in ironic disapproval.

By a tacit, unspoken agreement, certain words were forbidden in the Demestre family. It was as unacceptable to use them as it was to cry or to complain in public. As a result, their conversations always sounded like a collection of clichés, from which any genuine or meaningful words had been banished. Claire always said that through this excessive delicacy her husband and her brothers-in-law had reduced their vocabulary to words which, over time, had become gentle euphemisms. For them, as for many people, when they described someone as being "tired" it meant that in fact they were at death's door. She had whispered this to Augustin, who had smiled and murmured, "You're quite right, my dear!"

Theirs was one of those marriages that everyone acknowledged to be perfect: their politeness and mutual affection, together with a barely discernible hint of contempt in one of them, combined to present a smooth, impenetrable facade to anyone observing them.

Claire smiled. They understood each other well, she and Augustin. For a long time now she had been in the habit of talking like the Demestre family, while Alix on the other hand seemed to take pleasure in provoking them. Claire listened with astonishment to Alix's loud voice; when she was little she had talked quietly and shyly. Where did this harsh, almost vicious tone come from? When she and Alain turned toward each other, they appeared inexplicably hostile and angry. Even when she asked him to pass her the salt, it sounded like a furious accusation.

As they all left the table, the mother whispered to Augustin, "What's wrong with you children?"

"Nothing, Mother. Why should there be anything wrong?"

The three brothers remained together, leaving the women to go and have coffee in the salon.

Alain asked immediately, "Well, have you thought about it?"

"Yes."

"And you're not . . ." he stopped, took a deep breath, then started again, trying to control his husky voice. "Is it really impossible for you to help me? It's an excellent opportunity, you know, with great potential." He did not dare shout at them, "Look, listen to me! I'm finished if you don't help me. I can't stand Alix and the life I have any longer. I want to go, I must go! If only you knew! Who's going to understand me and help me if not my own brothers?"

Nervously he crushed an unlit cigarette in his fingers as he spoke. Even more brusquely than usual, he talked about the annual production of latex, in the faint hope that he might convince them of the soundness of a business he knew only by name.

"You're priceless," said Augustin, who never lost his temper, half-closing his eyes while a self-satisfied, faintly mocking expression crossed his face. "You can't see how hopeless it is, this plan of yours; it's typical of the Demestre family, and especially of Albert, our precious older brother. Naturally there are tobacco and tea plantations, factories, refineries, diamond and coal mines, and oil wells all over the world. But you have an infallible instinct for failure, a special nose for disaster—just like Albert in all his financial affairs—so you're going in search of rubber. With things as they are it's the most catastrophic choice you could make, the one most likely to lose you your—sorry, our—money."

"I want to go away," said Alain, through gritted teeth.

"You've got a perfectly good job here, and it's secure," said Albert.

"I want to leave. You don't know . . ."

"I do," volunteered Augustin.

Alain shot him a brief look. "We don't get along, my wife and I," he mumbled.

"Really?" replied Augustin, ironically. "I'd never have guessed . . ."

"It's your fault," said Albert firmly. "The way you talk to her, your moods, your lack of interest in the children . . ."

"That's my business, old man."

"Exactly so," said Augustin quietly. "Our life is our own business, it's ours alone. It's complicated enough without saddling ourselves with other people's lives, with those of our brothers . . . especially yours, Alain. I'd like to point out that no one's been helped and supported more than you. With your character, my poor fellow, marriage was the ultimate stupidity—almost a crime, in fact."

"But the day I want to get away from it . . ." Alain murmured bitterly.

"Too late," said Augustin, with unusual energy. "Even though it would be very convenient."

"Do you know what's held me back? You know that Alix has no money, no family, no one else in the world apart from your wife. You do know I couldn't abandon her to nothing."

"Yes, I do," murmured Augustin.

For a moment he seemed to hesitate, then closed his eyes wearily. Claire would never forgive him for contributing to Alix's unhappiness! Coping with her reproaches would be beyond him. And not to speak of the conjugal loyalty; it was a greater and more inflexible duty, he felt, than brotherly solidarity. To cut the whole thing short, he stood up, saying, "I just don't understand you, old man."

He was struck by the despairing look in his brother's eyes. "His tragic face," he thought with irritation and a strange feeling of remorse. He put his hand on Alain's shoulder.

"It'll work out in the end, old man, everything always does."

They went to join the women, who were obviously wondering what had kept them. Martine and Bernadette were sitting at a small side table playing dominoes. Claire murmured, "The coffee's cold . . ."

They drank it in silence. They heard the clock ticking. Each of them tried desperately to think of some news their mother might like to hear. Sabine talked about her servants. For a few moments the women became animated, then the conversation petered out again. During the longer and longer intervals of silence they could hear the gentle whispering of the rain pattering on the cobblestones and the occasional blast of a whistle from a barge on the Seine.

They were all feeling the overwhelming tiredness that overcomes members of the same family when they have been together for more than an hour. They were staving off a desperate desire to yawn, or go to sleep, which would vanish once they were outside. Even Alain longed to be in bed, forgetting that his wife would be there, too. But even her presence, with her tears and reproaches, would be better than this gloomy silence.

How impatiently they watched the hands on the clock slowly inching around! As soon as it got to ten o'clock they felt relieved and full of goodwill toward one another. Albert asked for more coffee, and drank it standing up.

"Good night, Mama, we don't want to keep you up . . . Good night . . . Good night."

She did not stop them. She was feeling tired herself. It was certainly a pleasure to see the children—these Sunday meals were a source of joy to her—but she did feel tired, especially tonight. She had caught a cold the previous day, and from time to time she shivered painfully. Then she felt stifled by the heat from the stove. She had once been used to living in the country for most of the year, in huge, cold rooms, and even here, when she was alone, she left all the windows open, in spite of the November rain; the smell of wet leaves, earth, and mist wafted up to her from the grounds of Sainte Perrine. But the children complained about the cold, and since midday the radiators had been spreading that dry warmth and strong whiff of paint characteristic of Parisian flats every autumn when the first fires were lit.

Albert said, "I can't take anyone with me. I've got to go and fetch the children. The car will be full."

"Of course, old man, that's fine! Good night, my dear fellow," said Augustin cheerfully.

He kissed his mother again.

"Don't forget me, my child. Why don't you come during the day sometimes—the days are very long."

"Of course I will, Mama," he murmured with impatient affection, not listening to her. "Claire will look in, or I will, one of these days. Anyway, we'll see you on Sunday, won't we? See you then."

As soon as they were outside they all went their separate ways. When Augustin and Claire were alone, she took his arm.

"Well?"

He shrugged. "Well, he won't go, of course. How can he go without any money? He's not going to leave Alix and the children on the streets. And he knows now that he can't expect anything from us."

This insane dream of Alain's had brought them closer together than usual; they talked in a remarkably similar low, rapid, affectionate tone.

"What does Alix say about it?"

"What can she say? He wants a separation without any tears or arguments. This ridiculous departure is just a pretext. What did he say to you?"

"He says he doesn't want to live in Europe any longer, that he can't put up with his office job, that he hates it and is not suited to it. He may be right, but why can't he just go off camping or fishing, instead of this? Abandoning his family, leaving them on our hands, no, absolutely not! We all have to manage our own lives! He's responsible for Alix and the children. I think it's outrageous that he's trying to get rid of them by dumping them on us," Augustin said angrily.

They fell silent as they walked in step together; their faces wore the same indignant expression. Each of them was thinking, "If it were only about money . . . but he's asking for our time, our peace of mind, our happiness." They would have to console Alix, calm down old Mme. Demestre. They loved them dearly, of course, as you do love your own flesh and blood. You want them to be happy, but you don't want to be forced to look after them.

Huddled together under one umbrella, they went toward the metro station: rarely had they felt so close to each other. They had reached that state of perfect understanding between husband and wife that meant that each could speak without listening to the other, at the same time knowing instinctively that their words were a response not just to the other's words but to their most secret, hidden, unformulated thoughts. They were soothed by this brisk walk in the dark and the soft rain. Wearily, Augustin said, "I don't want to talk about Alain anymore."

They stopped and sniffed the breeze blowing in off the Seine.

Claire murmured, "Poor Alix."

Then they went back to their own life: their plans, their worries, a chair in the flat that needed reupholstering, all those little preoccupations of daily life that unite married couples more strongly than love.

Meanwhile, their mother had closed the door after Alain and Alix, who were the last to leave. Alone, she went from one room to another, opening all the windows. How quiet it was! She did not usually hear the silence, but tonight, after her sons' steps had faded away and all the young voices had gone, it overwhelmed her. It was that terrible silence of old age, when everything seems to come to an end at the same time: the noise of life lived beyond her four walls, the inner excitement of youth celebrating its joy . . .

She moved slowly around the room, feeling a sort of self-pitying but benign anger as she tried to disguise her frightful boredom. "Men are lucky," she thought. "Even when they're old they have things to interest them— politics, war and peace, world events—and they have clearer and more vivid memories. Women are left with nothing apart from knitting or a game of patience. Oh!

What happy sounds there used to be in this house: children's voices, slamming doors, the sound of laughter and quarrels." All she could hear tonight were the maid's footsteps in the kitchen as her slippers brushed almost noiselessly across the floor, then a sigh, or the faint sound of a plate being placed gently on the sideboard, with a chink that echoed for a long time in the silence. She thought gloomily about her daughters-in-law. They had said this, done that . . . "Alix never says anything. She must make life difficult for Alain. Claire's a good little thing, she gets along well with Augustin. But then who wouldn't get on well with Augustin—the most intelligent and nicest of my children? Yet Claire herself . . . they never tell me anything. Do they think I wouldn't understand? Well, it's true, perhaps I wouldn't understand . . ."

She let out a deep sigh; her head felt heavy and she kept shivering. She must have caught a chill. She rang the bell for the maid, querulously reminding her that her hot water bottle was never hot enough, nor was her bed properly made. Yet she did not move away from the open window, enjoying the feel of the wind ruffling her gray hair as she breathed in the smell of wet leaves. Then she went to bed.

Almost straightaway she felt the beginning of a fever. She had been ignoring her malaise since the previous day, but now it had taken hold. The first deep shudder, which seemed to come from the very marrow of her bones, was followed by a burning wave, which she accepted patiently and almost with a sense of well-being; it warmed her up, her mood mysteriously lightened, and she recovered some of her lost liveliness and her sense of humor. She thought about her children, especially Albert. On hearing that his mother was ill, his first thought would be, "That's all I need." Poor boy! He assumed that family illnesses and all of life's misfortunes were deliberately sent to him by fate. She smiled. She imagined the reactions of Augustin, Alain, and Mariette. "They hoped I'd leave them alone until next Sunday." Her mind, which had become dulled through the passage of years, now grew alert, mischievous, almost lighthearted. She hadn't always been a bad-tempered old woman—the children had forgotten that—and she thought about them, not as she usually did with admiration, respect, and incomprehension, but with that indulgent and ironic tenderness a mother sometimes feels for her children while they are still small, not yet quite human beings, as comical as puppies. They were helpless, touching . . . How comforting illness and fever can be, as they spread throughout the body and let wisdom and a clearer understanding flourish in their warmth.

Nevertheless, her teeth chattered as she endured the icy little waves that rippled through her; her elderly body was giving in to illness, accepting the rhythm of the fever. Soon her head seemed heavier and she felt a dull ache behind her eyes. She had difficulty breathing.

It was as if the air was trapped in her chest, inside her ribs, and, moaning with the pain, she made an effort to drag it up from deep inside her. She wanted to move the pillow so that she could rest her cheek on the fresh linen of the bolster, but it was hot and heavy. All at once she realized how weak and tired she was. She closed her eyes, and the treacherous fever rose up like a slow, relentless tide of ice and fire, drowning her. There was nothing left in her now, no thoughts, no regrets, no desires. The images of the children grew faint. All that remained was an ill-tempered body, feebly fighting its illness. How long the night can be!

By morning, her temperature had gone down. She arranged for her sons to be told. Each of them took an hour out of his day to go and see her, to sit by her bed, to say with dismay, "But yesterday you were perfectly fine!"

The doctor came in during the morning. He said they would have to wait; it was too early to give an opinion one way or the other.

The three daughters-in-law had taken up their positions, one by the bed, the others in the little parlor. Soon they sent their clumsy husbands away; the mother was left in the cool, calm hands of the wives, who gently tucked her in. Only Mariette went from one to the other with a drawn, frightened face. She went over to the bed to look at her mother, but her sisters-in-law reassured her with a gentle shrug.

"It's a bad cold . . . It's nothing."

"It's the time of year for it," said Sabine.

"There'll be a nurse here tonight, Mother."

"What for?"

No one answered her. People don't listen to the sick. The young women arranged the room for the night: they drew the curtains, dimmed the lamp, lit the fire, and arranged the medicine bottles on the mantelpiece, with their labels clearly visible.

Then they all went home. But it was an anxious and sleepless night for everyone. They had telephoned the doctor before going home, and he had promised to come back the next day.

"It's flu, isn't it?" Albert had asked.

"Yes . . . but it's gone to her lungs. I could hear a rattle through my stethoscope. Well, we'll have to see how things are tomorrow."

Tomorrow . . . As they lay in bed, each of them closed their eyes, listened to the clock chiming, and gently stretched their legs between the icy sheets. It was a cold night. Occasionally Augustin would wake up with a start, muttering, "Wasn't that the telephone?"

"No, go back to sleep. Don't worry so much!"

At dawn he looked at his wife in the dim light coming through the shutters. She was sleeping peacefully, her wonderful dark hair spread over the pillow. "In spite of everything," he thought, "I'm on my own. Claire sympathizes; she doesn't suffer. But why should she suffer? She's looked after Mother well. She's always made a point of saying, 'Your mother's not easy to look after.' But now she's sound asleep."

He felt almost afraid, as he thought how far away from him she seemed, how unfamiliar. It was probably because of his dreams—a jumble of daydreams and nightmares that had sent him back to the years not so long ago when she had not been there. What was that idiot Albert doing? And Alain? He thought about them with irritation and scorn, yet he wanted to see them.

The second day went by very slowly. One by one they went into the room where the old woman was lying. She didn't move. They said, "She's sleeping," and tiptoed away. But it seemed to them she was better. She woke up during the day and ate a little food; they all breathed more easily, although the women did not allow themselves to be distracted or deceived by hope.

The women! How useful, rational, and practical they were! They spoke quietly, saying, "Poor Mama." They telephoned the doctor. They grieved as you would over the death of someone you are fond of but who is unimportant to you. When, at four o'clock, her temperature rose again, they were the first to say, "We must have a second opinion."

The two doctors took a long time to arrive and, growing colder by the minute, the family waited in a mood of solemn impatience. It was late. None of them had had dinner. The sons were incredulous. "Mama, dying? Oh, come now." They needed time to take in the idea of her death. But how quickly the women resigned themselves to it! They adopted a mourning attitude; they were intent on dispelling any hope, sighing, "She never looked after herself properly." "At her age, it's serious if you ignore a cold." "When my own mother died . . ."

They were troubled and upset, although they stayed very calm. What could be more natural, more to be expected, than the death of an old woman who was ill?

At last the consultant arrived. He listened to the patient's chest, questioned the nurse, then announced, "Bronchitis . . . not too serious."

He nodded at Albert and they left the room together. He said, "Look, it's a bit worrying. I fear there may be complications with her heart. She's getting pain and distress in the cardiac region. It's worrying!"

"It's not serious, is it?" asked Albert, bending his large, anxious face toward the doctor.

"If we manage to avoid complications in that area, I hope it won't be serious, but . . . well, we'll just have to wait, see how things are in the morning. I hope she may feel better in the morning."

Albert listened and—gradually, slowly—the thought took shape in his mind, "She's going to die . . . my mother's going to die."

[11]

THE EVENING DRAGGED ON SLOWLY. THE THREE
women sat knitting by the fire in the parlor; through the
half-open door they could see the patient dozing; her
cheeks were red and blotchy and her nose looked pale
and pinched. The women watched her, shaking their
heads. "Poor woman. She wasn't so bad. A bit . . . bad-
tempered, a bit spiteful . . . but at her age . . ."

They got up occasionally to go to the door and speak
to the nurse.

"No change."

"The doctor's worried about her heart, isn't he?"

"Yes. If it's that, there's nothing to be done."

"How old is she? I wouldn't want to live that long."

Eventually they began to discuss other matters. With
a sigh, one of them said, "Have you seen Adrienne? You
know that blue dress? I don't know whether to order it
now."

A pause, then: "Black is always so much more practical."

They were on their own. Their husbands were in the
dining room; they could see them sitting at the table,
smoking in silence. Mariette was with them.

Claire beckoned to them to come and join their
wives; Augustin got up and gently closed the door.

Every now and then the patient would moan, complaining that she couldn't breathe. She begged them to

open the windows, but they said, "Later, later . . . tomorrow, if the sun shines." They did not know that, for the sick, time does not move at the same pace as it does for those around them. There were so many long, drawn-out hours until the next day . . . You had to fight for breath and struggle toward nightfall as you would climb up a mountain.

She pushed away the hands that reached toward her—the cold arms felt icy; she shivered. "You can see she's cold." They pulled the blankets up higher, suffocating her; they closed the shutters and the curtains. The room was oppressive now, hot and stifling. All she could hear was the whistling noise coming from her chest. She closed her eyes. The hours passed slowly. First one, then another of her children came in quietly to sit by her bed. She did not need to look at them. She recognized Augustin's slow movements, Alain's lighter footsteps, and Albert's sighs. As if carrying a heavy burden on his shoulders, Albert sighed mournfully from time to time.

Each in turn slowly leaned over her, then left, walking through the parlor without answering the wives' questions, and went back to his brothers.

It was a relief to be together that night. They did not need to speak. Albert was the only one who talked, although nobody listened to him. "Just like the old days," thought Alain. Albert had always been treated with condescension by his brothers, but tonight this did not appear either to hurt or surprise him. In the early days, before he was old, rich, and important, he was just "fatty Albert" or "good old Albert" to his brothers, leaving the good looks and the talent to them and to Mariette.

From time to time Augustin stood up and went over to the window. As he opened the curtains to look out at the rain he felt his old spirit returning, that lighthearted impatience and inner fire that the years had extinguished. Mariette was smoking, her face hidden in the shadows. Some of the indefinable grace her brothers had loved so much could be glimpsed in her face.

In the little parlor next door the women could not hear what they said. Sometimes they pricked their ears, but no . . . they remained silent, waiting. Claire softly called out, "Come in here . . . you'd be more comfortable."

No one replied.

In a strained voice Alix murmured, "Whatever can they be talking about?"

Her sister gave her a surreptitious, pitying glance: she looked so worried and tense, haggard with jealous, unforgiving love. She listened, and said as she shrugged her shoulders: "I don't know. Something about Aunt Andrée or cousin Henriette, people who've been dead twenty years. As if they have nothing better to do."

She stood up, folded her knitting, and went into her mother-in-law's room, where the night nurse was helping her to sit up and drink. She asked, "Do you need anything, Mama dearest?"

The old woman did not reply. No, she did not need anything. Yet she felt worse; she was finding it more difficult to breathe. But she could hear the children's footsteps and their quiet, muffled voices. She knew they were there. She was sure, now, that she would not die alone one night, as she had so often feared, looked after by plump Josephine, waiting on her deathbed for her sons, who would be woken, summoned, but would get there too late. She had so often imagined that she would die alone in the summer in the empty flat, surrounded by shrouded furniture. The children had never understood why she was so miserable as the holiday season approached. Children didn't understand anything . . . But now she knew they were there, that they would leave her only when she was out of danger or, on the other hand, when death came to take her from them.

The night nurse complained to Claire, "She shouldn't slump like this. Her lungs are clogged up, but she won't sit up against her pillows. I keep trying to lift her, but every time she sinks back. If you could help me . . ."

Claire took the old woman by the shoulders and, with some difficulty, gently pulled her up, but as soon as they let go of her, her large body sank down into the bed, and her head fell heavily onto the pillow.

Claire went into the dining room. They were all sitting with their heads bowed under the lamp, talking in low voices. With a peculiar feeling of distaste she looked at Mariette's blonde hair, shining in the light, disheveled

and as pale and delicate as wisps of smoke. It was . . .
shocking, that beautiful blonde hair framing the worn-
out face.

"You must help me lift your mother," Claire said. "It's
bad for her breathing and for her heart to be lying like
that, but she won't make the effort to sit up. I don't
understand it. She's not fighting. You have to fight."

Augustin stood up and went to try to help pull the
patient up onto her pillows, but she slipped out of his
hands, as she had done with the others, moaning as she
sank down again. He looked at her silently and gestured
to Claire to leave her alone.

"But it's not doing her any good, as I told you . . ."

He left the bedroom without answering.

"One shouldn't let oneself go like that," Claire said
again.

"Ah!" said Alain softly. "They're all the same, those
little Hasselin girls."

Augustin smiled, remembering a time when Claire
and Alix were just the little "Hasselin girls," distant
strangers whom they greeted coldly, with a wary
reserve.

Alain murmured, "All the same. They're always
right there. They wave their arms around. They talk.
They think they can change the course of destiny . . .
they're very—energetic."

Augustin shrugged slowly.

"Yes, energetic, passionate and loyal."

They fought against illness, and even death itself, while the Demestres' instinct was to wait, to let things take their course. Augustin thought perhaps that was what was keeping them together that night, a need to be with one another, with family. They all felt the same weariness confronted with what seemed to them a futile commotion. They had tried to suppress their anxiety with useless words and pointless activity. But this had neither helped nor comforted them. Finally they resigned themselves to silence and to waiting.

Yes, it seemed to them that they should wait, stay out of the way, not say anything, shut their eyes. While the women . . . they had neither detachment, nor a man's superior wisdom.

"It's all so useless," murmured Alain, as a pained look flickered across his face. His brother guessed that he was thinking about Alix, who, after all these years, still had not given up trying to make him love her. And who knows? If she had not been so desperate to make him love her as much as she loved him, there could have been some tolerance and affection between them, whereas . . .

That was indeed what Alain was thinking. And his brothers could read his mind. They had stopped seeing one another simply as ghostly shadows, the way we see people whose behavior doesn't affect us and who bring us neither grief nor happiness. Perhaps their fear and worry that night made them more than usually sensitive to one another's thoughts. "Yet we haven't changed," thought Augustin in confusion. Their attitudes hadn't shifted enough to make them love one another. He, Augustin, still thought Albert was a fool and Alain withdrawn and selfish, just as they undoubtedly continued to judge him as harshly and intolerantly as only brothers could. In spite of this, they understood one another.

One of them asked suddenly, "How old was Grandfather when he died?"

In the parlor they could hear Claire's voice: "I'm telling you that the light is tiring Mama."

They did not reply. How old *was* Grandfather when he died?

For Claire, his was a name that aroused no echo in her heart. For the brothers, he was the man from whom they might have inherited the illness that would kill them one day.

Meanwhile, Claire and Alix were quietly talking together. Alix was complaining about Alain, about her children, about her life.

"Bernadette sometimes stands up to him; she's his favorite. Martine adores him, as I did, crawling to him. But he doesn't love them. He doesn't love his house, and he doesn't love me. I know there isn't another woman, which makes it worse. You can try to reach a man who has stopped loving you, but him . . . Oh, how I loathe the Demestre spirit; it's so elusive! They're all the same;

that's why we fell for them. When I was young, before I was in love with Alain, I think I was in love with the whole Demestre tribe. I loved that 'family look' they shared: their mannerisms, their peculiarities, their gentle voices, their beautiful hands . . . I loved Alain before I knew him, when he was just a name spoken by you and your husband and when I was still a child. Those Demestres! Do you remember, Claire?"

Claire did remember. My God, how glamorous they had seemed to her. She thought back to the summer when the house next door to theirs had been rented for the first time by the Demestre family, happy and well-off in those days. They, the little Hasselin girls, daughters of a lowly insurance clerk, spent their summer holidays in one of those awful little houses built, as pre-war villas often were, to look like a Swiss chalet, with a pointed roof, a wooden balcony, and the name written above the door in shells and pebbles. And there was the house next door, so beautiful, simple, and imposing, its garden merging into the damp pine forest. The night the Demestres gave a ball to celebrate Mariette's engagement, the little Hasselin girls stayed up all night, leaning out of their bedroom window, trying to make out the dancing shadows behind the dazzling lights. It was September, and already cold. They were frozen to the bone. Every now and then couples came out onto the balcony, and they would glimpse light, gauzy dresses and bare arms. Claire was then fifteen, and Alix barely ten. And now here was the legend of the Demestres, the Demestre world, regrouping itself slowly and quietly next to them.

"What are they talking about?"

They were talking about the house, the rooms they had as children, their mother's dresses . . . Alain listened. Casually, they said, "You won't remember any of that, you were too young, it was before you were born."

And Alain, usually so scornful of everything and everybody, was listening openmouthed, somehow becoming once again the "baby" of the family. His face took on the round-eyed, astonished expression of the youngest child allowed, as a special treat, to listen to the grown-ups. "You won't remember that, Alain." He thought he did remember but did not say anything, not wanting to contradict his elders. He realized that, deep down, the reverence and fear they inspired in him was still intact.

Augustin and Mariette were talking quietly, cracking nuts in their hands with identical gestures. Mariette sighed. Her face was lit up with that youthful, light-hearted beauty and grace they had never been able to forget. Perhaps they had never forgiven her for allowing age and life to spoil the reflection of their own youth in her face . . . Now, in the dark, they could see only her still-beautiful eyes and hear her gentle, slightly rasping voice. They forgave her for growing old, and loved her once more.

"Oh, do you remember? Do you remember?"

Remember what? Nothing. Sounds, shadows, such an ordinary past, but one the others did not know about, did not understand. The wives did not understand, that was all . . . They were not part of the family.

Albert listened, saying diffidently yet cheerfully, "Yes, you're right, Augustin, you're right."

Now they were discussing people whom neither Alix nor Claire nor Sabine had ever known. The women heard an indistinct murmuring, then suddenly a Christian name none of them had heard mentioned before. Georges? Henriette? Friends? Relations? They moved closer together. They knew, in their heart of hearts, that they did not really care about their mother-in-law's illness and her possible death. Although they passionately wanted to be involved in their husbands' grief, they were being gently rejected, with an obstinacy typical of the Demestres, rather like a dog discreetly slipping its head out of an uncomfortable collar. With the ruthless greed borne of love they wanted the men they loved to belong only to them. They wanted to console and to caress them, but above all make them realize that all they had in the world were their wives, their children, and their homes. That should be all they needed; it should replace everything else, be enough for them till the end of their days.

Sabine came and stood in the doorway.

"The light really is too bright. It's tiring for Mama. Come in here; come into the parlor."

They shook their heads, wanting to be rid of her.

Mariette turned out the lamps, leaving one burning by the fireplace. It reminded them of the nights when they used to be awake together while their mother slept, when they would look at the moonlit sky with a sweet, heartfelt longing. It was not their childhood that had scarred them so deeply, but their early youth and first, carefree love, before they took on the hateful burdens and responsibilities of forty-year-olds.

"You were so pretty!" said Alain artlessly.

Mariette sighed sadly. "I was, wasn't I?" she said.

"You really ruined your life, you poor old thing," said Augustin, with a curious bitterness, a strange anger, as if he were talking less to his sister than to himself.

Each of them was thinking, "We've all ruined our lives. But in any case, life is ruined just by living it." They said nothing. Whereas friends or a wife exhaustingly insist on talking, there comes a moment in which silence or a sigh or a brief look is enough among brothers and sisters. Each of them thought, "Poor old thing," and then went back to thinking about themselves; yet through some miracle of kinship, thinking about themselves did not distance them from the others.

"Do you remember . . ."

They smiled at one another trustingly. "You can't rely on a woman," thought Augustin. "She listens greedily to her husband's memories, collecting every crumb from the past of the man she loves, accepting or rejecting it forever according to how it relates to her: 'Was that before you knew me? Was that after we were together?' "

Nothing else exists. A man's life can begin only on the day, at the moment, when his wife takes possession of him.

[III]

THE NIGHT PASSED VERY SLOWLY. THEIR MOTHER appeared to be sleeping. She no longer had the strength to lift her head. She wanted a drink, but the thought of having to call the nurse, force her lips apart, and make the effort to swallow some water was too much for her. It was very late. She opened her eyes and gazed at the gleaming brass rails of the bed as they caught the light from the lamp. The pain had gone. She felt utterly detached from everything. She was not worried about her illness; she was no longer thinking about the children. She was resting. She had forgotten about her daughters-in-law's appearance and Alain's unhappy life. She looked at each object in her room in turn, as if trying to recapture a memory of something that escaped her. Her pulse slowed. The nurse got jugs of hot water ready and prepared capsules of camphor oil.

It was Mariette's turn to look in. When she came out of her mother's room she said in a shaky voice, "She's very weak."

They all rushed into the bedroom and gathered around the bedside. The nurse sent them away. "There are too many people in here."

Tears ran down Mariette's face. Augustin sighed. "Poor girl. It will be hardest for you."

"I'm all alone!" she murmured.

"Yes," said Alain quietly, "but we all are, you know . . ."

Augustin thought, with both irritation and pleasure, "How well the swine understands me! He's always understood me better than I do myself."

"Well, I'm not unhappy with Sabine," Albert said timidly, "but the children . . . ah, the children!"

At last he voiced his bitterness, his anger, and his love: "Children . . . you do everything for them, give them everything, in the hope that in exchange, one day when you're dying, they'll be there like we're here now . . . unhappy, yes, upset, of course, but . . ."

They fell silent. They looked pityingly at their mother's face, just visible in the shadows. With a moan and a sigh, she had refused an injection. She was calmer now, and careful hands had moved the lamp away from her.

"Yes," Augustin said, "it's not much, but at least we're here, aren't we? That's something, isn't it?"

"I suppose we won't see much of each other now," said Albert abruptly. "It's a shame. I just wanted to say that, in spite of everything, we are brothers; we are fond of each other . . . We should see each other from time to time, don't you think?"

"Yes, yes, of course, old man," Augustin said, almost tenderly. "You see, the trouble is that we have no reason to hate each other. Nothing binds a family closer together than the passionate hatred which used to make brothers fight each other over a field or a vineyard. We don't even have that. All we have is a very special, brotherly feeling of irritation: Albert's sighs and your bad moods, Alain."

"The way your lips move when you're being sarcastic and not really listening, which makes me want to punch you," said Alain.

They both smiled.

"And yet," added Mariette, "we were so close, such good friends . . . Then love happened and it was all over."

"It wasn't love so much as marriage," said Augustin. "Love is just a peculiar, fleeting affair that isn't very important, but in marriage there is always hostility between two different tribes of human beings. There are two opposing forces, who fight each other until one of them wins, and you and I, my poor old Alain, have been knocked out too easily . . ."

"You can laugh," Alain said quietly. "You can't know . . . But when you don't love one another?"

"Your wife loves you," Albert said.

"Well, I don't love her," said Alain in despair. "It's not

my fault. Love doesn't beget love, or, at least, and that's what's so terrible, it only induces an illusion, an ersatz love."

"Yes," said Augustin gently, almost in spite of himself.

"You wake up to see a woman sleeping in your bed and the first thing you ask yourself is: 'What's she doing here?' That's how I've felt for years and years."

"There's that overwhelming depression," said Augustin, "at the thought of going home in the evening."

"Only breathing freely far away from her."

"Yes."

"Knowing that you're being cruel, untruthful, wicked, and hypocritical but not being able to do anything at all about it. I couldn't say this to anyone else in the world. I'd be ashamed. But you must understand me. Did you ever know why I married Alix? No? I was in love with a woman, never mind her name. She is dead. You, Augustin, had married Claire. Alix was living with you. I saw her constantly. I knew she loved me and it made me feel grateful to her. There's something overpowering about a woman who wants to be loved: that face always lifted up to you, that anxious look, that obsessive desire. It gives you a feeling of limitless power. I thought it could replace love."

"It does," said Albert.

"Sometimes," murmured Augustin.

"Yes, but in that case both of you have to be disappointed and resigned, like you and your wife," said Alain sharply as he turned toward Augustin, who flinched and said nothing. "But when one of you still loves, still suffers, and the other can only watch the loving and the suffering—ah, that's hell! I've been thinking about going for years, dreaming about leaving her! For years, do you understand? But I can't leave them wandering the streets; they only have me . . . If only I could make her happy, but she'd be a hundred, a thousand times happier if I were far away. Oh, if only you could, would dare, help me! We were young together, and our lives are similar. Do you want to punish me?"

"Alain," said Augustin, raising his head, "you lied just now . . . This woman isn't dead, is she? Are you going away to be with her?"

"Yes. She's married. Her husband's taking her away. I want to live with her. I must. I've only ever been happy with her. I married Alix in despair, out of spite; then I found her again; she's been my mistress for more than eight years. If I have to stay here, I'll never forgive Alix. Our life would become a living hell. You're my brothers: you should love me above duty, above morality. Yes, I know what I'm asking seems cruel and senseless— abandoning a wife who is beyond reproach, abandoning my children. But what can I do, if they're like strangers to me? I've tried desperately to love them, without being able to. The other one . . . the other one. I love her! She has a child by me. My life is with her. Think about it . . .

I'm asking you . . . for some money, Albert, and for you, Augustin, to put up with Claire's reproaches and Alix's tears. If I stay, what will happen? Nothing but misery for my wife, my mistress, and myself. If my sacrifice would make Alix happy, perhaps I'd give in and resign myself, but what will happen if I stay? More scenes, more sordid quarrels, more agony for her and me, and for the children."

"The children," said Albert.

"The children? Who are you to talk about children? What have your children ever given you in the way of happiness, gratitude, or affection? Are they happy to be with you? Do you think they need you? You talk about making the children happy: what do you actually do for Jean-Noël and Josée that's worthwhile, that actually has an effect on them? You would like to, yes, with all your heart. But what can you do for them? Give them advice? They don't listen. Tell them about your own experience? They despise it. Offer them friendship? They reject it. My children don't need me; they've got their mother. They love her; they're like her. For the last eight years there hasn't been a single night when I've gone to bed without praying that it would be my last. I waited for the children to grow up. I hoped for a miracle. I've even been waiting for Alix's death to set me free. The only reason I've been able to get through the last eight years is that the other . . . this woman . . . was in France. Not in Paris, but in France. Sometimes she would come to see me, and I would escape for a couple of days to go to see her and the boy. He belongs to another man, but I love him. I would spend the night in a train, kiss the boy, then come back the next day."

"Won't she leave her husband?" Mariette asked quietly.

"No. Because of money. Anyway he loves her, he loves the child. There's no way out."

"Who is she?" asked Mariette.

He did not respond. His brothers tried briefly to guess who the woman was but did not say anything, choosing not to intrude any further.

Augustin stood up and walked slowly to the closed door. Through the glass pane he watched the women in the next room. Alain's words had made him see his own life in a new light. He thought about his brother with that mixture of clear-eyed contempt, irritation, and the odd, almost primitive attachment that binds brothers together. Apart from one's family, one's own flesh and blood, there is no one else for whom one can feel that attachment, and even then, it is felt only rarely. "At least let him be happy. I'd prefer it if it were me, but if it can't be me, then let him . . ."

He came back to Alain and murmured, "It's completely idiotic, your plan . . . But what the hell? At least you should have the life you want!"

Albert raised his large, anxious face. "You won't regret it, will you? You won't blame us for anything?"

"No," Alain said dully.

"Well, what do you need?"

Alain looked up; he let out a faint sigh. "Do you mean it?"

"I'll do what you tell me to do," said Albert.

"I'll speak to Alix myself," said Augustin.

They sat down again, huddled together in the dark. Each of them was feeling emotional. "After all, that's the one thing we have among us, a bit of human warmth," they thought.

It was late. The night was passing. Mariette shivered as she thought about the rain outside and the bed that awaited her, in which she would sleep alone between cold sheets.

Silently, half-asleep, they waited for morning.

Alain threw himself onto the sofa. His long body looked suddenly weak and childlike. He whispered, "Call me if I'm needed."

He fell asleep almost at once. At first he sighed restlessly and moaned, but sleep had a soothing effect, taking away the sad, ironic expression that twisted his lips. From time to time first one and then another would wake, get up, and tiptoe to their mother's bedside, watching her still face as in a dream you might look into a dark pool where a man is struggling, but you can't reach out to help him.

At last, at dawn, she seemed to come back to life.

Augustin said softly, "I'm not sure, but she seems a little better."

At first she did not recognize him. She pushed him away, wanting to say, "The children . . . where are the children? Who's looking after the children?" Then she saw the night nurse coming.

"Are you feeling better? Do you feel àny stronger?"

The old woman's lips moved, but no sound came out of them. Yet she had heard, and after a moment she understood and remembered. Better? As life returned to her, she felt thirsty, feverish and hot, and became aware of the weight of the blankets and the light hurting her eyes. Painfully, she turned her face away.

The nurse touched her hand and smiled. "She's feeling better."

Albert came to join them. They waited for the doctor. Gradually their mother's face lost its look of repose: it twitched, and she muttered some indistinct words in a plaintive, querulous tone; her cheeks were still ash gray, but she was breathing more easily, and the dreadful whistling noise that had echoed through the room all night had stopped at last.

Augustin laid his cool hands on her forehead. She found his touch gentle and soothing. As he lifted the strands of hair that had fallen over her eyes, he said in a low voice, "Well, Mama darling . . . are you feeling better?"

Her lips smiled at him, but her eyes looked troubled and anxious, full of shadows. She managed to murmur, "Yes."

Augustin turned toward Albert, who was standing absolutely still.

"Well, old man . . ."

He did not finish his sentence. The brothers looked at each other and did exactly the same thing: they slowly inhaled, as if swallowing a mouthful of cold water, then quickly turned away. It was over. The night was over. Their mother was getting better. For a moment they were filled with a heavenly peace.

But then straightaway they felt cold and exhausted. Augustin stretched and yawned nervously. In the gray light they looked with distaste at the dreary mess in the sickroom. The nurse went back to sleep. Each of them in turn touched their lips to the patient's forehead and left.

Augustin realized that he had not had any sleep and that he was hungry.

Sighing deeply, Albert said, "That's over, thank God, that's over! What a night!"

"You going home?"

"Yes. I'm dead. A bath, then bed."

"You lucky bastard!" Augustin said, making a faint effort to smile.

Alain seemed well rested. He had managed to sleep on the hard sofa without any sheets; although his face was pale, it was smooth and relaxed.

"He's younger than I am," thought Augustin. "And in love, the fool!"

"Mama should get some sleep now. We'll come back this afternoon."

They went downstairs together. Augustin was shaking with exhaustion. He waved at Alain and Albert as they went off, and got into a taxi. It was raining; a sharp wind blew in through the open window. He stopped at the Régence for a black coffee and was then driven to his office. He telephoned home: Claire had come back but was still asleep. Gradually he was overtaken by a deep sense of sadness. He thought about his mother, muttering vehemently, "Thank God, thank God." But his heart was heavy. "Who dares admit that even the most devoted love contains a small amount of boredom and irritation?" he thought. At this time of physical exhaustion and mental upset, what did his mother's recovery mean to him unless it was to reveal how vulnerable he was and how fragile and upset this made him feel? "All in all, what is there to be happy about? Life's a fine thing . . . But what has she got to look forward to? All this business of Alain's that she'll have to cope with . . . Oh! I suppose she's happy enough in the way old people can be, happy to know that we're in good health and believing we're happy. Because she does think we're happy."

He was struck by a thought. "She can't carry on like this . . . At her age she won't recover fully from such a serious illness. She'll be weak. She can't go on living alone with Josephine. So the best thing would be for Mariette to go and live with her. I should think this would be the cheapest, the most sensible, and the pleasantest thing for both of them. Yes, that would be best," he said to himself, with a feeling of relief. He made a mental note: "I'll talk to them about it this evening." Yes, arrange it all for the best, so that everything worked out well and they were all happy, then forget about anything to do with family for as long as possible.

At lunchtime he went home. Claire was sitting in their bedroom doing her hair. She held out a cheek to him, which he touched with his lips.

She asked gently, "Is she really better? It's hard to believe . . . I'm so happy, my darling!"

"When did you all leave this morning?" he asked.

"It must have been about four o'clock. I could see, through the door, that Alain was asleep on the sofa, and you looked as if you were sleeping as well. I didn't want to disturb you. When are you going back to Mother's?"

"Immediately after lunch."

They ate quickly and in almost complete silence. Augustin thought, "Let's not spoil this fragile truce." Alain's departure was going to cause such havoc and lead to so many quarrels! All that would have to be said, all that would have to be left unsaid . . . How peculiar and cowardly it was, the desperate need to hold on to this fragile marital peace above all else! How much one has to sacrifice in order to be spared a woman's reproaches, in order not to see her tears! "I've never asked for much from life," he thought, with uncharacteristic self-pity. "Or, rather, I asked the same as everyone does, but as I didn't get anything, or only very little,

I've become resigned to it. That fat idiot Albert has his money, Alain has his romance, and me, what have I got?"

Abruptly he said aloud, "If Alain left, what would Alix do?"

They exchanged that look of complete and silent understanding, which often, in a married couple, is the only remaining evidence of their love.

"He won't do that," she murmured. "You won't allow it, will you?"

He shrugged.

"How can I stop him? Supposing he talks to Albert?"

"Albert! You know your brother . . . He'll promise anything in a weak moment, then the next day his English or Australian shares will drop by three points and everything will fall on you again! Remember Mariette's divorce, the court case, all the trouble you had? Your brothers have always been ready to make a sacrifice out of you."

"She's right," thought Augustin.

He said nothing more and left. He went back to his mother's, where he stayed for about an hour. The doctor had visited; she seemed to be out of danger, but it would be a long convalescence.

Alain arrived in his turn after the bank closed. Like his brothers he began by talking in an animated, warm tone before relapsing into silence. The old woman was complaining, "I don't like this doctor. He spent two seconds listening to my heart, then went away. I had a thousand questions to ask. My leg is swollen. Who found him?"

"I don't know. Augustin . . ."

"Ah! So it was his wife? Probably his wife."

Alain replied absentmindedly. He looked at his mother and thought about the woman whom he was about to go and meet, the wife he was about to abandon, the child . . . That very morning he had given a formal promise that he would leave, that he would pay for his share in the purchase of the plantation. What he had not dared to tell his brothers was that the plantation was owned by his mistress's husband. My God, how vile it all was! But what could he do? It had gone on for eight years. The husband liked him, suspected nothing, trusted him. He adored the child. He was perfectly happy. The remorse, the suffering, even the jealousy— all these were his, the lover's.

"Aren't you going home?"

"No, Mama."

"Aren't you eating?"

"No, Mama."

"What's wrong, my child?"

"Nothing. I'm not hungry, that's all. And I'm waiting for Augustin and Albert. They should be here at eight."

"But Josephine can make you something to eat!"

"No, really, Mama!"

"What did you say? I can't hear anything; I don't

understand. You mustn't neglect your health; you've always been delicate."

He let her talk, barely listening; he was unable to focus on her. "How cruel we all are, deep down," he thought despairingly. He bent down to kiss her cheek. Agitatedly she said again, "Please. Just to make me happy. Eat. Go and eat."

What else could she say? A mother's words, once a sign of love and wisdom, were now useless and ineffectual: "Eat, sleep, don't cry," was all she could say.

Alain did not say anything. He took out a cigarette, put it to his lips, then remembered that you shouldn't smoke in a sickroom and let his hand fall. He waited. He watched the hands on the clock. He was waiting for his brothers. They had promised to help him. They had seemed to understand. "But that was last night," he thought sadly. A strange night, out of time, made unusual and solemn by the specter of death. Tonight, however, was like any other, like a thousand other evenings that had brought them and their wives together in this house with an elderly mother they loved, a mother who was now reasonably well, who would get better. "I trust them," he thought anxiously. "Yet maybe I've given my trust too quickly and easily?"

The purchase of the plantation had been concluded that very morning by his mistress's husband, who, relying on his assurances, had committed him to his share of a hundred thousand francs, a fortune . . .

If his brothers refused to help him, he would be the man's ruin. And what about her, the woman he loved? His brothers did not know that she, too, was leaving that very night. "I'm leaving, I'm leaving," he repeated to himself, like an incantation. "Whether or not they keep their promise, I'm leaving with her and I'm never coming back. I'll never see my wife again. I just can't carry on any longer. I'll follow Elizabeth as far as Marseille. I'll see the child once more. I'll spend another hour with her before the ship goes. Then I'll wait till she's gone; I'll wait till the evening. I'll stay until her warmth and her perfume have faded from the room. I'll wait until the evening for a miracle to happen. Then . . ."

He closed his eyes. The rest was easy: a bullet or, even better, pills dissolved in a glass of water. Then he could enjoy a peaceful, dreamless sleep before dying. It had been such a long time since he had slept peacefully. Asleep or awake, he always had a picture in his mind of both of them, Alix and the other. If only he could sleep forever, sweetly and deeply . . .

He started, and the ashtray fell to the floor. He looked around him, shaking. His mother! How could he leave her . . . ? But it was just one more knot to unravel. There were so many of them, each so tightly fastened around his heart.

He heard his brothers' voices outside the door and stood up.

They came in, Albert first, Augustin and Claire behind him. They kissed their mother, then Claire said, "We mustn't make Mama tired."

As on the evening before, they left Claire alone in the parlor with a book, and the three men and Mariette settled down in the dining room, huddled together behind the carefully shut glass-paneled door.

"Hasn't Sabine come?" Mariette asked.

"No. She's tired. She's sleeping."

Augustin sighed. "Well, what are we going to do? We've got to make a decision. Mama doesn't want to keep the nurse."

"That's madness!" said Mariette, looking anxiously at them as she realized that they expected her to step in.

"You know what Mama's like. She's given me three days to sort something out. Anyway, she's useless, that nurse," Augustin muttered irritably. "Who found her?"

"I did," said Albert.

"There are other nurses in Paris," said Alain.

He was standing by the window, hidden by the folds of the curtains. He was watching the rain falling.

"That's not the point. I'll say it once more—you know what Mama's like. Once she's better she'll send the nurse away, whoever it is. She can't live here alone with a housekeeper who sleeps on the top floor. Mama's old. She's fragile. She should have had one of us living with her a long time ago; suppose she has a sudden, more serious illness, some kind of attack, I don't know what. Or a simple cold that turns worse during the summer while we're away. She can't live alone."

"That's what I think, too," Alain said. He looked tenderly at his mother's face, hardly visible in the shadows, only her white hair lit by the lamplight.

"That's what you think, is it?" muttered Augustin. He thought, "You don't care. You're off . . ." He shrugged his shoulders. "It's obviously the best thing to do, but how do we organize it? I wonder if you, Mariette?"

"No," Mariette said in a low voice. She looked at each of her brothers in turn. "I can't. I love Mama with all my heart, but I can't live with her. I mean it. I wouldn't know how to look after her, nor . . . and anyway, I've got my life, just as you have yours. I don't have much that's mine, just two rooms where I can be on my own."

"On your own?" Albert interrupted.

She did not reply. At last she said quietly, "Albert, it seems to me that you could easily look after Mama. You're well-off. Your house has more space than you need."

"Me?" Albert asked bitterly.

Of course he would happily have his mother, but why was it always him? After all, Augustin wasn't exactly penniless; he earned a good salary. His wife was better dressed than Sabine. He could have suggested looking after their mother. But there was no danger of that! It was always him, thought Albert, and then nothing he did was any good. They didn't even like the nurse, just because he'd chosen her. His brothers were so . . . discouraging.

Mariette was crying.

"Oh, come on," Augustin said irritably, "don't cry. There's nothing worse than a woman's tears. It's so . . . feeble."

Almost in a whisper, Mariette said, "Maybe when Alain's gone, Alix and the little ones could come and live here?"

"No," said Alain.

"Why not?"

"Mama and Alix don't like each other."

"How can one not like Mama?" asked Mariette.

"I'm telling you, they'd be unhappy. It would be impossible. I'm thinking of both of them."

"How very honorable!" snorted Albert.

"Listen," Alain went on quietly, "you've got to think about me now. I need to know if what you said yesterday, what you promised yesterday . . ."

Augustin sighed. "Just wait a moment, my dear boy. We must finish deciding about Mama. It's just as important, isn't it?"

"It's getting late, very late," said Alain in a low, strange voice. "I want to go tonight."

They looked at him in amazement.

"Are you mad, Alain?"

He did not answer but pressed his face against the windowpane.

"But that's impossible!" Augustin said gently.

"You're . . . you can't be serious. Leaving like this, forever, and . . . and your wife? Mama?"

"Yes. My wife. My mother. I know exactly what
you're going to say. But there's someone else who's waiting for me, who's getting desperate. I have to go today,
this very evening," he repeated dully. "You promised
you'd help me."

"Listen," said Augustin wearily, "let's be quite clear
about what each of us can do for you. I can give your
wife a thousand francs a month. And let me tell you,
that's a huge amount for me. I don't need to remind you
that both Mama and Mariette are supported almost
entirely by us. I can't leave my wife with nothing. It will
be up to Albert to sort out the rest."

"I was waiting for that," said Albert. "Why is it me,
always and only me? Look here, it's simply not fair! You
keep telling me I'm rich and that you're . . . But the
money's not mine! It belongs to my children. My savings
are their security. I've got a daughter, you know! I need
a dowry for her to safeguard her future. I love you all—
I love Alain, I love Mama—but the children must come
first. It's my duty. It's up to Alain if he doesn't want to
acknowledge his! The truth is, I've always been sacri-
ficed for you two. You laugh at me; you think I'm
clumsy, stupid, unintelligent, but you certainly know
how to make use of me. When Father died, didn't I give
up my share of the inheritance to Mariette?"

"I did, too," said Augustin. "It appears that the ties of
flesh and blood cost rather a lot in the Demestre family."

"It's not just my wife," said Alain. "I've bought my share of the plantation by borrowing money from . . . a friend, and now I owe him a hundred thousand francs. You simply have to advance the money against any guarantees you care to ask of me."

Albert shouted, "A hundred thousand francs! Are you out of your mind? And you want it tonight, at once? You're a . . . well, you're a lunatic!"

"You promised!"

"I promised, and I'm ready to keep my promise, to give your wife and daughters a certain amount every month, on condition that it's on absolutely equal terms with Augustin: it's a matter of pride and of principle. As far as the rest goes, I can't do anything about it now. You seem to forget that it's not just me, there's my wife. The money is my wife's. I have to talk to her, get her agreement, work out how to give the money to you without depriving her. She has some shares we can't sell without taking a hit, just for you, just to be kind to you. If you don't believe me, go and find Sabine and . . ."

"I'm not going to go and beg Sabine for her money! It's you I'm talking to, my brother, not an outsider!"

"Don't shout. Are you crazy?" Albert said angrily.

Augustin held up his hands to silence them.

"Alain, don't forget that we are responsible for Mariette and our mother. What we will be giving you, what we will guarantee your wife, will cut brutally into their share, which is already modest. Alain? Are you listening? Don't you care about that either? Are you happy to wreck everything, abandon everything, for a whim?"

"It's my life I'm fighting for," said Alain obstinately.

"Don't be so melodramatic. You've still got the mentality of a child of twenty. You're not twenty any longer. There comes a time when you have to accept that your life has been a failure, a time when actions become irrevocable. So you're unhappy with Alix? What about me? Do you think I'm happy? But I don't say anything. I don't complain. I put up with my life. I am responsible for it. You should do the same . . . Do as I do."

"I swear to you," said Albert, "as God is my witness, I would give everything I possess to save you from death or poverty or dishonor, but you're asking us to deprive ourselves in order to make you unhappy, as well as your wife, your poor children, your mother . . ."

"We're prepared to help you," said Augustin quietly, "but within the limits of reason and decency. For there's something else you appear to have forgotten: my wife and Alix are sisters. I can't openly take your side. Only time and patience can unravel a situation as upsetting as this one."

"Now I understand," murmured Alain with a painful feeling of humiliation.

He had cried in front of his brothers. He had implored them for help. He had believed in them, implicitly, as in the old days. But it had all been in vain. How quickly they had rallied! How grimly they defended what was theirs! His loneliness was more bitter, more stifling than ever; and there was no remedy for his failings . . .

"It's late," he said again. "If you agree, say so. If you refuse, say so. But say it at once, at once. I can't wait."

"We're not refusing. But we can't do more."

"Fine," said Alain.

He got up and moved toward the door. Augustin stood in his way.

"Where are you going?"

"I'm going home. Where do you expect me to go?"

"Oh, I see! Well, good night," Augustin said in a tired, irritable tone. "You're lucky, being able to go to bed. I'm the one who's got to wait until the doctor comes. Aren't you going to say good night to Mother?"

"She's asleep," said Alain in a hoarse voice. "Good night!"

He left. Their mother, meanwhile, was awake and had been listening to the muffled sound of their quarrel. She heard Alain's footsteps fading away, then Augustin and Albert coming nearer. They entered her room on tiptoe.

"Good night, Mama. Do you have everything you need?"

"What's wrong, children? What were you talking about? What did Alain want?"

"Nothing, Mama, nothing at all! There's nothing to worry about; don't upset yourself."

"Are you angry, Albert? Are you, Augustin?"

"Angry? Of course not! Try to sleep, go back to sleep. We're waiting for the doctor."

The doctor arrived and reassured them. Their mother was better; she was going to recover. Plump Josephine came in when they had all gone.

"Madame is better tonight? Madame won't be worried anymore?"

She did not reply. She shut her eyes and listened to the silence in the flat, to the slow footsteps of the nurse as she prepared her black coffee for the night ahead, the long, lonely night. She was no longer worried about being ill. She knew that now she had recovered.

Fraternité

[BROTHERHOOD]

HE WENT BRIEFLY INTO THE DESERTED FIRST-CLASS waiting room; the stoves were lit, but he could feel a cold draft coming up through the thin floorboards. He went back outside. The station was very small, surrounded by bare fields. It was an icy October day: a faint pink glow was fast disappearing from the sky, for summer time had ended the day before and the clocks had gone back. He walked up to a bench under the gabled roof, hesitated, then sat down. He wished now he had listened to Florent, his driver, and spent the night in town. The hotel hadn't been that dirty . . . Now he had to wait on the empty platform, and then crawl along until evening in some horrible local train . . . He wouldn't get to the Sestres' until after eight o'clock. The car had smashed into a pylon and was unusable. He shouldn't be driving anymore; he was worn out, and his reflexes were slow. It was a miracle he'd gotten away without being hurt. He hadn't had time to see the danger, and he could have died. Afterward he had pulled himself together enough to conceal his fear from Florent and had managed not to display any emotion. At least, he hoped so! Now he was shivering . . . perhaps from the cold. He dreaded the open air and the wind.

He was a thin, frail, hunched man with silver hair; his narrow face had a yellowish tinge; his dry skin looked starved of nourishment; his nose was excessively long and pointed; his lips, also dry, seemed parched by a thousand-year-old thirst, an affliction passed on from one generation to the next. "My nose, my mouth, the only specifically Jewish traits I've kept." He gently cupped his hands over his thin, almost translucent ears, which were quivering like a cat's; they were particularly sensitive to the cold. He tightly fastened the collar of his coat, made from the best English wool, dark, thick, and soft. Yet he didn't move. This deserted station platform, its lights almost invisible against the bright evening dusk, this solitude and sadness held an inexpressible charm for him. He was a man who took a deep and per-verse pleasure in melancholy, in regrets and bitterness, too clearheaded—*self-conscious,* he said—to believe in happiness.

He looked impatiently at the time. Not even five o'clock . . . He felt for the cigarette case in his chest pocket but immediately let his hand drop. He smoked too much; he had palpitations, insomnia. He sighed. He was rarely ill, but his heightened senses, acutely conscious of any pain, were alert to the slightest twinge, to every movement his body made, to his blood's ebb and flow; rarely ill, but he had a weak throat and a delicate liver; his heart was tired and his circulation bad. Why? He had always been sober, prudent, and moderate in all things. Ah! So prudent, even when he was young, even at the time of his blind, unforgettable folly . . . He didn't miss his youth. It had been uneventful. At the time he had felt only the natural sorrows inherent in the human condition: his parents' death, disappointments in love or work, nothing comparable to the pain caused by the death of his wife ten years before. He knew his family was surprised that his grief had lasted for so long. In fact, he had married Blanche without love and their union had been placid and lukewarm, but he was the kind of man who was faithful. A home, with its warmth and lamplight, that feeling of stability and peace in and around him: that's what he had sought, that's what he had loved, that's what he had lost when he lost Blanche. For him there would never be another woman. He was not a man who found love easily: he was too reserved, too touchy, too shy. "A coward," he thought. He lived as if everything were conspiring to rob him of life and happiness. In the depths of his heart he felt contrite and humiliated; he was constantly anxious, timid as a rabbit . . . And then, an hour ago, on the road, another minute would have meant the end of all his worries. "I always said that car was no good. And it was a heavy lunch. I was sleepy, had no energy; my reactions were slow." What, exactly, had he eaten? Some pheasant, a mushroom omelette . . . what else? A bit of brie . . . "It was too heavy for me. Eggs don't agree with me. Ah! This sedentary existence, at my age! I'm fifty years old. From one end of the year to the next I get barely a month of fresh air—the rest of the time it's the bank, home, or the club."

Once again he thought that, as soon as he could, he would stop working and be able to live more in the country. Gardening, golf . . . Golf? He imagined feeling the wind stinging his face on a day like today, on a golf course . . . Of course he'd hate it! Of course he knew equally well that he hated country walks, sports, riding, cars, and hunting . . . He was happy only at home, alone or with his children, safe under his own roof, safe from human beings. He didn't like people. He didn't like society. Yet he had always been welcomed everywhere and greeted with friendship and goodwill. In his younger days, some charming women had loved him. Why? Why? It always seemed to him that he hadn't shown enough affection, enough tenderness. How he had made Blanche suffer at the beginning of their marriage, asking her, "Are you happy? Not just in your heart but in your whole being? Do I make you happy?

Completely? Uniquely?" His own heart throbbed with frustration. The strangest thing was that everyone thought him so self-possessed, so calm. He sometimes used to think that only extraordinary good looks, fame, or genius could have made him happy, quenched his thirst for love. But he had no exceptional gifts. Nevertheless he was rich, comfortably settled in life, happy. Happy? How could anyone be happy without absolute peace of mind? And who could have peace of mind these days? The world was so unstable. Tomorrow might bring disaster, ruin, or poverty. He had never been poor. His father had been comfortably off, and he himself was rich. He had never known need or dread of what the next day would bring. Yet he had always had this fear and anguish inside him, always, always, taking the strangest and most grotesque forms . . . He would wake in the middle of the night, shaking, fearing that something was going to happen, had happened, that everything would be taken away from him, that his life was as unstable as scenery that was about to collapse and reveal he knew not what abyss.

When the last war began, he thought that was what he had been waiting for, had even expected. He had been a soldier, a conscientious one, carrying out his duties punctually and patiently, as he did everything. After a few months he had been sent back behind the lines; he had a weak heart. After the war, life was easy; his business affairs flourished. But there was still this anxiety, this latent worry that poisoned his life. Such anguish. His health wasn't good, for a start, and then there were the children. Ah! The children. His elder daughter was married. Was she happy? He had no idea. Nobody ever told him anything. And then there was the financial crisis and ever-increasing taxes, business getting more difficult and surely soon disastrous? Political uncertainty? . . . He was one of those people who, after every speech given by this or that politician or dictator, would visualize war not in the next month or the following year, but tomorrow, immediately. Yet in conversation he never allowed himself to give in to panic, as his rich bourgeois colleagues did. However, it was all very odd: even while they predicted the most appalling disasters, they somehow appeared to remain in good health, stayed cheerful, and did not either lose a wink of sleep or forgo a single meal. He was the only one who was eaten up inside and worried sick. He was the only one to believe that misfortune could strike him personally, whereas for the others misfortune was a ghost without substance, a shadow. They referred to it all the time but didn't believe in it. He was the only one who did! And everyone around him said, "Christian Rabinovitch? The steadiest and calmest of men."

Now and again the wind was icy. The thought of this hunting party at the Sestres' was hateful. But he had to go . . . He had to see his son, Jean-Claude, and the young Sestres girl with his own eyes. He sighed heavily. He was slow to admit what truly hurt him, what really pained him—it was one of his defining characteristics. As a result, when he was preoccupied by something he stayed awake for hours, his heart thumping, brooding about some unpleasant encounter or some tedious journey. He hated stations, ports, steamships . . . Better not to go anywhere, better to live and die in his own little corner of the world. Then, toward morning, it would be as if an invisible dam deep in his heart had finally given way, and a real wave of distress would unfold, rising to the surface, stifling him. Well . . . now . . . it was all about his son; it was always about him. How he loved him! He loved his two daughters: the elder married, a mother, the younger one still in short skirts. But this son of his, who had given him more sorrow than joy . . . so lightweight, anxious, and dissatisfied, a brilliant student, his studies soon abandoned. Frivolous? No. Dissatisfied, that was it . . . dissatisfied. And now he was in love. He wanted to marry the Count of Sestres's daughter. Ah! How difficult. His race . . . "He won't be happy, I know it. He won't be happy." In any case, would Sestres give his consent? Or insult Jean-Claude, and himself? His heart was bleeding already, but he would cut off his own two hands to prevent the marriage! They wouldn't be happy, Jean-Claude and this girl. They could never truly understand each other. They would be united in the flesh, but each would have a solitary and an unfulfilled heart. But what could he do? He was sure that no one would listen to him. His children already thought of him as someone from another age, an old fogy. He was one of those men who aged quickly. No—were born older than their years, already burdened with experience. Ah, why did Jean-Claude want to get married? Wasn't he happy? Not a moment's peace on this earth!

He looked at the time. He had been brooding so much, yet only twenty minutes had elapsed. Such a gloomy autumn, such a wretched evening . . . It was then that he noticed that a man was sitting next to him on the bench: a badly dressed, thin, ill-shaven man with dirty hands. He was looking after a child. The child kept going to look at the rails, fascinated by them. He was wearing an ugly, worn-out little coat and a cap, and he had big ears, curved like French horns, on both sides of his head; his wrists and red hands stuck out of sleeves that were far too short for him. He moved about restlessly. Then he turned toward the bench; his huge, liquid black eyes, which dominated his thin face, seemed to jump from one object to another. He took a step forward and, even though the track was completely empty, the man leapt anxiously from his seat, picked him up, and came back to sit down, holding him tightly against his chest. He saw that the eyes of his prosperously dressed neighbor were on the child, and he immediately gave him a nervous smile.

"Could I ask you the time?"

He spoke with a hoarse, foreign accent, which distorted his words.

Rabinovitch, without replying, pointed out the clock above their heads.

"Oh yes, I'm so sorry! Only twenty past five? My God, my God! The train isn't due until six thirty-eight. Forgive me . . . are you waiting for the Paris train, too?"

"No."

Christian stood up; at once the man started muttering, "Monsieur, if you would be good enough . . . it's the child. He's been ill, and the third-class waiting room isn't heated. Please, could you allow us to follow you into the first-class waiting room? If we go in with you, they'll let us wait there."

As he spoke, his features moved comically fast, so that he looked almost like a monkey. It wasn't just his lips that moved, but his hands as well, and the lines in his face, and his shoulders. His black eyes, feverishly bright like the child's, seemed to leap from one thing to another, turning away, searching anxiously for something they could not see, would never see.

"If you like," Rabinovitch said, with an effort.

"Oh, thank you, monsieur, thank you! Come, Iacha." He took the child's hand in one of his and with the other picked up Christian's bag, although Christian tried to stop him, embarrassed.

"Leave it, for goodness' sake."

"Let me, monsieur, what does it matter?"

They went into the first-class waiting room, where a central light with three gas lamps was now lit, shedding a pale, flickering glow. Christian sat down in one of the velvet chairs, and the man sat gingerly on the edge of a bench; he still had the child on his lap.

A melancholy little bell jingled interminably in the silence.

"Your son has been ill?" Christian finally asked absentmindedly.

"He's my grandson, monsieur," the man said, as he looked at the child. "My son's just left. I went with him to the boat. He's going to live in England, in Liverpool. He's been promised a job, but he's left the boy with me until he's sure."

He sighed deeply.

"He used to live in Germany. Then for four years I had him with me in Paris. Now we're separated once again . . ."

"England," said Christian with a smile, "is not that far away."

"For people like us, monsieur, whether it's England, Spain, or America, it's one and the same. You need money to travel; you need a passport, a visa, a work permit. It's a long separation."

He fell silent, but it was clear that talking soothed his distress. He started again at once. "You were asking if the child had been ill? Oh, he's sturdy, but he catches colds easily, and then he has a cough for months. But he's strong. All the Rabinovitches are strong."

Christian started.

"What's your name?"

"Rabinovitch, monsieur."

In spite of himself, Christian replied in a low voice, "My name's the same as yours . . ."

"Ah! *Jid?*" the man said slowly. He said a few more words in Yiddish. Christian had recovered himself and murmured curtly, "I don't understand."

The man gently shrugged his shoulders, with an inimitable expression of disbelief and mockery, mixed with affection and even some tenderness, as if he were thinking, "If he wants to show off, he can please himself . . . but to be called Rabinovitch and not understand Yiddish!"

"A Jew?" he repeated in French. "Left a long time ago?"

"Left?"

"Well, yes! From Russia? Crimea? The Ukraine?"

"I was born here."

"Ah, so it was your father?"

"My father was French."

"So it was before your father. All the Rabinovitches come from over there."

"Possibly," Christian said coldly.

The short-lived emotion he had experienced on hearing his name spoken by this man had now evaporated.

He felt awkward. What did he have in common with this poor Jew?

"Do you know England, monsieur? Yes, of course you do. And Liverpool, this city where my children are going to live?"

"I've passed through it."

"Is the climate good?"

"Certainly."

The man let out a long, inflected sigh, ending it with a plaintive *oy-oy-oy*. He gripped the child more tightly between his knees.

Christian looked at him more closely. How old was he? Between forty and sixty, that's all one could say! Probably no more than fifty, like him. His narrow chest seemed compressed, crushed by a heavy and invisible burden that weighed on his shoulders, dragging them forward. Occasionally, if there was an unexpected noise, he shrank back against the bench; yet, frail and thin though he was, he seemed to possess an unquenchable spark. He was like a candle alight in the wind, barely protected by the glass of a lantern. The flame beats against the glass, the light flickers, fades, almost goes out, but then the wind dies down, and it shines again, humble but tenacious.

"I worry so much," the man said quietly. "You spend your life worrying. I had seven children but five died. They seemed sturdy at birth, but they had weak chests. I've brought up two. Two boys. I loved them as much as

my own two eyes. Do you have children, monsieur?
Yes? Ah! You see, I look at you and I can't help compar-
ing myself to you. It's a consolation, in some ways.
You're rich, you must be a successful businessman, but if
you have children you'll understand me! We give them
everything and they're never happy. That's how Jews
are. My younger son . . . it started when he was fifteen:
"Papa, I don't want to be a tailor . . . Papa, I want to be a
student." You can imagine how easy that was in Russia
at the time! "Papa, I want to leave home"—"Now what
do you want, you miserable child?"—"Papa, I want to
go to Palestine. That's the only country where a Jew can
live in dignity. That's the Jewish homeland." Well, I said
to him, 'I respect you, Solomon, you've studied, you're
better educated than your father. Go, but here you could
have a decent job, a gentleman's occupation; you could
be a dentist or a businessman one day. Over there you'll
be clearing land like a peasant. As for Palestine,' I said to
him, 'the day you can catch all the herrings in the sea
and put them back in their mothers' bellies will be the
day Palestine can be called the Jewish homeland. Until
then . . . but go, go . . . if you think that will make you
happy.' So finally he left. He got married. 'Papa, send
money for the wedding . . . Papa, send money for the
baby . . . Papa, send money for the doctors, the debts,
the rent.' One day, he started to cough up blood. The
work was too hard. Then he died. Now I'm left with the
elder, the father of this one. But as soon as he was grown

up, he left me, too. He went to Constantinople, then to Germany. He had begun to earn a living as a photographer.

"Then along comes Hitler! I'd left Russia because at the time of the revolution—that's the luck of the Jew!—for the first time in my life I made a bit of money. I was scared, so I left. Life is worth more than riches alone. I've lived in Paris for fifteen years. That'll last as long as it lasts . . . And now there's my son in England! Where does God not cast the Jew? Lord, if only we could have a quiet life! But never, never can we settle! No sooner have we achieved, by the sweat of our brows, a bit of stale bread, four walls, and a roof over our heads, then there's a war, a revolution, a pogrom, or something else, and it's good-bye! 'Pack your bags, clear off. Go and live in another town, in another country. Learn another language—that's no problem at your age, is it?' No, but you just get so tired. Sometimes I say to myself, 'You'll get some rest when you die. Until then, carry on with your dog's life! You can rest later.' Well, God is the master!"

"What is your occupation?"

"My occupation? I do a bit of everything, of course. For now, I'm working in the hat trade. As long as I have a work permit, you see. When they take it away from me, I'll start selling again. Sell this, sell that, wholesale furs, automatic cameras, whatever turns up. I stay alive because I sell at a tiny profit. But to have had the luck to be born here! Just by looking at you, I can see how rich it's possible to become. And probably your grandfather came from Odessa, or Berdichev, like me. He would have been a poor man . . . Those who were rich or happy didn't leave, you can be sure of that! Yes, he was poor. And you . . . maybe this one, one day . . ."

He looked tenderly at the child, who was listening without saying a word, his face twitching with nervous spasms, his eyes glittering.

Ill at ease, Christian said, "I think I can hear my train."

The man immediately stood up. "Yes, monsieur. Allow me to help you. Don't call a porter. What's the point! No, really, monsieur, it's nothing! Come, Iacha, don't run off! He's like quicksilver, that child! We have to cross the tracks."

The train did not arrive for another ten minutes. Christian walked silently along the platform, the man following behind, carrying his suitcase. They did not speak but, in spite of themselves, Christian and the Jew could not help looking at each other as they walked beneath the station lamps, and Christian, with a strange, painful feeling, thought that this was how they understood each other best. Yes, like this . . . with no words, but by their expression, the movement of their shoulders, or the nervous twist of their lips. At last they heard the sound of the approaching train.

"You just get in, monsieur. Don't worry about the

case. I'll pass it to you through the window," said the Jew as he lifted the English gun in its deerskin sheath.

Christian slipped a twenty-franc coin into the man's hand. He looked embarrassed and quickly put it into his pocket, then waved and grabbed the child's hand; the train left. Christian at once turned away and went into the empty compartment; with a sigh he threw his things into the luggage rack and sat down. It was completely dark outside. The small ceiling lamp shed hardly any light; it was impossible for him to read. The train was now speeding through the bleak countryside; the sky was cold, almost wintry. It would be nearly eight o'clock when he got to the Sestres.' He thought of the old Jew, standing on that icy station platform, holding the child's hand. What a wretched creature! Was it possible that he was of the same flesh and blood as that man? Once more he thought, "What do we have in common? There is no more resemblance between that Jew and me than there is between Sestres and the lackeys who serve him! The contrast is impossible, grotesque! There's an abyss, a gulf between us! He touched me because he was quaint, a relic of a bygone age. Yes, that's how, that's why he affected me, because he's so far removed from me, so very far . . . There's nothing to connect us, nothing."

As if trying to convince an invisible companion, he repeated in a low murmur, "Nothing, there's nothing. Is there?"

Now he felt outraged and resentful. There was certainly no common ground between him and that . . . that other Rabinovitch (in spite of himself, he made an irritable gesture).

"By education and by culture I'm closer to a man like Sestres; in my habits, my tastes, my way of life, I'm much further away from that Jew than I am from an oriental peddler. Three, or even four, generations have elapsed. I'm a different man, not just spiritually, but physically as well. My nose and mouth don't matter, they are nothing. Only the soul matters!"

He did not realize it but, carried away by his thoughts, he was swaying forward and backward on the seat in a slow, strange rhythm, in time with the motion of the train; and so it was that, in moments of fatigue or stress, his body found itself repeating the rocking movement that had soothed earlier generations of rabbis bent over the holy book, money changers over their gold coins, and tailors over their workbenches.

He looked up and caught sight of himself in the mirror. He sighed and gently put his hand to his forehead. Then it came to him in a flash: "That's what I'm suffering from . . . that's what's making me pay with my body and my spirit. Centuries of misery, sickness, and oppression . . . millions of poor, feeble, tired bones have gone toward creating mine."

He suddenly remembered one or two friends who had died, nobody quite knew why, after retiring to a life in the country and playing golf; they felt uncomfortable being rich and idle. The familiar yeast of worries started fermenting, poisoning his blood. Yes, for the moment, at any rate, he was free from exile, poverty, and need, but their indelible mark remained. No, no! It was humiliating, impossible . . . He was a rich French bourgeois, pure and simple! And what about his children? Ah! His children . . . "They'll be happier than I've been," he thought, with deep and passionate hope. "They'll be happy!"

As he listened to the train rumbling through the sleeping countryside he gradually dozed off. Then, at last, he was there.

The train pulled into the little station at Texin, the stop for the Sestres' château. He had asked his driver to send a telegram to tell them when he was arriving. Three of his friends were there: Louis Geoffroy, Robert de Sestres, and Jean Sicard. They gathered around him.

"You poor man! How appalling! You could have been killed!"

He walked among them, smilingly answering their questions; they all spoke the same language, they dressed in the same way, they had the same habits and the same tastes. As they approached the car together, he began to feel happier and more confident. The painful impression left by his meeting with the Jew began to fade. Only his body, shivering with cold in spite of his warm English clothes, and his oversensitive nerves acknowledged their ancient inheritance.

Robert de Sestres sighed deeply. "What fine weather!"

"Isn't it?" said Christian Rabinovitch. "Isn't it? A bit cold, but so bracing . . ."

And surreptitiously he covered his icy ears with his hands and got into the car.

La femme de don Juan

[DON JUAN'S WIFE]

August 2, 1938

Mademoiselle,

I hope that Mademoiselle will forgive her old servant for addressing her in this way. I know that she's married, and I saw in *Le Figaro* the happy news of the birth of little Jean-Marie and his sister. I respectfully congratulate Mademoiselle. The babies must be two and four years old now. I'm sure they are very sweet! It's the nicest age, when children belong entirely to their mothers.

To me, however, she will always be Mademoiselle Monique, as I haven't seen her since she was twelve, when I was in service with her parents. I apologize again for taking this liberty.

Mademoiselle, I have hesitated for a long time before deciding to write this letter. The things I have to say are so serious and so important to the Family that it would certainly be better to say them in person. But Mademoiselle lives in Strasbourg and has two small children. It's a difficult time for everyone, and I don't think she would leave Strasbourg for Paris in order to go and see an old servant she's probably forgotten, even if I do have things of the utmost seriousness to tell her about her Parents. After all, the dead are well and truly dead, and one couldn't expect anyone to make such a long and expensive journey to listen to old stories that may not affect Mademoiselle anymore. She can rest assured that I don't blame her. Life is life, and everyone has their own to live.

As for coming to visit Mademoiselle, I cannot, as I am ill in the hospital. In a few days I am to have an operation on a nasty tumor, which I do not think I will survive. I was very upset about it at first. I'm fifty-two. I'd put some money aside and have a little house in my native village, Souprosse, in the Landes. I always thought I would work until I was fifty-five and then live quietly at home. You get tired of living in other people's houses in the end, especially when you're no longer young. But, as they say, Man proposes and God disposes, and that's so true.

I know that I have only a few days left, so I decided to put it all down in writing. Mademoiselle will do as she pleases—it's her Family business, nothing to do with me—but I'll have a clear conscience and no fears about what might happen after my Death, as I do at the moment with the worry about those letters I have.

In order to explain everything properly to Mademoiselle, I'm going to leave this letter and then come back to it and finish it gradually during the week. When you think about the past, you want to describe everything, but you can't avoid a choice. It's very difficult. But I have a week ahead of me: the operation is next Tuesday. They could have done it sooner but, as it's summer, there are not many patients; and as the insurance companies pay them by the day, they like to keep patients in longer, which is what they're doing. So Mademoiselle Monique will, I hope, be patient enough to read this letter right to the end.

August 3

Mademoiselle was so young when poor Monsieur died that I ask myself what she knows and what she doesn't.

I came to the Family when we still lived on the Avenue Hoche. Mademoiselle Monique was six, Monsieur Robert two, and Monsieur René was not yet walking. Monsieur was very handsome, so handsome that the pictures Mademoiselle certainly has can't give any idea. Since, after what happened, Mademoiselle and her Brothers were all brought up by Madame's

Family, I imagine she knows everything there is to know about Monsieur's behavior. The Countess, Mademoiselle's Grandmother, did not like her son-in-law. In some ways you can understand it. It's the natural jealousy of a Mother. Oh! Mademoiselle Monique, if God had given me children, I would have been jealous of their love, so fearful for their happiness, that I would have killed the man who betrayed my daughter! Mademoiselle, when I took up my place at Avenue Hoche, all the chambermaids stayed six or seven months, never longer. Can Mademoiselle understand why now she's married and knows a bit about life?

I was already thirty-four. I had had some education; I went to school until I was fourteen, thanks to my poor mother's sacrifices. I can never be grateful enough to her, even now, although I've forgotten so much. I wasn't like those poor girls who don't know anything. They believe everything they're told and think life is like in the films. If I'd looked at anyone, he would have had to have been from my world and not a Rich Man who can only give a poor girl kisses that are paid for later with bitter tears. I wasn't tempted. The truth is, I was always quite at ease with Monsieur, but it was impossible not to see how handsome and seductive he was, with his devil-may-care manner, his magnificent teeth, and the little mustache he had above his beautiful lips. He was generous and, Mademoiselle Monique,

generous Men are rare. He loved women, and it wasn't
just to have a fling or to boast about his exploits; it was
a grand passion, every time. He got bored quickly, but
at the beginning the flames burned intensely. He was
still very youthful. He was, in fact, very young: two
years younger than Madame.

Mademoiselle certainly knows that he and Madame
were first cousins, brought up together, and that all the
Money was on Madame's side of the family. Otherwise
he would never have married anyone, and certainly not
Madame, who, poor thing, was not at all pretty. I know
she was ill after the terrible event and, until her Death,
lived mostly in Switzerland. Mademoiselle probably
doesn't remember what her mother was like before?
She was no plainer than anyone else. She even had
beautiful eyes. But her body was clumsy, too tall and
too thin, and her arms and legs seemed to get in the
way. She walked with long strides in flat shoes, like a
man. She had no confidence, no grace. She was neither
stylish nor charming. The Countess reprimanded her,
even at her age, as if she were a little girl, telling her she
was ugly and awkward. She must have really
tormented Madame when she was young. The
Countess, who had been beautiful in her youth, was
annoyed that her daughter was so unlike her and
worried about what would become of her. The truth is,
Mademoiselle Monique, a woman has to be pretty to be
happy. Madame knew that she wasn't at all beautiful,

poor thing, and it made her despair. But as she was also very intelligent, she realized you have to have a Role in life, and that her Role could not be that of the pretty little wife. She was very serious-minded and very well educated, she played a lot of Music, and she was highly regarded, both in Society and also in the Family, which is always more critical than Society. People said, "She's a Saint," and that she put up with Monsieur's escapades like women used to in the old days, whereas now it's divorce straightaway, I'll go my way, you go yours, and never mind the children!

Madame behaved as though she did not see anything, and that was very sensible, people said, since she loved her Husband. Nobody doubted her love for him. All the women ran after Monsieur. When he abandoned them, they were even crazier about him. Does Mademoiselle understand what women are like? People said it was perfectly natural to adore a Husband as handsome and popular as he was. He was nice to her. He made her unhappy with his Affairs, of course, but he was always very polite and respectful: "Yes, as you wish, Nicole, you're right, Nicole." He never spoke in any other way to her, at least not in front of other people, and I often heard him say to Mademoiselle and her little brothers, "You must love your mama, my dears. She's the best mama in the world. You must obey her and please her in everything." His beautiful eyes sparkled as if he was laughing at what he was saying, but I think that was just the way he looked, he couldn't help it, and that really he spoke from the bottom of his heart. He respected his Wife very much. You couldn't say he was horrid to the children. But he didn't take much notice of them, although when they were ill, I saw how worried he was. He didn't know how to play with children, nor how to speak to them. A kiss, a lump of sugar dipped in his coffee when he ate at home, one couldn't ask more of him. Children bored him, to tell the truth. Say what you like, they're rare, Men who like children. For mothers it's their flesh and blood, but for them . . .

As for Madame, they said she lived only for the children and that later on they would worship her as a Saint. But she was as cold and stiff with the little ones as she was with everyone else. It wasn't her fault: she was shy and dreaded being laughed at. But one could say that you didn't have a very happy childhood. That's maybe why I loved Mademoiselle, who was as affectionate and sensible as a little woman.

August 5

Mademoiselle, I didn't write yesterday because I was very tired, but mainly because I am reaching a very painful time for Mademoiselle. I fear I may distress her by talking about it, yet I must, so that Mademoiselle can understand properly what happened. I ask for Forgiveness with all my heart if I hurt her.

It must have been just twelve years ago this autumn.

It started with an affair with Baroness Debeers. I saw in *Le Figaro* this summer that she lost a twenty-year-old son in a flying accident. I read the Society and Domestic Situations columns in *Le Figaro* so as not to lose track of people I knew when I was young. It's nice, in some ways, to follow people through life; but how short it is, Mademoiselle Monique! It's frightening to read about a young girl one knew as a kitchen maid looking for a position as a pastry cook, along with her daughter as chambermaid. Life goes past in the twinkling of an eye. Although you never think about it when you're young, and so much the better!

As for the Baroness, it's unbelievable she's lost a son who was already twenty years old. I can see her still! Now there was a woman who knew how to dress! I can remember one evening at home, the Baroness had come to dinner. I was helping the butler to serve cocktails, and I could see her clearly. People were talking about Monsieur and the Baroness, saying they'd been together since the previous spring. It had never lasted that long with Monsieur. So I had a good look at them. My goodness, that woman was beautiful! She was wearing a red dress that covered her modestly at the front, but showed her bare back. She had just returned from Biarritz and her skin was golden. The effect created by having a dress cut high at the front and décolleté at the back has since become quite common, but then it was the first time anyone had seen it in Society

and, Mademoiselle Monique, the eyes of those
Gentlemen . . . I feel as though I can see them still. Men
are animals, it has to be said.

Nobody believed that it would be serious for either
of them. In High Society—and I've seen a great deal of
it, Mademoiselle!—love affairs were more for public
display than showing real feelings. A bit of fun, some
pretty dresses and fine underwear, a few pinpricks to
one's pride and a bit of jealousy here and there, then
good-bye and on to another one. But it must really have
been love for Monsieur and his lady friend. After all,
love comes like a thief, grabs us by the heart, and we
don't even know its name. For Monsieur, who'd had so
many women, it seemed as though it was the first time.
Always cheerful and mocking, he had become all pale
and sad. As for her, she devoured him with her eyes.
We were starting to tell each other we could feel a
divorce on the way.

They must both have wanted a divorce, but the
Money on Madame's side held Monsieur back. And
maybe the children. I wouldn't want to make
Mademoiselle think badly of her poor Parents, nor
allow her to believe that she and her brothers were
forgotten in all these complications. I'll say it again,
Monsieur was definitely not a bad man. I'm sure the
thought of divorce scared him because of the children,
but more especially, it has to be said, because of the
money. It's not that Monsieur loved money. He was

much too well brought up for that. But since his marriage he had never been without it, and we are slaves to habit. Anyway, whether it was that or something else, even if it seems sad to Mademoiselle and makes her think bitter thoughts about her parents and her childhood, the fact is they are both dead. God has judged them, as He alone has the right to do since we should not judge anyone, especially not our Parents, who should be sacred to us; and now that Mademoiselle is a mother, she must believe the same thing.

Naturally, Mademoiselle Monique, in front of the servants people tried to hide things, but it's impossible. A snatch of conversation overheard as you go to make the beds, a tearstained handkerchief under a pillow, a trace of powder on a jacket, that's all you need. They think we're spying on them and that we're prying into their affairs . . . but I can assure Mademoiselle that we're not interested in our employers' business. Often things disgust us to the point where we would prefer not to see them, but if they are staring you in the face? Unless you're a machine, you can't help taking an interest in the people who give you your daily bread. That's why Mademoiselle need not worry. Everything I'm telling her, everything I have to say, is the truth, I swear before God.

August 6

Mademoiselle Monique, it was November 2nd twelve years ago, I'll never forget it. The weather was very bleak. Not exactly raining, more a sort of misty drizzle. I don't like weather like that; it's depressing and ever since that day I've not been able to stand it. We'd been in the country since September, at Madame's Parents', for the hunting, like every year. There were fires in every room. It was the end of the season. All the guests were leaving. We were due to go back to Paris a fortnight later. But the Baroness was, of course, still there.

It all started that morning. Monsieur and his Lady Friend were in the park, in a part of it where nobody ever went. As the house was sold after everything that happened, neither Mademoiselle nor her brothers probably remember it. All three children had chicken pox and were sleeping in a separate part of the house, which in some ways was a blessing, as they didn't know straightaway what had happened. We could tell them a little bit at a time, very gently, since everyone tried to be as kind as possible toward those poor innocent little children. A Tragedy like that is sad when there are children.

So the undergardener told me he'd seen Monsieur and the Baroness walking together in a deserted part of the grounds. They were close together and talking quietly as they walked. It wasn't a lovers' conversation; they looked far too serious. They were almost certainly discussing divorce and money. The Baroness wasn't rich. With her, it was the opposite of the situation in our house—it was her Husband who had the Fortune. Nevertheless, she was ready to follow Monsieur, which makes one understand how madly she loved him. Of course, for a Woman in Society, she was making a huge sacrifice for him.

We have lunch. After the meal, Madame follows Monsieur and says (there was nobody left except for the butler clearing the table—I heard it all from him), "I need to talk to you, Henry."

"I don't have time," says Monsieur. "I'm sorry, Nicole."

"But it's very important," says Madame, detaining him.

Still with his eye on the doorway through which the Baroness and the other guests have just gone out, he then replies, "This evening, Nicole, without fail."

Madame insists. Monsieur says he'd ordered the car, that he's in a hurry, that he has an errand to run in Le Blanc, eighteen kilometers away.

"I'll come with you," says Madame.

Madame goes upstairs. Everyone can see she looks distraught. The butler then says that she must have seen the two of them together that morning, and that's what was tormenting her. As for me, I stay silent.

So Madame goes up to her room and rings for me to

get her coat. I bring her good vicuña coat. It was still raining, and there was very little light. I help her get dressed and she pulls on a little purple felt hat. I can see her still: she shook so much in front of her mirror she couldn't get her hat on.

She takes something out of the drawer of the dressing table and leaves. I have a sudden thought: I go and see if the revolver that was always kept in Monsieur's study is still there. It isn't! I feel as though my heart has stopped. I go down to the servants' hall. They are just about to sit down to eat. There are sixteen of us, including the servants the guests had brought. They tell me I am deathly pale. I don't say anything but force myself to eat. How I reproached myself afterward. The car had not yet left. Monsieur could have been warned but I didn't know what to do. If there had been servants from only our family there, I would have told them what I thought I'd seen and asked for advice, but the Baroness's chambermaid was there and four chauffeurs who were strangers. Family matters are sacred. That's part of maintaining the Family's honor, and you have to know when to hold your tongue. Anyway, whether I acted badly or stupidly, I meant well, as the good Lord knows when he reads our minds, especially when you are at the end of your days on earth, as I now am, alas.

So I pretend to eat. The chauffeur, Auguste, gets out the car, and Monsieur and Madame leave.

Everything that happened afterward, I got from the

chauffeur, Auguste. What a Drama! We discussed it over and over again. From the moment they left in the car, I was shaking. That is to say, I could feel disaster in the air. When you've spent time with many Families and in many Houses, each one with its stories, its sorrows, and its secrets, I can assure Mademoiselle Monique that you can sense if a household is happy or unhappy. I used to know a butler—he drank, that's probably why he was so sensitive—and if he went somewhere and felt an unhappy atmosphere, he thought, "No, I'm not staying here!" To my knowledge, he guessed correctly at least twice. Once it was a bankruptcy, the other time a robbery, both being most unpleasant for the servants.

August 7

I went up to see Mademoiselle, which proves how upset I felt. Perhaps Mademoiselle remembers? She was already twelve years old. I had no business in her room at that time of day; that wasn't my job, but my heart was so full of pity for the children that I wanted to see them, especially Mademoiselle Monique, whom I'd always liked better than her brothers. I prefer girls. They're much sweeter. Mademoiselle was in bed with a book, some cutting-out, and her knitting, like a little grown-up. She was working so well and so nimbly! I was the one who had taught her how to knit and

Mademoiselle was making a vest for my little niece; Mademoiselle Monique always had a kind heart.

I'd been with her for five minutes when we heard the car come back, then doors slamming, then nothing! I thought, "Blessed Virgin! It's happened!" Alas, I was right. It was all over.

According to Auguste, this is what happened: he had left the grounds and was speeding toward Le Blanc. He couldn't tell me anything about the beginning of their conversation. Suddenly their voices grew louder and Auguste heard Madame say, "I beg you, I beg you."

"No," answered Monsieur, and he started to laugh, said Auguste, but quietly to himself, as if something was amusing him. That laugh seemed to drive his wife mad. She screamed loudly and almost immediately Auguste heard the shot. He couldn't believe his ears. In fact, a revolver only makes a slight popping sound. He wondered what he'd heard, whether it might have been a burst tire, but in the mirror he saw Monsieur fall backward, blood pouring from his mouth. Poor Monsieur! He'd laughed for the last time.

By the time Auguste had stopped, opened the door, taken Monsieur in his arms, and laid him by the side of the road, he was no longer breathing. Then Auguste went back to Madame. She hadn't moved; she was still holding the revolver; she clung on to it and he had to tear it from her hands. She didn't say a word. Poor Auguste didn't know what to do. He waited a good five

minutes, hoping that a member of the Family might
come past, but nobody came and it was raining. As for
Monsieur, it was obvious he was dead. In the end,
Auguste gathered up the body again, put it in the car
next to Madame, and came back to the Château. He
said that during the whole journey Madame did not
look at Monsieur once. Going around a bend, the body
leaned forward like a live person and started sliding
onto the floor, but Madame made no move to pick him
up. When the car stopped in front of the steps,
Monsieur had half-fallen out of his seat, his head bent
toward the ground, and the trickle of blood that had
been oozing from his mouth was making everything
sticky. It made Auguste ill to see it, and still Madame
said nothing, looking straight ahead, her head held
high.

And that, Mademoiselle Monique, is what the whole
world knows and what the papers at the time said
about the terrible Tragedy which, you could say,
created three orphans, since their father was taken by
death and their mother would also be taken—by
prison, by the trial, and by everything else, and after
that her death, poor thing, at the age of thirty-eight.

Of course, the reply to everyone who asked, "What
will happen to her?" was: "She'll be acquitted. It was a
crime of passion; there's absolutely no reason to doubt
it'll be an acquittal, with their Money and their
Connections."

It is true, that if any murderer had an excuse, at first sight that one certainly did. Here was a woman who had been a perfect wife and a mother beyond reproach, with a husband who deceived her, who had put up with everything silently for the children's sake, who had suffered for thirteen years; then one day along comes another woman who, not content with taking her Husband's affections, wants to remove a father from his children . . . Ah! Mademoiselle Monique, poor little Mademoiselle Monique, never before had so many people talked about the three of you! Your pictures were in all the papers, along with one of Madame hugging you, and another of Madame in prison weeping for "her poor children," and then, finally, at the trial, her lawyer had shown, as clear as daylight, that Madame had gone mad at the thought of her Husband wanting to abandon the Family he no longer loved, and after putting up with so much, she couldn't tolerate the latest blow! He was a brilliant lawyer. The Family had spared no expense. I was told he had cost them a great deal, but he certainly earned his money. Everyone wept during the trial, even the women who had done their best to separate Madame from her husband were in tears, saying she was a Martyr.

Now that it's all coming back to me, I can remember lots of things I thought I'd forgotten. I can't stop myself from wanting Mademoiselle Monique to think of them, too. One should not let memories disappear just because they are sad. When you're old or ill like me and you can't work any longer, it's too sad thinking about tomorrow. Blessed Virgin, what would one do if there were nothing to remember? And here's a funny thing: the memories I thought were happy ones, like the games with my friends at school and the orange my poor mother always gave me on New Year's Day, are the ones that make me cry, and others that were so important—a boy who courted me and married another girl when I was twenty—just make me smile when I think of my grief at the time, as if there's any man in the world worth crying over. So what I'm writing may make Mademoiselle sad for now, but one day it will matter less. She must believe her old servant!

It was the week after the Tragedy. Mademoiselle had recovered from the chicken pox, but she was very tired, so she was sent to bed at seven o'clock and had supper brought to her on a tray. One evening, as I went past the children's room, I thought I heard someone crying. I opened the door quietly. Mademoiselle didn't see me come in. She was lying on her side, hunched up against the wall, like a poor, shivering little bird! She was crying and, oh, Mademoiselle, she was scared of making any noise. She was holding back her tears with all her might, but a child can't cry silently. You learn how to do that later.

I go in and say as gently as I could, "Why are you crying, Mademoiselle Monique?"

The children couldn't have known anything about what had happened. Everything had been hidden from them, even Monsieur's death. They weren't yet going out and so it didn't matter if they didn't have any black clothes. There was plenty of time for that. They were told that Monsieur and Madame were traveling, which was easy, as of course Madame was in prison and Monsieur's body had been taken back to Paris, where he had been buried two days earlier. I am absolutely certain that not a word could have reached the part of the house where the three children were living with their things and their toys and their nanny, who was very nice for an Englishwoman. However, that evening I realized you had guessed everything.

Mademoiselle wouldn't answer me and made a huge effort to stop crying, but in vain.

I go even nearer and gently ask, "Are you ill, Mademoiselle Monique? Would you like a nice cup of sweet lime tea?"

Mademoiselle gave me such a sad look as she shook her head.

So I ask again, "What's wrong, Mademoiselle Monique? Tell your old Clémence who loves you dearly."

But Mademoiselle, always so sweet and polite, said, "No, there's nothing wrong, really, my good Clémence."

So I tuck her in and stay for a while, so as not to

leave her alone. Mademoiselle watched me, but was much too proud to ask for anything. I say, "Would you like me to stay with you until Miss comes back up?" (She had gone to have her dinner.)

Mademoiselle looks at me without smiling, but her face lights up and, very quietly, she says, "Oh, yes please, you're so nice, you . . ."

So I hold her hand and stay like that, on a little chair next to the bed. I try to tell silly stories to make Mademoiselle Monique laugh. But she didn't feel like laughing, poor little thing! She says, "Tell me about what you did when you were little. Talk to me about your papa and mama."

I began to tell stories to cheer Mademoiselle up, but after a while I feel like crying myself. We had all been very tense since the Tragedy, and in any case no one ever shows any interest in the servants, or wonders if they're happy or unhappy, nor even where they come from, where they lived, or who their Parents were; it's as if you give up your past when you go into service.

Mademoiselle becomes calmer. I can hear Miss coming back up. I get up to leave. Just by the door I hear, "You'll never leave, will you, Clémence?"

Then I understand that Mademoiselle had guessed everything and the poor little thing was hanging on to what was left of her childhood.

"Of course I'll never leave."

I left two months later. It was four months before the

trial. Because of the children I didn't want to leave. But putting up with the Countess, who was now managing everything—and I thought it would be a lot worse when Madame came back—that was beyond me. The Countess actually wanted me to wait at table! Mademoiselle well knows that wasn't my job! I was senior chambermaid and seamstress. I was offered a position in the Rue du Bac, which meant I would have to move but would be nearer a friend who was a cook in the same part of Paris: we used to go out together every Sunday. It suited me as I didn't have to pay the cost of transport when I visited her. It was a good position. I accepted it; I stayed five years and was very happy there. Leaving Mademoiselle Monique broke my heart. But I did it.

The day of the trial came. I was in a terrible state, the reason for which Mademoiselle will soon understand. I was a witness, but with nothing much to say. They wanted to make me declare that Madame had lived only for her children. I realized that the lawyer wanted to impress that on the jury, so I said, "Madame was an excellent mother. Even though I am no longer in Madame's service, I hope that she will soon be returned to her poor children and to the household which needs her, and so I sorted out everything, her room and even the cupboards, before I left. Madame need not worry."

I knew that I was making a fool of myself. My God, how they laugh, people who don't understand, and luckily nobody did. Except for Madame. She understood immediately! She stood up and, pale as she was, went even paler, and collapsed with a loud cry. In some ways nothing could have been better for her than that cry and the long fainting fit that followed. It made an excellent impression on the jury. In the public gallery people were murmuring, "Poor woman. How she must have suffered."

I won't repeat what the lawyer said or any of the things Mademoiselle can read in the newspapers of the time, if she's interested. What they said about Monsieur! Women, Madame's friends, chambermaids, immoral women, the lot! No doubt there was a lot of truth in what they said, but a lot of lies as well, I shouldn't wonder. But the lawyer was right: Monsieur was dead and it made no odds to him, to say nothing of the fact that a man can have as many women as he likes—with no stain on his honor. Quite the opposite. The lawyer was right to think only about saving the woman who was left behind from disgrace and condemnation. Anyway, that's what he was being paid for. He had to do his job.

He did it conscientiously and she was acquitted, just as everyone thought she would be.

August 8

I'm hoping to finish my letter today, Mademoiselle, but what's left is the hardest to say.

A year before the Tragedy, I had begun to notice a
change in Madame. It was the way she dressed. There
was a spring in her step and there was a sense of hope
in her face and the way she spoke. It's quite true what
they say: What Woman wants, God wants. There was
no doubt that she wanted, as never before, to be pretty,
and she had almost become so. Before, she dressed
conventionally, austerely, as if, you might say, she was
afraid of being noticed. Suddenly there were lovely
dresses and pretty underwear. Another time, it was a
new hairstyle. I thought she wanted to get her husband
back. I did my best to help her. A good chambermaid
or lady-in-waiting can do a great deal, Mademoiselle,
for a Lady's appearance and sometimes I had made so
bold as to offer her advice. When I was young, I
worked for a Kept Woman and I knew about beauty
treatments and how to help her show off her
complexion and figure to best advantage. Madame had
perfect skin. But when I said, "Madame must listen to
me, Madame should do this or that, she's still young,"
she shook her head sadly.

"There's no point, dear Clémence!"

She was a very unhappy woman. It was in her
character not to be able to accept things as they were,
but her pride wouldn't allow her to try to change them.
It was the same with the children: she tried to console
herself with her little ones for not having the love of a
Man and, aware that they didn't console her enough,
she took it out on her innocent children. She never

found them beautiful enough, bonny enough, or well behaved enough to make up for all that she had lost.

Mademoiselle Monique, one day Madame had had an argument with Monsieur. He had left the drawing room and she stayed there alone. Then Monsieur's secretary, Monsieur Jean Pécaud, arrived. He went into the room. Mademoiselle can be quite sure that, whatever happened between the two of them that day, nobody said anything to me and I saw nothing; but, all the same, it's strange that, after going in there at three o'clock, he didn't come out until five.

After he'd gone, Madame rang and told me to tidy the room. I found Madame's handkerchief, soaked with tears, underneath the cushions on the armchair. She'd certainly been crying when Monsieur Pécaud arrived. What he did or said to console her, no one will ever know, for Death has claimed her, and Monsieur Pécaud won't brag about it now that he's married and rich, or so I'm told.

I would like to tell Mademoiselle that she mustn't believe from all this that it was her Mother who was to blame. Her loneliness was what pushed her toward Monsieur Pécaud. But her affections were misplaced.

I think that if Mademoiselle saw this Gentleman when she was little, she will remember that he was small and thin; he looked like a fox with his ginger hair and pointed ears; and his whole face was as scrawny, red, and alert as a fox's muzzle. Thanks to his Wife

Monsieur had many investments, and Monsieur Pécaud looked after everything. Looked after things rather too well, as Mademoiselle will see.

Now, as soon as Monsieur had turned his back, we had Monsieur Pécaud at the house. But even that didn't last long. Madame was out all the time, coming back cheerful and happy. No one knew anything, because it seemed beyond belief that a Lady like her, married to such a handsome man, a Don Juan, should prefer such a plain and insignificant fellow. Women would have had themselves chopped into little pieces for the sake of just one hour with a lover like Monsieur, and would have accepted every rebuff and thanked him yet again for an hour of love, whereas his wife . . . Say what you like, Mademoiselle, women are strange creatures.

I should also say that Madame was certainly not abandoned by Monsieur, as they said at the trial. Monsieur never forgot what a man owes his wife before God. That's just to say to Mademoiselle that he did have his good side.

But he was too handsome, too striking compared with Madame. People had eyes only for him and, as a result, nothing he did could be kept secret. At home, he was like the sun. People saw only him. People discussed his every movement, but nobody saw what was being plotted in the shadows. Witnesses stated that he was in the park with the Baroness on the morning of November 2nd. They thought they were quite alone, but a number of people were ready to report, or invent, what they had whispered to each other, their words of love, and the way they looked at each other; but nobody in the world knew what Madame was doing that morning, because nobody was interested.

On the morning of November 2nd Madame got up earlier than usual. She went to the window and stayed there for a long time watching, no doubt waiting to see Monsieur leave. She dressed to go out. She said, "I'm going out, Clémence. I'll be back at eleven. I've got a headache."

Everyone saw her go and nobody found it odd that, in the awful weather I've described, Madame should have calmly gone off for a walk, whereas everyone had smiled to see Monsieur pacing up and down on the terrace, in spite of the rain, and suddenly rushing off when he saw his Lady Friend's blue coat under the trees. It was always like that. Monsieur would say that he wouldn't be in for dinner and everyone thought, "He's having a good time." Madame would go out at two o'clock and we wouldn't see her again until eight; it seemed perfectly natural that she should have been delayed at the dentist. In some ways, she had luck on her side.

So off Madame went. But she didn't go far. I'd followed her several times. She went across the park and into the little summerhouse, by the greenhouse where the children kept their toys. Does Mademoiselle

Monique remember it? No one ever went there except for the children, and of course all three of them were ill. So I saw her going in, and ten minutes later Monsieur Pécaud. I went quietly into the greenhouse, where you could hear everything. I'm telling the truth as before God, Mademoiselle.

Monsieur Pécaud was repeating frantically, "Help me, Nicole, help me!"

I can't repeat word for word what they said, as it's twelve years since I listened to that poor, unhappy victim of her passion (or of her pride) and to that dishonest man. I can remember the sense of the words but not the words themselves. I certainly understood what it was all about. Monsieur Pécaud had falsified Monsieur's documents to procure money for himself: he was playing the Stock Market. Madame had several times paid for the losses. The latest debt was huge; he had not dared to tell her about it before. Monsieur had found out about it and was going to dismiss him and take him to court.

"So what do you want me to do?" she asked him.

He replied, "You have proof of his infidelity. Offer him your silence in exchange for his. He'll have to agree to that."

"He has to agree!" she said, after a moment's silence, in such a tone of voice . . . Ah! If, the jury, the lawyers, the judge, and the public could have heard that tone of voice when they were talking about the love Madame

had for Monsieur! She hated him, Mademoiselle
Monique! I had often thought so, but now I was sure.
Now Mademoiselle will understand what must have
happened in the car. Each wanted to outsmart the
other, Madame offering her silence if he didn't destroy
Monsieur Pécaud, and Monsieur realizing that he had
her cornered and that he could lay down his conditions
for divorce; but Monsieur refused and, witty and
sardonic as he was, he couldn't help laughing at the
idea that the wife he had discarded, older than him,
plain and neglected by him, could be having an affair.
But he didn't laugh for long.

It must have been that laugh that sent her mad, poor
thing! I can't help but pity her. I think you can do
anything to a woman: deceive her, beat her, and
abandon her, but whereas a man might forgive being
laughed at, a woman never would! Naturally you can
mock a woman for her ignorance or the way she
dresses and how she leads her life; you can mock her
work as much as you like, but never her body, her face,
or her lovemaking. Mademoiselle, I've always thought
she sensed contempt in Monsieur's manner toward her.
Maybe even before they got married. Perhaps it went
back to when they were both children: he was so
handsome, spoiled by everyone, charming and brilliant,
and she was so inconsequential and awkward. And
after they were married! I'm certain he never laughed
at her like a workman or a farmer might have done.

He was a well-educated Gentleman. But a woman can sense what she's not being told, and suffers for it. When they were alone in the evening, which didn't happen very often, Monsieur would look at her with a bored smile. And she . . . well, I often thought, Mademoiselle, that if her eyes had been pistols, poor Monsieur would have been dead.

I think it's quite wrong to make first cousins like them marry. They didn't treat each other as man and wife, but felt the same about each other as they had when they were children, with Madame's jealousy and Monsieur's scorn. How, or rather why, they married, and what pushed them into something as serious as it can be joyful (as I hope it has been for Mademoiselle Monique) but more often than not turns out to be a disaster, we'll neither of us ever know. No doubt it was money for Monsieur, and for Madame the triumph over her friends in at last catching her handsome cousin for keeps. The poor woman may have been guilty, but she certainly suffered.

Mademoiselle, when the Tragedy happened, I quickly realized that if nobody knew anything about Madame, she'd be acquitted; but she had a great deal to lose if ever the story of what really happened came out. All those women crying over her, calling her a Martyr, would have ripped her to pieces, just like the bitches women so often are to each other.

In Madame's wardrobe, under the pink crêpe de

Chine dresses, there was a bundle of letters from
Monsieur Pécaud. I took them and hid them even
before I went down to see Monsieur's body. My first
thought was to ask Madame what to do with them, but
the doctors, the police, and the family wouldn't let me
near her. I wanted to keep them until after the trial.
Everything was in those letters: the business with the
money, their love affair—I hid them in a trunk, right at
the bottom.

I thought that Madame would come home that
evening, after the trial and acquittal, and that I would
go to see her one day, when she had recovered. But then
she fell ill, and the Countess took her to Switzerland,
where she lived for three years before dying. As for
Monsieur Pécaud, he got married almost at once. Poor
Madame never had any luck. What was I to do,
Mademoiselle? I carried on waiting. After all, the
letters were safe in my house. I'd hoped to give them
back to her when she was better, but she died in the
sanatorium over there, alone and abandoned by
everyone, apart from the Countess, who stayed with
her until the end, as it was her duty to do, although I
imagine that didn't make poor Madame any happier.

When I heard about her death, I felt very uneasy. At
first I thought I'd tear them up. Then I didn't dare.
After all, they're not mine. It's one thing to act as I did
to help out but quite another to take on such a
responsibility. I thought, "If ever one of the children

needs money—and who knows what might happen—
here's the proof that Madame gave almost a hundred
thousand francs to that Monsieur Pécaud, who's now so
rich . . . It's all very delicate." I would die if I thought I
could have deprived any of the children of a single
penny, I who loved them and have never deprived
anyone of a penny, as God is my witness.

Mademoiselle was living in Strasbourg; otherwise I
would have come to see her. But Mademoiselle
Monique must understand: when you don't have
anyone to look after you and you've had a hard life, you
have to be careful with your money. I had almost made
up my mind to come last summer, but the train fares
increased again. I don't know what the world is coming
to. Then I suddenly fell ill. I was taken to the hospital
where I'm now waiting. The letters are in my trunk,
with my things, in my married niece's house in Nice.
At first, I thought I'd write and ask her to send them to
me here, but I know my niece. She and my nephew,
who lives in Belfort, are furiously jealous of each other.
She would never part from the trunk, as she would
think it contained jewelry or valuable documents that I
might be going to give to my nephew instead of to her.
They'll be very surprised when I die, as I spent
everything I had on building my house in Souprosse,
where I thought I'd end my days, and they'll never
agree about selling it. Well, I can't worry about that!
Money isn't the most precious thing when you consider

where I am now. They've got their lives ahead of them, but mine is over.

Mademoiselle Monique, I'm sending the key to the trunk with this letter. I could not have allowed my niece to rummage through it: she'd have read everything. Mademoiselle must go to Nice. I think she'll decide to go now that she knows everything. She must tell them I sent her. The address is: Madame Garnier, 30 Rue de la République. She must ask for the trunk and open it. In the left-hand corner, under the woolens, she'll find all her poor mother's letters, neatly folded in my great-nephew's christening box, which also contains a rosary blessed at Lourdes. It would make me very happy if Mademoiselle would send me the rosary. I'd like to have it with me when I die. The letters belong to Mademoiselle and she can do what she wants with them, but if she will allow her old servant to give her a bit of advice, she shouldn't read them. There are some things in life it's better not to know. The people who wrote them are dead, or will die one day, like us. Mademoiselle must let God judge them. That's not for us to do.

Good-bye, Mademoiselle Monique. I hope your children are a source of great comfort to you.

Believe me, Mademoiselle, your most respectful and devoted servant,

Clémence Labouheyre

Le sortilège

[THE SPELL]

IT IS THE ELEMENT OF MYSTERY IN CHILDHOOD memories that gives them their power. The people and events of the past seem to have been disguised; you thought you knew what was happening but, years later, you realize your mistake. What seemed simple was in fact masked by secrets and shadows: what intrigued you then was just an everyday matter of inheritance or adultery. A child's ignorance creates a world that is only half-understood and partly concealed. Perhaps that is the reason it remains so vivid in the memory.

When I was eight, in the Ukrainian town where I was born, there lived a family I often used to visit with my young aunt. The father was a retired soldier. I have forgotten his rank and his name, but I can still visualize the house, the furniture, and the faces.

Their home was a long way from ours; we lived in the center of the town, and they were on the outskirts. Getting there was quite an excursion. I remember the old brown walls, tin roofs eaten away by rust, and countless drainpipes. The first time I went there it was a day in spring. The snow was melting, trickling away with a lively, joyful sound like the clinking of silver coins, surrounding the house with its shimmering sparkle as it flowed over the paving stones. I went inside, but then felt shy and hung back. A little girl came and took me by the hand. She was called Nina and later would become my friend. I stood in the hall while my aunt unwrapped the shawls and capes I wore against the cold. The little girl smiled as she looked at me; she had a wide mouth and dark eyes.

"Go and play in the nursery," said my aunt, who was impatient to be alone with Nina's older sister, Lola, so they could talk about their suitors.

Both my aunt and this young woman were twenty years old. My aunt was pretty, with soft skin and a trim figure, and no more intelligence than a flower. Nina's sister was a tall, pale, thin girl, with a fine, sharp profile and such beautiful grass-green, almond-shaped eyes that one never wearied of gazing at them. Nina took me through the drawing room. I had never seen such an old house. There were many rooms, all of them small. To get from one to another you had to go up and down uneven, rickety brick steps. It was great fun. Signs of disorder, dilapidation, and neglect were everywhere, yet at the same time it was full of life and the most welcoming home I have ever been in. There were cobwebs and dust everywhere, wobbly little armchairs and ancient, overflowing trunks all over the place. The house smelled of strong tobacco, wet fur, and mushrooms, for it was damp. The walls in the nursery were gray and sweating.

"Don't you worry about Nina's health?" asked Mademoiselle, my nursemaid.

My friend's mother shrugged her soft, plump shoulders.

"No. What can I do about it? The children are well. It's God who sends us illness and health, my dear Mademoiselle."

It was true that Nina was never ill. She ran barefoot over the cold floors and wet grass; she ate what she wanted; she went to bed after midnight; she was beautiful and strong. Sometimes I stayed in the house for a couple of nights. It might be raining and I would have caught cold going home in the evening, or the rising wind meant the coming of a storm: any excuse was good enough for my aunt and me, and I was always happy to pretend to have a sore throat or to feel tired when convenient. It was wonderful living there! I slept in Nina's room; we would get up at dawn and run through the sleeping house; we hardly ever washed. When the grown-ups weren't playing cards or sleeping, they were rather vaguely tidying up. Visitors would turn up throughout the day, for morning coffee, dinner, supper, tea after supper, at midnight, it didn't matter when. Friends would sleep on sofas. Toward noon you might meet a tousle-headed boy wandering around the corridors in his nightshirt, who would introduce himself, "I'm one of your son's friends."

"Hello, make yourself at home," would come the answer.

The table was never cleared; the food was heavy, but it was excellent. Some of the guests would be finishing their dessert as others were beginning their soup. Barefooted servant girls were constantly running between the dining room and the kitchen, bringing plates and taking them away. Then someone would exclaim, "I'd really like something sweet . . ."

"Nothing could be easier," the mistress of the house would reply affably and, yet again, cakes would appear, then an omelette, a cup of hot chocolate, or some milk for the children. "Some more borscht?" And people started to eat again, as cigar smoke swirled around them, while in the same room a game of whist would start up and the sounds of a piano and violin would filter in from the next room.

"Don't these people ever work?" asked Mademoiselle who, being foreign, had strange ideas about life.

But these Russians expected to get their daily bread from the czar, from their land, or from God. It was he who conferred good fortune and poverty, just as he conferred health and sickness. What was the point of worrying?

Sofia Andreïevna, my friend's mother, seemed old to me; she could not have been more than forty, but she did not use makeup and did not wear a corset; she was a plump, faded blonde, soft and white as cream. When she pulled me toward her to greet me with a kiss, I breathed in a smell that reminded me of a high-class pâtisserie—orange flower water, vanilla, and sugar.

The father was very tall and thin but, perhaps because of his height, I don't remember his face. I would have had to lean my head right back to see him properly, and I wasn't interested enough in him for that. He lived a little remotely from his family, often having his meals taken to his room on a tray. If he happened to see me, he would stroke my cheek with his large cold hand. He had known Chekhov well; I don't know why, but I remembered the grown-ups mentioning it one day. On his desk he had a box of letters from Chekhov. He had ordered them to be burned after his death. He was ill and knew he was going to die. That was the reason he had retired.

"Why burn Chekhov's letters? They belong to posterity," a young man once said in my hearing.

Looking at him grimly, the father said, "Trampling on a man's soul with their big boots, that's what they like doing. No, everything precious must be a secret."

Friends, poor relations, elderly governesses—they all lived in this house. A student had come ten years before, as a tutor for the two boys, Lola and Nina's brothers; he was supposed to stay for a month, but he had never left and was still a student. He didn't have a room of his own; the old house, although enormous, was completely full. He had been sleeping for the last ten years on two chairs in the hall, and this surprised nobody.

The second place at the table, near the samovar and next to the mistress of the house, was reserved for a certain Klavdia Alexandrovna, one of Sofia Andreïevna's childhood friends. She seemed to me a pale, ageless woman, but one day I saw her doing her hair—in the garden.

"These people," said Mademoiselle, "sleep in the drawing room, eat in the bedroom, and get dressed on the terrace."

On stormy days the rainwater was collected in tubs, and all the women of the house would wash their hair in the open air, then let it dry in the sun; that's how I saw Klavdia Alexandrovna's hair. It was like a golden cloak. I stood quite still admiring it. Her hair came down to her knees, and it shone in the light. Sofia Andreïevna was there, too, half-stretched out on a wicker chaise longue; she was wearing a lilac housecoat, which fell open to show her deep, creamy bosom. She caught the look on my face and started laughing. When she laughed, her chin quivered slightly and she looked nice—gentle and wise.

"You should have seen her twenty years ago," she said, pointing at her friend. "She was so young; she had her hair hanging in two long golden plaits, and when she leaned her head back a little she could stand on them with the heels of her shoes."

She sighed and turned toward Mademoiselle.

"Life is simpler than you think. When Klavdia and I were young, we both loved the same man and he was very . . . yes, he was very fond of her because of her hair and her lovely figure. But, you see, she didn't have a dowry. What can you do when God refuses to make you rich? The young man's parents would not hear of their marrying. There were quarrels, tears; his mother went to see Klavdia and said, "Make my son happy. Go away. Make a sacrifice." She appealed to the finer feelings of the girl she had brought up in her own home. It was no use. So one night she called all three of us together, told us she was going to die, ordered her son to marry me, and told Klavdia to give up her love; but she made us both swear before God that we would never abandon the orphaned girl, that she would live under our roof. And in the end that's what happened. I married the young man. You know him: he's my husband. We kept the promise we made to his dying mother and Klavdia found a home with us."

I saw Klavdia Alexandrovna turn toward her friend.

Tears were running down her face. She wiped them away and, in a voice breaking with emotion, said, "You are my benefactress, Sofia. You know that I'd give my life for you and your children. I've been so happy. What would have become of me without you? No home, no food, possibly even compelled to give lessons in order to survive! Ah! One day I'd like to return your kindness."

Both of them were crying now, and Klavdia took Sofia's hand and kissed it. Sofia gathered Klavdia into an embrace and traced the sign of the cross on her forehead. "May God watch over you! You help me so much keeping this house in order."

It was true that, when cakes were brought to the table, Sofia Andreïevna would seize the silver knife and, with a deep sigh, plunge it into the middle of the thick crust; but then the effort seemed too great and she pushed the plate toward Klavdia, who finished what she had started and said to the guests, "Eat. You haven't eaten anything yet. Please eat . . ."

And when people helped themselves, she added, "Bless you." The same as when one sneezes. That's what Russians do.

Klavdia Alexandrovna had other talents. She could read tarot cards. She knew all sorts of superstitions and strange rituals . . . On the eve of Twelfth Night she would slip mirrors under young girls' pillows so that in their dreams they would see the man with whom they would fall in love. On the same evening she would shut herself away with Lola and my aunt, and they would throw burning wax into a basin of water: the wax would take on the shapes of rings, crowns, rubles, or crosses, and these would predict the future. Sometimes she would teach them how to do table-turning. A saucer was placed on a sheet of paper covered in letters, signs, and numbers; you touched the edge of the saucer with your fingertips and it would race across the table, forming words and sentences, sometimes skidding about so quickly you had to catch hold of it with both hands to stop it from falling off. Nina and I, the youngest of the children, would watch these séances, and I was never able to discover their secret. Klavdia would recite incantations that, she said, were for the dead, or to make thunder go away. I wondered how much she believed in them herself, but for us she was surrounded by an aura of mysterious charm. We respected her; children were drawn to her. At her age, and in her position as a poor relation dependent on others, she could have been despised; but, on the contrary, there was no fun without Klavdia.

"She knows a spell to attract love," Lola said to my aunt.

"She knows a spell to attract love," little Nina repeated, mimicking the grown-ups even though love held no interest for an eight-year-old child.

My half-French education saved me from believing

in the supernatural, and I was the only one to respond skeptically. "That's what you think! If she really knows the secret of finding love, then why isn't she married?"

I will leave you to guess how many times young girls tried to persuade Klavdia to reveal the secret of her spell. But she shook her head. "Later, my little ones, when you're older."

It was winter. The garden was buried under deep snow. A lamp on the terrace lit up the lower branches of the trees with a soft, white, shimmering glow.

The dogs would come in covered with snow. In the drawing room people played cards, drank tea, or played music. I remember a tall lamp on a bronze base with a red shade. Klavdia would read the cards, a large, fringed silk shawl draped over her shoulders. This shawl was almost the same color as the lamp shade and, to my eyes smarting for lack of sleep—for at home I was not used to going to bed so late—the drawing room ended up seeming a dark, rather frightening place, with two burning flames. I would doze off, then wake up, and surreptitiously play with the crimson silk, holding it up to my eyes so that the light in the room took on the delicious color of raspberries and wine!

All this time Klavdia would shuffle the cards, muttering, "What is in the mind, what is in the heart, what happens in the house, what was, what will be . . ."

Another regular visitor was a man we called the doctor; thin and fair, he had a short, pointed ginger beard that he would stroke with a distracted, dreamy air. He had a peculiar but attractive gaze: his heavy eyelids were always half-lowered and the expression in his eyes was thoughtful, ironic, and sad.

I wondered when he went to see his patients. One saw him at the house at all hours of the day and night; in fact, we saw him more often than we did the master of the house, whose seat at the dining table was often left empty. Nina called the doctor "Uncle" or "Uncle Serge," although I knew they were not related in any way; but he was an old family friend and, in any case, Russian children called the adults they met at their parents' house "Uncle" and "Aunt." And, it is true, I would not have suspected anything about the doctor's constant presence at Sofia Andreïevna's side, their long conversations, their silences, had it not been for my aunt's stifled laughter when she mentioned it, or Mademoiselle's frown as she discreetly gestured in my direction, saying, "Oh for goodness' sake, be quiet, that's ridiculous."

Poor Mademoiselle! She was curious, as well as being scandalized and, above all, she was astonished: this mature woman trailing around all day in a rumpled housecoat, this courteous, silent man, absorbed in his thoughts, were not, it seemed to her, a likely pair for an adulterous liaison. And then there was the husband, so clearly in the know yet resigned to it! Ah! Where were the Parisian bachelor flats, afternoon assignations, the suitably elegant setting for civilized love affairs? The most virtuous of women, Mademoiselle searched for descriptions of such scenes in novels, much as an exile listens to songs of his homeland. These people, in this part of Russia, were uncivilized. In fact, I think she and my aunt were wrong and that the doctor and Sofia Andreïevna had never had an affair. Though it's certainly true that these people *were* uncivilized. Perhaps through laziness, or realism, or an innate coolness, or some other reason, they were perfectly content with platonic relationships; yet it was clear that there was real love between Sofia Andreïevna and the doctor. Even as a child, once I was aware of it, I recognized it. Sofia Andreïevna's voice would crack, then become higher and more resonant when she saw the doctor. It was customary in the Russian provinces for a man to kiss the hostess's hand after a meal, whereupon she would lightly put her lips to the man's bowed head. When the doctor approached Sofia Andreïevna, she would look at him with . . . oh! I can't describe that look . . . An inexpressible tenderness was mingled with a sorrow that I guessed at without understanding, but she did not kiss him. She would smile and he would move away from her. My aunt would observe the performance with great curiosity, while Lola seemed to see nothing; her magnificent green eyes were bright and indifferent.

So the winter passed and spring arrived. How lovely spring was in that part of the world! The streets were lined with gardens and the air smelled of lime and lilac blossoms; a soft dampness rose from all those lawns and from the trees that grew close together, their sweet perfume filling the evening air. Slowly the sun would set. Out in the open the heat was intense, and in May there were frequent thunderstorms. How good it was to run around in the wet garden afterward! Nina would take her shoes and stockings off, flattening the soaking wet grass with her bare feet. We would shake the branches of the syringa so that our hair was sprayed in a shower of water.

Sometimes a storm broke out at night, and then we ran out onto the terrace to watch the sulfurous lightning as it suddenly lit up the garden. Once we were out there when it was almost dark, and we happened to be just outside the drawing room; the rain had stopped but we could still hear a gentle rumble of distant thunder, moving away toward the river Dnieper. I heard my aunt saying to Klavdia, "Klavdia Alexandrovna, didn't you say that the spell works the night following a storm in May?"

All the girls, all the young people who were there, surrounded Klavdia, laughing and pleading with her. Sofia Andreïevna had stayed in the drawing room, but the doctor followed us outside.

"And the moon has to be out," cried Lola. "Look, there it is!"

A glimmer of moonlight could be seen through the clouds.

"You also need a river or a spring," said Klavdia.

Someone called out, "There's a stream at the bottom of the garden!"

"But it's always dry."

"Not after a storm like this one."

"Well . . ." began Klavdia Alexandrovna.

She wasn't allowed to finish. Everyone dragged her off, and we little ones ran behind them, shrieking.

The garden was in deep shadow. We slid about on the wet grass, holding on to tree trunks; the girls were all laughing. The stream flowed through a clearing. Sometimes the clouds parted and the moon could be seen clearly.

"We must wait until it's shining brightly," said Klavdia.

She knelt down at the edge of the stream. I was right next to her and watched curiously. She looked worried, and her nostrils were pinched. She was obviously caught up in her own game.

"Look, little ones, here's the spell," she said, as the last of the clouds dispersed and we were bathed in a greenish light from the moon. "Watch carefully."

From her finger she took a little ring that she always wore and that I had often noticed. It was a simple silver circle decorated with a dark red stone from the Caucasus. She turned it around so that it gleamed faintly in the moonlight. She hesitated for a moment, then murmured a few words I didn't hear and briskly plunged the ring three times into the stream, each time breaking the moon's reflection. A small frog hidden in the grass started croaking and others answered it. I saw Lola shiver suddenly.

"Oh, how noisy those frogs are; they scared me! Is that your spell, Klavdia? Give me the ring, I want to try. How does it go?"

Klavdia whispered something in her ear. Lola took the ring, at first repeating the incantation so quietly that nobody could hear it. Then, at my aunt's insistence, she recited out loud:

> *Flower of the lime, wild oats, and black mandrake*
> *Thrice, thrice, thrice,*
> *Joy, I reject you,*
> *Innocent happiness, I reject you,*
> *May blind passion bind me forever to . . .*

She stopped.

"To whom, Klavdia?" she asked, laughing.

And in a strange, cold voice, Klavdia answered, "Oh, to whomever you like. You know it's only a bit of fun. Choose anyone. The one you *cannot* love, for example: the doctor."

She was silent, and everyone went quiet, holding their breath. The doctor suddenly threw the cigarette he was holding into the water.

"What are you doing?" cried Klavdia sharply, close to tears.

"The only thing missing was fire. Water, fire, and moonlight are the three vital elements. Finish the spell, Lola."

After a silence, the young girl's voice could be heard again: "May blind passion bind me forever to Serge."

"Go to him and put the ring on his finger," ordered Klavdia.

Serge gently pushed her away.

"Leave me alone, Lola."

But Nina and I danced around the couple like devils possessed. "Yes, yes, Uncle Serge, let her put the ring on your finger. Are you scared of spells? Are you scared of witchcraft, Uncle Serge?"

He shrugged and held out his hand. Of course the ring was too small. All the same, Lola managed to slide it as far as the joint of his little finger. But the doctor immediately tore it off as if it had burned him.

"Oh, give it to me now!" cried my aunt. "Let me have a go."

Then in a faint voice, Klavdia answered, "There's no point. The spell only works once."

After this scene, she refused to have anything to do with any magic games. But we hadn't forgotten the incantation, and ten times a day Nina and I would plunge a ring made out of woven grass into the stream, laughing wildly as we repeated, "Flower of the lime, wild oats, and black mandrake . . ."

Then, "May blind passion bind me forever to . . ."

And we would finish with the most ridiculous names: old Stefan, the *dvornik* who swept the courtyard; Ivan Ivanich, my mathematics tutor; or Jouk, the black dog.

But one day, Lola heard us. She rushed at us, grabbing Nina by the shoulders. "I won't allow it, do you hear, you horrible child! I . . . forbid you . . ."

She was stammering; her face was convulsed; she pulled her sister's ears and burst into tears. Nina was reduced to silence, her eyes wide with astonishment.

"Is she mad?" she asked me, when Lola had fled. "What's the matter with her?"

I had no idea. I suggested a game of hide-and-seek.

Time passed. I cannot remember if it was two months, or six months, or more. One evening, we needed some material to make dolls' clothes: we usually got some from Klavdia Alexandrovna. I went running into her room. She was standing by the window, her hands clasped to her breast, looking out at the dark garden. The lamps had not been lit. I saw Lola and Uncle Serge sitting next to each other on the sofa, not speaking. Lola was repeatedly rearranging a stray lock of hair that fell over her eyes.

When she saw me, Klavdia Alexandrovna seemed all at once mad with rage; she had these sudden, inexplicable moments of fury.

"What are you doing here? Go away!" she shouted,

stamping her foot. "Do you always come into someone's room without knocking?"

I had in fact tapped on the door, but they hadn't heard me. I tried to say so. Then Lola got up. "Leave her alone, Klavdia," she said.

She lit the lamp. I saw that she was a bit unsteady on her feet, in the way you are if you're woken suddenly in the middle of the night. There was a red mark on her neck. I saw it clearly: it looked like the mark of a bite. However, fearing another rebuff, I said nothing and slipped away. Behind me, the door was banged shut and then locked.

After that I don't remember anything until an evening when we all met as usual in the drawing room. Sofia Andreïevna, Uncle Serge, and some other friends were playing cards; Klavdia was at the piano making Nina and me practice a duet. The door opened and Lola appeared. How pale she was! She crossed the room, stopped by the table of cardplayers, watched them for a few moments without saying anything, then at last spoke to her mother and said, "I'm going to a friend's house."

It was nine o'clock in the evening. Her mother made no objection, asking neither who the friend was nor when her daughter would return. I told you that everyone in that house did as they pleased. She replied calmly, "Well, go with God."

Those simple words—an everyday expression in Russian—had an extraordinary effect on Lola. She kept twisting and untwisting her hands, looking at us all in despair. Nobody noticed anything. Our duet came to an end. Klavdia played a few bars of "The Happy Farmer," and then immediately switched to a gentle, sensuous tune, which, as you listened to it, made you want to cry, laugh, then hide in a dark corner and stay there the whole night long without moving. Lola left the room. A little later Uncle Serge threw down his cards. "I have to visit a patient this evening," he said.

He bowed to Sofia Andreïevna, let his lips linger a long time on the hand she held out to him, and left. Klavdia Alexandrovna stopped playing and disappeared to her room.

Uncle Serge's departure brought the game to an end. Sofia Andreïevna was soon left on her own and began to play patience. Mademoiselle, in her severe black dress with its little white collar and a gold chain hanging on her thin chest, was sitting very straight in the armchair opposite embroidering a fine linen handkerchief. I could hear Sofia Andreïevna: ". . . Well, that's youth, my dear Mademoiselle. You wait, you search, you make a mistake, you weep, you get over it . . . How can we help them? Parents can only pray to God."

"God helps those who help themselves," said Mademoiselle.

That night I slept in Nina's room. I was woken by footsteps and slamming doors. I opened my eyes, saw that it was barely light, and went back to sleep.

Nina and I had planned to build a hut out of branches

at the end of the garden, first thing in the morning. We left the house very early without seeing anyone, taking our breakfast with us. At lunchtime, as we were coming back, happy and messy, the first person I met was Mademoiselle.

"I've been looking for you everywhere," she said. "We're going home."

"What, now! Why?"

She didn't reply, but dragged me off to the hallway. I could see Sofia Andreïevna through the open door, sitting in an armchair, her head thrown back, tears coursing down her pale, ravaged face and an opened letter on her lap. Then I suddenly heard Klavdia Alexandrovna laughing: it was a sharp, false, convulsive sound, which ended in sobs and curses. Sofia Andreïevna sat up.

"Help! Help!" Klavdia exclaimed, distraught.

Mademoiselle, who always had a little flask of English smelling salts on her—I had often amused myself by unscrewing the silver stopper, breathing in the smell, and making myself sneeze—rushed to Klavdia and, delighted by the drama, I followed her.

Klavdia's arms were flailing about: this wasn't a pretend collapse. At least, I don't think so. She seemed to be suffocating. She kept repeating, "It's my fault, all my fault! May God punish me!"

"What could you do, my dear friend," said Sofia Andreïevna, stroking her hair. "What even a mother couldn't see or guess, how could you be expected to know?"

Still, Klavdia repeated, "It's my fault, mine alone. I shall die."

After administering the smelling salts, Mademoiselle was now standing next to her, gazing at her coldly.

"I fear for her," Sofia Andreïevna said to Mademoiselle.

"If I were you, Madame, I wouldn't be too worried."

"Ah, but she's so devoted, so warmhearted . . . This tragedy will kill her . . . as it will me," said Sofia Andreïevna, in an exhausted voice.

I caught sight of Nina in the hall, making signs at me through the half-open door. I went to join her. "What's going on?"

"I don't know," she whispered. "I don't understand. Apparently Lola has run away with Uncle Serge. Maybe they will get married? I don't understand why Mother is crying. If it were me, I'd be very happy."

We discussed it for a moment and concluded that Sofia Andreïevna was angry because it had been done in secret, without consulting her.

Then, as all this really did not concern us, and as we were actually a bit embarrassed by it, we took advantage of the upset to carry out a plan we had been hatching for a long time and endlessly putting off. We crept into the kitchen to put a few changes in place: we swapped the sugar for salt, put coal in the icebox, and the cat and her kittens into the big casserole dish.

"Cook will lift the lid and the cats will jump out at her, she'll put fish in the icebox and it will come out all black. She'll think someone has put a curse on her. She's always accusing Klavdia of witchcraft."

That suddenly made me remember the spell with fire, water, and moonlight. I did not say anything then, but later on, in the tram on the way home, I slid closer to Mademoiselle and whispered, "I know why Klavdia Alexandrovna was in such a state."

"Why?" asked Mademoiselle, no doubt too interested to remember to give her standard reply: "Irène, you pry too much into the grown-ups' business."

I told her the story of the magic game by the stream after the storm.

"Is it true, Mademoiselle? Did she know a spell?"

"No, it's just silliness."

"So why hadn't Lola and Uncle Serge thought about each other until that moment?"

"Well, for a start, how do you know they'd never thought about each other before?"

Now it was my turn to surprise her. I shrugged self-importantly. "I'm sure they hadn't—it's not as if one can't tell when people are in love!"

Mademoiselle sighed and said nothing. I carried on, flattered by her attention.

"It was certainly all because of her. And now she's full

of remorse because witchcraft is forbidden by God. She's crying because she's sorry, that's all."

Mademoiselle looked down at me with an expression I could not quite work out, but which I did not like: I hate irony when it is directed against me, and anyway, what had I said that was so amusing?

"That must be it," she said.

Le spectateur

[THE SPECTATOR]

THEY HAD EATEN WELL. THE CREAMINESS OF THE quenelles brought out the deep, dark flavor of the truffles: not too overpowering, but mingling with the tender flesh of the fish and the delicate white sauce, just as the deep notes of the cello had harmonized with the sound of the piano in the delightful concerto he had heard yesterday. If one used one's imagination and experience it was possible, thought Hugo Grayer, to extract the maximum pleasure from life, and innocent enjoyment. After the exquisite and complex taste of the quenelles, the Chateaubriand steak with potatoes had an austere simplicity reminiscent of classical design. They had drunk a small amount of wine—Hugo had a delicate liver—but it was a 1924 Château Ausone. What a bit of luck it had been to discover such a rare wine in an apparently simple restaurant on one of the Parisian quays. With a smile Magda said, in English, "You are a marvel, Hugo dear!"

She took his arm. He was short and very thin, and looked as if he had been created by a particularly refined artist using only a limited palette of colors: gray for his suit, hair, and eyes; a touch of pale ocher for his face and gloves; a few spots of white on his stiff collar and forehead; and a gleam of gold in his mouth. His companion, taller than he, solidly built and rosy-cheeked, was wearing a little hat, fashionably and jauntily perched on top of her silvery curls like a bird on a branch. She walked by his side with long, confident strides that rang out on the old cobblestones.

It was an August day in Paris, on the Quai d'Orléans by the Seine. Hugo kept congratulating himself that this year he had postponed his departure to Deauville: the weather was fine and Magda quite entertaining. He did not like dining with pretty girls; at his age it was better to keep his pleasures separate. For a lunch like this what he needed was a hard-boiled, cynical old American such as Magda, who appreciated her food and had good taste in wine. She admired him, but that left him indifferent: he had always been admired for his taste, his wealth, his splendid collection of porcelain, his knowledge of ancient Greek writers, his generosity, and his intelligence. He did not need other people's admiration, yet Magda amused him. It was better, and more unusual, to be amused than admired . . . better and more unusual to be amused than loved.

"Egoist."

A weeping young woman had called him that once. The sensual memory of her tears still touched his heart pleasurably: she had been so young and so beautiful. He had been young then, too. Egoist . . . he might have replied that in this world of mad, brutal men and their stupid victims, the only harmless people were egoists like him. They did not hurt anyone. All the misery suffered by human beings, thought Hugo, is unleashed by those who love others more than themselves and want that love to be acknowledged. Whereas he just wanted to lead a peaceful, quiet life. There was no great secret about it. One had to think of life as an interesting theatrical production, every detail of which deserved praise, and then it all acquired great beauty. He showed Magda a dank little street between two old houses, where a girl was standing by a gate clutching a crusty loaf of bread to her chest. Hugo looked at her kindly: a few basic elements—an anemic child, a pale golden loaf, some ancient stones—had by chance come together to form a graceful, touching picture that pleased Hugo Grayer.

"I've had my share of sadness, like everyone else," he said to Magda. "Old Fontenelle used to insist that no sorrow, however wretched, could survive an hour's reading. But for me it isn't books or works of art that console me; it's the contemplation of our imperfect world."

"Fontenelle must have led a peaceful existence like yours," said Magda, laughing.

Her laugh was the only thing about her that Hugo did not like; she laughed like a neighing horse.

"It's not that peaceful," he replied.

He did not know why, but he felt both proud and annoyed when it was implied that he was happier than other people. He was like a pedigree dog pulling on its lead, trying, for a change, to get at the food of lesser breeds.

"I've had my share of misery," he said, thinking of his mother's death. They had often quarreled: she was a horrible woman. But her last moments and the death-bed reconciliation had been brief; there were no tears or shouting, and due to their measured, almost aesthetic observance of convention, all had been forgiven. And he thought about his divorce twenty years ago, and about De Beers, which had just dropped a hundred points. Well, a man like himself had worries on a spiritual plane that the mass of humanity could not possibly grasp. He had suffered, truly suffered, because of certain books, unsuccessful journeys, silly women, dreams, and gloomy premonitions. A night spent in an ugly hotel room overwhelmed him with sadness. Some gaudy wallpaper, in an inn where a cold had kept him in bed for a week, had been at the root of a chronic melancholy, a tendency to migraine, and gloomy speculation about the future. And now this remark of Magda's had irritated him: she was too down-to-earth to be able to understand him.

But Magda had stopped at the spot on the quay at which the Seine gently curved around to the right. Hugo thought how ugly and sharp the usual expression, "the river's elbow," was, evoking the image of an old beggar woman lifting her arm to ward off a blow. In fact, it was a graceful and exquisitely elegant movement. The Seine twined itself around Paris like a woman putting her arms around her lover—a very young woman, affectionate and blushing, Hugo said to himself, as he watched the water glitter. How he loved its flow, its pale color . . .

Nearby there was a quiet little square.

"It's all so beautiful!" murmured Hugo. "Europe has the charm of those who are going to die," he said, stroking the river's gray stone parapet as he went on walking. "That's what makes it so seductive. For several years I've felt particularly drawn to these threatened cities: Paris, London, Rome. Every time I leave I have tears in my eyes, as though I'm saying good-bye to a terminally ill friend. It was the same in Salzburg before the Anschluss . . . God, it was so moving, listening to Mozart's music on those cold summer nights and thinking of Hitler a few miles away, tormented by insomnia and greed. One was witnessing the end of a civilization. One was watching a country shudder and die while singing, just as one might feel the beating heart of a wounded nightingale in one's hand. Poor, charming Austria . . . And then all this," he said, pointing at Notre

Dame, "destroyed in air raids, ruined and in ashes, how horrible! And yet . . ."

He felt a little out of breath. He could not keep up with Magda, who was walking too fast for him, but vanity would not allow him to admit it. (Magda was, in fact, older than he but considerably more robust.)

"Women are indestructible," he thought.

He suggested sitting on a bench in the square; the weather was too nice to be shut up in a car.

"So do you believe in this war?" she asked, as she looked at herself in her little handbag mirror and rearranged her curls, which resembled the carved chunks of solid silver decorating a Victorian soup tureen. A young street urchin, fascinated by so much glamour, stopped in front of her and stared. She smiled.

"So do you believe in this war?" she repeated.

"My dear friend," said Hugo emphatically, "do you believe in the bullet that comes out of a loaded revolver when the trigger is pulled?"

They contemplated Notre Dame with compassion.

"The fate of those old stones affects me more than that of human beings, Magda."

The little boy was still standing in front of them. Hugo Grayer took some small change out of his pocket.

"Here you are, child, go and buy yourself some barley sugar."

Surprised, the child looked down, hesitated, then took the money and walked away.

"After all, it took centuries to build an irreplaceable cathedral and it takes only a few seconds to create a man, similar to all other men, for they are interchangeable, alas, with their vulgar passions and pleasures and crass stupidity."

"Yes," said Magda, "at mealtimes during the Spanish War, when I thought about the El Grecos that might be destroyed, I couldn't eat a thing. I could truthfully hear a voice repeating in my ear, 'the El Grecos, the El Grecos you'll never see again!' "

"There were certain scenes from the Spanish War in the cinema that could match the El Grecos." Hugo sighed.

Magda gazed at the sky, trying to look as if she was thinking about the war in Spain. Actually she was wondering if her stockbroker had managed to sell her Mexican Eagle shares in time. Dear Hugo was so detached from worldly concerns, unsurprisingly since he possessed one of the largest fortunes in Uruguay. Then she thought about the two big rooms on the first floor of her home in New York, briefly considering the best combination of colors: purple and pink, perhaps? That could be fun, with her Italianate mirrors painted with birds and flowers . . .

Hugo smiled in the sunlight. Even though it was the height of summer, the light wasn't too bright, but soft and gentle. He would go to the Louvre and look at *L'homme au verre de vin,* one of his favorite paintings,

205

before going home to dress for dinner. He had been invited to dine outside Paris by a Brazilian woman friend who lived in Versailles. Yes, it was strange to watch old Europe sinking like this, like a ship taking on water from all sides, plunging into those terrible depths where God's voice ceaselessly resounds. In a few weeks or months would the ancient towers of Notre Dame be blown up by bombs, hurling their martyred stones to the heavens? And all those beautiful old houses . . . What a pity! He felt compassion, as well as a suitable indignation, and the comfortable peace of mind one experiences when watching a play. There is a lot of blood, and a lot of tears, but they are flowing a long way away from you and will never affect you. He himself was a neutral; "a citizen of no man's land" was how he smilingly described himself. There was a handful of people on earth (Magda was one) who, by virtue of their birth, ancestors, family ties, and a quirk of fate, had so many different racial strains within them that no country could lay claim to them. Hugo's father was Scandinavian, his mother Italian. He had been born in the United States but had become a national of the small South American republic in which he owned some property.

Young men and women strolled slowly along with their arms around each other's waists. How would they all feel if one day . . . ? What curious conflicts of emotion and duty they would have! And their poor bodies, made for pleasure! No, the human body was certainly *not* created for pleasure, thought Hugo; he put his hand over his eyes, for the sun suddenly shone brightly between two dark clouds that had come from nowhere: man had been created to endure hunger, cold, and exhaustion, and his heart was made to be filled with primitive, violent passions—fear, hope, and hatred.

Benevolently he watched the pedestrians strolling by. They didn't understand the resources within them, or that the human species could endure almost anything. Hugo Grayer was deeply convinced of this. The way things were at the moment, it took courage to come to Europe every year as he did. He might find himself trapped, an innocent man, among these nations going up in flames, just like some poor rat in a burning house. So what? He would leave in good time. With some difficulty he wrenched his thoughts back to Magda, who was asking his advice about the house she had recently bought in New Jersey. Then they got up and walked back to the Boulevard Saint Germain, where the car was waiting for them. Then they went to Versailles for dinner, and Hugo went back to his hotel. He was still asleep the next morning when the citizens of France were reading the announcement printed in capital letters on the front page of their newspaper: AUGUST 22, 1939. THE OFFICIAL GERMAN NEWS AGENCY STATES: THE GOVERNMENT OF THE REICH AND THE SOVIET GOVERNMENT HAVE DECIDED TO AGREE TO A PACT OF NON-AGGRESSION.

There were those who thought, "Things will sort themselves out again."

Others thought, "There's nothing to be done this time; we'll have to leave."

It was like hearing a knock on the door in the night, warning you that your sleep is over, that you must set off again, and for a moment your heart seems to stop beating. Women looked at their husbands, or at sons old enough to fight, and prayed, "Not that! Have pity! Lord, remove this cup from me."

That same morning a thousand candles were lit in churches "for peace." In the street people stopped at newspaper stands, and strangers talked to one another; their faces looked calm but very solemn. Hugo had lived in Europe long enough to be able to interpret warning signs like this. He asked for his bill. He was sad to be leaving, but of course there was nothing he could do here. He handed out generous tips.

"Monsieur is going?" asked the chambermaid. "It's because of what's happening, isn't it? Everyone wants to go back to their own country. It's only natural in a way."

Where would Hugo go? Well, first to America, where he had heard there was to be a sale of antique ivory: he was beginning to get bored with porcelain. After that, he'd see. It was very disappointing to think that he wouldn't see Cannes this year.

"Of course, I'd love to stay," he said, "but there'll be air raids . . ."

When he looked at all the strong, handsome men who might be going to their deaths, he felt a sort of ironic affection for himself, for his fragile bones, his narrow spine, and his long, pale hands that had never in his life done any ordinary, rough work; they had never touched an ax or a weapon, but they knew how to stroke old books, look after flowers, or gently rub boiled linseed oil into some valuable piece of Elizabethan furniture.

However, the weather was so beautiful that he decided to put off his departure until the next day, and still he lingered. War was declared on a radiant September day. That day, on the Alexandre III bridge, Hugo came across a middle-class family going for a walk: father, mother, and a son—still young, but almost old enough to join up. The father looked at his watch and said, "We've been at war for twenty minutes."

"It's remarkable how resigned these Europeans are," Hugo Grayer thought. Some pigeons flew away with cheerful squawks.

Hugo would leave the next day. He sighed. He was starting to think that Paris would not be bombed . . . not straightaway . . . but there was the potential inconvenience, gasoline rationing, the best restaurants being closed . . . Yet how interesting it would have been to see the beginning of this war! What would everyone feel? How shaken they would be! What would come out of this terrible crisis? Heroism? A longing for pleasure?

Hatred? And how would it manifest itself? Would men become better? More intelligent? Or worse? It was fascinating, all this, fascinating! Behind each human face lay a mystery that, until now, had been seen only in works of art. Yet, above all, he felt a kind of detached pity, like that of a god who, from the empyrean heights, watches the futile activities of mankind. Those poor people! Poor mad people! Never mind—the human body was made for suffering and death. And maybe these monotonous, gray lives would be livened up by enthusiasm, by passion, by new experiences. Like all fortunate, intelligent men, Hugo was inclined to be pessimistic about his own prospects but optimistic on others' behalf. It was nevertheless quite clear that he could do nothing to help them and it would be madness to stay.

He left France at the same time as Magda. Their ship was neutral, of course. It sailed serenely across a blue sea. It was moving farther away from Europe. Soon they would not think about it anymore. It would be like the stage after you have left the theater, like a blood-soaked Shakespearean tragedy when the curtain comes down and the footlights are turned out. The horror was unreal, but the memory of it still held a certain beauty. Sometimes, on a fine evening, in the bar or on deck, people competed with one another to recall these historic moments: "When I knew it was about to start, I wanted to see how the French were taking it: I went to Fouquet's."

"Well, I went all around Paris; it was a historic moment. I stopped in all the cafés in Montparnasse. It was so moving! And, as it was dark, there were people kissing each other in every corner."

But by the second evening Europe was already forgotten.

In his cabin Hugo was undressing. On a tray next to his bed there was a bowl of fruit, some iced tea, and a book. He wanted desperately to go to sleep. He was one of those men who would continue to enjoy some of their childhood pleasures until the day they died: deep sleep, the subtle taste of little cream cakes dusted with icing sugar, the best fruit. He greatly missed his French servant, whom he had been forced to leave in Paris in the first hours of the war. The poor devil had been called up. They had almost cried as they parted.

"He stole so much from me that in the end he became as attached to me as a peasant does to the ox that provides him with a living by working the soil. Poor Marcel . . . I'd send him some sweetmeats, but he'll be dead before they reach him. His health was bad and, after eight years' service with me, he was very spoiled. It's funny to think of him having wartime adventures," he thought to himself, as he carefully chose a peach.

He usually fell asleep like that, half-undressed, one hand on his book, the other luxuriantly squeezing a piece of fresh fruit as if it were a woman's breast. He would then wake up fifteen or twenty minutes later, put on his pajamas, cut an orange or a grapefruit in half, drink a few mouthfuls of the delicious iced juice sprinkled with a little sugar, put down his book, and sleep until morning. But tonight a prolonged earsplitting blast of sound disturbed his sleep. He listened to it incredulously at first, thinking that he was dreaming about Paris and was imagining he was one of those wretched Parisians who were probably just then listening to the sirens in their beds. But he was Hugo Grayer, a neutral, on a neutral ship on a sea that belonged to no one! The call of the sirens reached Hugo's ears from the depths of the sea and the pinnacle of the heavens, like an echo of those ringing out in a sorrowing Europe: it was a harsh, inhuman voice, quivering with anguish and concern, calling out to all mortals, "Watch out! Be careful! I can do nothing for you except warn you!"

He leaped out of bed and began to dress. Were they being shipwrecked? Impossible, the sea was so calm . . . Was it a fire, a submarine attack? Doors banged. People ran along the corridors. He put on trousers, socks, and a pullover. He had never felt so alert before, and yet he was very calm.

However, he could not get his jacket on; he could not find the sleeve. But so what! It was warm and "is not the body more than clothing?" This thought stunned him for a moment. From what buried memories did those ancient words come? In shirtsleeves, his life preserver correctly fastened but his soul uncertain and angry (it wasn't fair; he was a neutral. He wasn't mixed up in their arguments. Why had they disturbed him?), Hugo Grayer went up on deck. He was not afraid. Perhaps a very intelligent, well brought up man can't experience panic-stricken, primitive, animal terror? He was furious. It seemed to him that there must be someone to call to account, someone who had not done what he should, the captain of the ship perhaps, or the company that owned it? He had an acute sense of how ridiculous his situation was. It was vulgar, hateful, to be walking around in shirtsleeves, wearing a life preserver, on the deck of a torpedoed ship.

For now he knew. He had heard other passengers talking as they ran: they were being pursued by submarines. "A mistake they won't make again," Hugo Grayer had said at the bar the previous night, forgetting that human nature is fallible and man's memory short.

He felt reduced to the level of a savage. It was as if, tattooed and with a ring in his nose, he had suddenly been forced to dance! He was a civilized man! He had nothing to do with their war! There were moments when he thought he was still dreaming. Yes, this all had the incoherence, the brutal speed, and unreality of a nightmare, right down to the colors that one sees only in dreams: the purple ink of the shadows, the livid brightness of torches, the blinding light of reflections in the swirling water. Split into small groups, the passengers were waiting at the embarkation points where the lifeboats were to be lowered from the upper deck. In the darkness Hugo could see diamonds twinkling on bare hands. That's where his people were; he went to join them. The women had put their fur coats on over their nightdresses and were wearing their jewels safely next to their skin, believing this to be more secure than leaving them in a case that might be dropped as they jumped into the sea.

Mechanically Hugo adjusted his life preserver and looked at the black water. The first boats were just being lowered when there was a blast of gunfire. A smell of gunpowder wafted past Hugo's astonished nostrils; it was a smell he had never experienced, but something in him recognized it; it was a coarse, violent smell that aroused a muffled excitement rather than terror. A shudder ran right through him, from his narrow feet to his pale hands, and it seemed to him that death was touching him, blowing in his mouth, and grabbing him by the hair. Nearby there were screams of pain and fear. There was a second, then a third burst of gunfire.

An invisible hand was shuffling, shaking up and mixing all these hitherto separate groups of people, as if they were ingredients in a cocktail shaker. First- and third-class passengers, women in mink coats, young German-Jewish children on their way to an Uruguayan orphanage with an American charity: they were all running together now, bumping into one another as they rushed toward the boats that were slowly being lowered into the sea. A shell whistled past Hugo. It did not hit him, but someone nearby who pulled him down as he fell.

At that very moment the moon rose with a horribly theatrical brilliance, just like a spotlight over a stage. Hugo saw a woman who had been cut in half. Her head with its dark hair, her ears with their silver earrings, and her torso were intact, but her legs had been blown off. There were cries of "the torpedo!" and everyone crowded onto the starboard side, away from the expected point of impact. The crowd was now behaving as one, quivering like an animal about to be whipped. Hugo got up and ran farther off. The first torpedo had missed them. The second arrived. It seemed strange still to be alive. The second went through the bow of the ship.

There were very few boats left that were of any use: some of the lifeboats had been smashed and several sailors killed by the shelling. Hugo realized that he would not get a place on one; there were too many women and children on board. He jumped into the sea. He didn't know how to swim. Buoyed up by his life preserver, he made futile and exhausting efforts to get away from the ship. The waves played with him, tossing him from one to another with ironic condescension.

A lifeboat went past, but no one saw him. At last he was noticed by some sailors on a raft. They had picked up some women and children floating in the sea, and now Hugo. They wanted to get away from the torpedoed ship, but the wind was blowing them back. They were still close, horribly close . . . They did not have time to worry about the survivors lying at their feet. Hugo had injured his hip jumping into the water. He was lying among people as drenched as he, as frozen as he, and as dazed as he, none of whom could help him. There were two little girls beside him. They must have been part of the group of orphans traveling to Uruguay; their wet hair hung limply over their pale faces. He could give them nothing. He tried to talk to them, to reassure them. They did not reply; they did not understand. Like him, they were awaiting death, for although the ship was still afloat, it would soon capsize and the raft would go down with it, sucked in by the backwash.

Hours passed, as slow and confusing as a night of fever. He was shivering with cold. The wind that had seemed so soft was in fact bitterly cold. It would soon be daylight.

He asked one of the sailors, "Are there many dead?"

He did not know. A woman sitting near Hugo, probably one of the chambermaids, as she addressed him formally, answered, "Monsieur cannot imagine how many bodies I've seen."

The ship was still afloat. Fascinated, he watched the black hull that, like a careless fish, would soon dive below the water, taking them with it. Was Hugo afraid of death? He had always thought not—but it's one thing to see death at the end of a long road, a natural end to a long and happy life, quite another to think that this very night, this very morning, these very moments, might be his last. And what a death! In the dawning light he looked at the water.

It was terrifying. It was being churned up by the wind, bringing to the surface a sort of scum that could not be seen in broad daylight or from the top deck of a ship; foam, seaweed, and the thousands of bits of rubbish floating there since the previous day, or since time began, created a greenish sludge that Hugo contemplated with horror. Where was the fresh sea of a September morning on a French beach? Was this what it concealed in its depths? The waves rose and fell all around him, and he was surrounded by steam, shadows, and ghosts.

Occasionally he became confused again. What was he doing here? Hugo Grayer, a victim of the war, how ridiculous! With every wave, he thought, "This time, it's the end!" But the raft was solid. It was not sinking, but it was not making any progress.

"If I could row, it would help," Hugo thought.

But where would he find the strength to pick up oars? His hip was so painful . . . He felt as if he had been lying there for weeks, or even months, although in moments of lucidity he realized that it was barely daylight, that the torpedo had struck in the middle of the night, that he had been suffering like this for only a few hours—the period of time that had once separated lunch from dinner, or a concert, or one pleasure from another. Five or six hours at most! How short that was! How long! How long it was when every second trickled by in beads of anguished sweat! How cold he was! Suddenly his stomach heaved and he vomited. He wanted to turn his head away out of a sense of decency, but he found his neck was too stiff to move; he remained lying down, vomiting over himself like an animal.

"Monsieur is ill," the woman next to him said compassionately. The awful retching had relieved him for a moment and he was able to reply, "No, it's nothing."

He suddenly remembered that once—a century ago, or was it yesterday?—he had said to someone—Magda? Someone else?—that he was curious to know what sort of emotions would be aroused by extreme danger. Now he knew. He also knew that everything was not immediately lost, that shame, pity, and human solidarity stayed alive in people's hearts. It gave him some comfort to know that he had answered with a measure of dignity. He wanted to do better. Painfully, he breathed, "Thank you."

"You're very cold, monsieur . . ."

She was no longer speaking so formally. She took Hugo's pale, inert hands in hers and held them; she squeezed them, gently rubbing each one as she lifted it . . .

There was no end to the suffering his poor body could endure. His hip was being stabbed cruelly and relentlessly, as if a wicked and intelligent lobster were digging at him with its pincers. Seasickness added to his appalling feeling of cold and abandonment. The day was passing. He dozed, cried out. No one could help him. They looked at him with pity; that was all they could offer him. To hell with their pity! He, too, had watched with compassion as French soldiers went off to fight. Enough, he'd had enough! It was time for these horrible waves to stop! It was time for some warmth! Time to stop seeing those little girls' faces in front of him, as pale and lifeless as dead fish! How tolerable misfortunes appear when they affect only other people! How strong the human body seems when it's another man's flesh that bleeds! How easy it is to look death in the face when it's another man's turn! Well, now it was his turn. This was no longer about a Chinese child, a Spanish woman, a Central European Jew, or those poor charming Frenchmen, but about him, Hugo Grayer. It was about his body being tossed about in the spume of the waves, his vomiting; it was about his frozen, lonely, wretched, shivering self! How often, before going to bed, had he casually crumpled the newspaper he had been reading, in which there were stories about air raids, torpedoes, or fires—oh, so many of them that he wearied of pity? So tomorrow, decent, untroubled people would briefly consider the picture of a calm, smooth sea with its floating wreckage and would not lose an hour's sleep over it or pause over their breakfast. His body would be bloated by the water, eaten by sea creatures, while in a cinema in New York or Buenos Aires the screen would show "The first neutral ship torpedoed in this war!" Then it would be old news, of interest to nobody. People would be thinking about other things, their ailments and their little irritations. Boys would grab hold of girls' waists in the dark; children would suck their sweets.

It was appalling; it was unfair! The whole lot of them were behaving like chickens that allow their mothers and sisters to have their throats cut while they carry on clucking and pecking at their food. They did not understand that it was this passivity, this silent acquiescence, that would, when the time came, also deliver them up to a strong, merciless hand. Hugo thought suddenly that he had always proclaimed his hatred of violence and how it was one's duty to be opposed to evil. Hadn't he said that? Perhaps he had not had time to say it, but one thing was certain: he had always thought it, professed it, believed it! And now here he was in this terrible situation, while others . . . others, in their turn, would maintain their fastidious scruples, parade their well-meaning neutrality, and enjoy delightful peace of mind.

Meanwhile the hours dragged on . . .

Monsieur Rose

[MR. ROSE]

HE WAS AS ALOOF AND SELF-CONTAINED AS A CAT.
He had an easy life; he had never married; and he
was rich. Ever since he had been a child his face had
had a condescending, mocking expression that inspired
respect. He seemed to think that the world was peopled
by fools; that, in fact, was what he did believe, and there
was little to be said in response. He was well into his
fifties, with nice plump cheeks, a sharp, authoritative
voice, a sensitive and discreet manner, and a pointed wit.
He had a good wine cellar and gave excellent dinners
for selected friends. To get to know a man, you have to
see him at the table or with a woman he finds attractive:
whether he was peeling a piece of fruit, or kissing a
woman's hand, Monsieur Rose showed the same fastidious, coaxing attention.

He cared for no one; he hated no one. The general opinion was that he was the most easygoing man in the world. He managed his fortune remarkably well. He had traveled a great deal in his youth, but this no longer gave him any pleasure. He lived on the Boulevard Malesherbes, in the house where he was born. He slept in the same room, in exactly the same corner that his bed had been as a child. His monotonous, reclusive life held joys known only to him. He approved of simple pleasures: long walks, strolls, reading, the same liqueur drunk at the same time every evening in the same quiet bar, children's treats—fondant creams, chocolates, soft-centered sweets; he never picked out a praline rashly but, through half-closed eyes, would look thoughtfully at the pink bag and then, with a little sigh, choose one and delicately put it in his mouth. He thought that one should plan ahead, weigh things up, be wary of the unknown. He was happy to admit that this was not always easy, but patiently he tried to ward off misfortune.

His greatest concern was where to invest his money and how to avoid heavy taxes. He had anticipated the war of 1940 when it was still only a shadow on the horizon, before the time came when every evening, in every Parisian drawing room, twenty or so false prophets in tails and evening dress began glibly to declare that the end of the world was upon them. He had been taking precautions since 1930, although these were not always successful. "I've lost a few feathers," he confided to his close friends in 1932, "but better a feather than the whole bird." Very early on he decided to sell the buildings he owned in Paris, one of which was the house in the Boulevard Malesherbes. He was a little ashamed to admit that he was frightened of air raids. In any case, his reasons were no one else's business. Quietly, without any rush, he finalized some deals, as always without making or losing too much money. He chose a delightful spot in Normandy, not far from Rouen, where he bought a comfortable and well-appointed house with a large garden. After the Anschluss in 1938 he had his collection of porcelain sent there and arranged it in two glass-fronted cabinets in the ground-floor drawing room. When German troops marched into Prague, Monsieur Rose had his glassware and pictures packed away; the books and silver had left shortly before Munich. He was also one of the first Frenchmen to acquire a gas mask. In spite of all this, he remained an optimist, and declared cheerfully that everything would be fine.

MONSIEUR ROSE HAD A MISTRESS, whom he had chosen astutely: she was pretty, elegant, silly, and well-meaning. Monsieur Rose preferred to forget that once, just like other men, he had almost let himself be trapped by a woman. It had happened in Vittel, in 1923. He had fallen in love with a young girl. For the first time in his life, Monsieur Rose's eyes fell on a girl of twenty. She was the niece of the doctor who was looking after him, an orphan who had been taken in through charity; because they didn't much care for her, they wanted to marry her off as soon as possible. She was healthy and brown-haired, with smiling and submissive eyes and a pretty mouth. He was attracted to her immediately; she awoke in him a curious feeling of tenderness and lust, along with a rather unsettling feeling of pity. She wore simple pink dresses, straight as a child's shift, and a round comb in her hair. One day, after a charity event, she wrote to him, signing herself Lucy Maillard. Monsieur Rose had smiled when he saw the "y," which she must have hoped would be an improvement on Lucie, a perfectly good lower-middle-class name: her bad taste enchanted him, he did not know why. It was naive, laughable, delicious: in Monsieur Rose's eyes it symbolized a step toward her dream, a timid attempt at disguise, or a longing for escape.

When he saw the girl again, he teased her about the way she spelled her name, and about the red polish on her nails. She sometimes bit them with a little girl's ferocious energy, then, remembering her age, blushed and asked Monsieur Rose for a cigarette. She did not inhale, but made a face and, as she blew out the smoke, pursed her young girl's lips, which Monsieur Rose found as fresh and sweet as a praline. He did once kiss her. He had met her in the public gardens; it was evening and they were alone. He had kissed her very quickly, wondering how she would react. Lifting her eyes to his, she had asked in a shaky voice, "Do you like me?"

She seemed so uncertain about herself and wanted so much to be reassured, flattered, and loved, that again he could not help the pity he felt when he was with her. He said, "My darling." When he put his hand on her thin neck, he could feel her heatbeat gently under his fingers. It made him think of the warm, palpitating body of a bird, and he whispered, "My darling little bird." They walked on together and he kissed her again. This time she returned his kiss. Softly she asked, "Do you love me? Really? Really and truly? At home, nobody loves me."

After that he invited her to where he was staying. His intentions were honorable; he wanted only to kiss her, but she looked at him and said, "If you were to marry me . . . Oh! You wouldn't want to, I'm sure. I know I'm neither pretty nor rich enough, but if you wanted to . . ." Seizing hold of his hand, she added, "How I would love you!"

She bent her head and kissed his hand. Monsieur Rose was so overcome by this, by her perfume, by her dark hair, that he caught hold of her and, pulling her close, told her that he would marry her and that he would love her.

"Are you unhappy at home?"

"Yes," she said. "Oh, yes!"

"Well, from now on you'll be happy, I promise. You will be my wife. I shall make you happy."

An hour later, when she left, they were engaged. But then he was alone once more, and gradually he came to his senses. What had he done? He wandered through the public gardens; the beautiful evening had misted over and it was raining. He went back to his rooms. He imagined his flat on the Boulevard Malesherbes with a woman whom it would be impossible to get rid of in the evenings. There would be a woman at mealtimes, always. A woman in his bed, whether he wanted her there or not. When he bolted his bedroom door, as he did every night, he was struck by the thought that a wife could perceive this simple act as unusual and almost insulting. He would never be on his own. He was still young and might one day be persuaded to have a child. Then anything would be possible: a wife, children, a family.

"Ridiculous," he said out loud, "ridiculous."

He fell into an armchair, closed his eyes while he collected his thoughts, and then reached a decision: "Impossible."

With one bound, he was on his feet. Never had he moved so fast. He dragged his suitcase into the middle of the room and started to pack. The next day, he fled. It was strange. He forgot the episode at once. For the next ten years no thought of Lucie Maillard ever returned to haunt him. Even so, in 1925 he heard about her marriage and, three years later, her death. He had learned about both events through the doctor: the first left him indifferent and the second aroused only a brief feeling of compassion. But recently he had begun to dream about her, and as he got older he did so more and more often. Yet, thank God, dreams vanish quickly, and these left just a faint feeling of unease, like a distant migraine, which went away as soon as he had sipped a few mouthfuls of his weak morning tea.

Then it was 1939 and Monsieur Rose stopped having dreams. In fact, he slept less and less. How difficult it was, in this shifting, unstable world, to steer a course with certainty, as one used to do. Monsieur Rose foresaw disasters ahead. He regretted them very much, but as he could neither avoid them himself, nor help anyone else to do so, there was only one rational response: his only concern was for himself, for his own well-being and his own fortune.

He would not have admitted this to anyone; the feeling remained, unformulated and troubling, deep down in his heart. Monsieur Rose was not in any way a cynic. Along with everyone else, he talked about necessity and paid homage to the nobility of sacrifice; he was happy to·talk, forcefully, about the citizen's obligations and rights, but in his mind there was an essential difference between himself and other people: he left the obligations to them, keeping only the rights for himself. It was a natural reaction for him, almost an instinctive one. He could not help but relate everything he saw, heard, or read to himself; he saw the world through the prism of his own preoccupations. As these depended on the fate of the world, this was hugely important to him. Thus his conscience was clear. He was able to convince himself with no difficulty that it was Europe's destiny that was preventing him from sleeping, and that by abandoning his peace of mind in this way he was sacrificing what he held most dear. What more could he do? He was no longer young and had no children. In any case, he was overburdened with taxes. That was enough.

One day he decided he must rescue as much as he possibly could.

How could he protect his money? Neither England nor America was, in his view, a safe haven. He deliberated for a long time, using all his experience, caution, and skill to make a careful comparison of every country in Europe, as well as in the rest of the world. None of them seemed to be well enough defended or secure enough to act as his strong room. Finally he chose Norway, where he had financial interests.

At the outbreak of war he was at home in Normandy. He drank fresh milk and tended his roses. When he reappeared in Paris in November he was able to smile at some of the stories he was told about other people who had left.

"Really, my dear fellow, you sent your wife off to the Hérault? What a strange idea!"

"So what did you do?"

"Oh, I just prolonged my holiday. September was so beautiful! I have to tell you that I feel perfectly calm, perfectly indifferent to whatever happens to me. An old bachelor like myself . . ."

Absentmindedly he picked up a paper bag tied with gilt thread that had been left on the table, took a sugared almond from it and, chewing thoughtfully, went on: "I'm no use to anyone, not even myself. Sometimes I feel I've had enough. Now I've seen two wars. This violent and bloody world disgusts me."

And so the winter passed. It was now springtime and Paris had never looked so lovely. There was something melancholy, tender, and luminous about the atmosphere—such a rare and precious beauty that, in spite of himself, Monsieur Rose kept putting off the day of his departure.

He had, in fact, made very specific plans: he would spend this summer of 1940 quietly in Normandy. Then he would take a short trip to England. He had been feeling weary and overwrought for some time; the fighting in Norway had hit him hard. He hoped, indeed was fairly sure, that all was not lost. Nevertheless . . . Yet he had behaved reasonably, with thought, logic, and caution. But reason and caution were gradually losing their hold and their traditional value. As they came into contact with this insane world, they were overturned and came adrift—just as scientific instruments go off course in extreme atmospheric conditions.

Happily, Monsieur Rose's fortune had been only

diminished by the disaster in Norway; it had not disappeared altogether. And he still had his house in Normandy, his china, his pictures, his valuables, and his gold. Nevertheless, he felt angry and bitter, rather like a betrayed lover. Feeling as he did, he dreaded the solitude of the countryside. This splendid Parisian spring suited him better.

It took the night of the tenth of June finally to make him leave. He had slept badly; the sirens had woken him twice and, although he had not gotten out of bed, his sleep had been shattered by their wailing, by the sound of his neighbors hurrying downstairs, and by antiaircraft fire nearby. At dawn he fell deeply asleep and dreamed that he was looking for something, he knew not what, in a strange house, where the doors banged and there were wisps of straw and scraps of wrapping paper all over the floor; someone outside the room shouted at him to hurry up, while he searched desperately for a very dear and precious object or person that he could not find; but he had to leave, and in his dream he was weeping. He was in such anguish that when he woke up his heart was beating furiously. When he discovered what had happened in the night he became very thoughtful. It was time to leave.

THINGS WERE NO BETTER in Normandy. It was ridiculous, he knew. What danger threatened him in this peaceful countryside? In any case, it was not anxiety he felt but a kind of sadness. He felt old, far older than his years. He was out of place in this world. He was a survivor, in fact, of a species that had almost disappeared; his habits and his tastes were leftovers from another era. Something else was needed, he did not know what—youth perhaps? But he was no longer young. He had never been young.

And so he waited.

He did not have to wait long. With one bound the war pounced on Monsieur Rose's peaceful retreat, like a wild animal bursting from its lair. Once more he had to leave. All his silver, books, valuables, and gold, which he had taken such trouble to arrange so carefully, to hang, label, or lock away, were now in chaos: some were buried in the garden, and the rest piled into the car when Monsieur Rose finally decided to go.

"We should have left yesterday," said Robert, the chauffeur.

Monsieur Rose had employed him only since the outbreak of war as a replacement for the previous one, who had been called up. He was a short, ginger-haired, puny man who was exempt from military service. He drove well and did not seem to be dishonest. But Monsieur Rose could barely tolerate him and did so only because he couldn't find anyone else. He spoke with a working-class Parisian accent and was offhand, if not insolent, in his manner. Monsieur Rose liked him less and less. He grumbled, shrugged his shoulders, and was almost rude when spoken to.

They drove all day. When evening came Monsieur Rose was hungry. He was surprised that, in the midst of such a disaster, he could feel such normal, healthy emotions.

"Stop as soon as you see a village," he said to the chauffeur.

He could see only the back of Robert's neck, the ginger hair under the blue cap.

Robert said nothing, but his big red ears quivered; his back seemed to hunch and the back of his neck to crease; impossible to know how he did it, but seen from behind, and without saying a word, he managed to express so much disapproval, such sarcasm, that Monsieur Rose went purple with anger and shouted, "Stop at once!"

"Here?"

"Yes, here. I'm hungry."

"And what is Monsieur going to eat? I can't see a restaurant."

"I can see a farm. At times like these," Monsieur Rose said sadly and severely, "one shouldn't make difficulties."

"It's not difficult to stop," Robert said with a smirk (the car had been stuck for an hour in an unimaginably bad traffic jam). "The problem will be to get going again."

"Do what I tell you," Monsieur Rose replied. "Get out

of the car and run to that house. Buy whatever you can, bread, ham, fruit . . . oh yes, and a bottle of mineral water; I'm dying of thirst!"

"So am I," said Robert. Pulling his cap down over his eyes, he climbed out of the car.

"Well," thought Monsieur Rose, "I'll get even with him tomorrow."

Tomorrow . . . where would he be tomorrow? He knew there was an airfield not far away, and an army camp a bit farther on. Even farther away there were railway lines, bridges, and large factories. It would soon be dark. Every section of the road hid dangers. He had heard that Rouen was burning. What would have happened to his house? He had left it only that morning and was still quite close to it, yet perhaps it was now nothing more than ashes? Strangely, however, as the hours went by he thought less and less about what he had left behind. If he had lost everything, so be it! He still had his life. His life would be saved. At times like this the future shrinks with dizzying speed. He no longer thought about next year or next month but only about today, tonight, the next hour. He looked for nothing beyond that. He was hungry and thirsty; all he wanted was a bit of bread and a glass of water. To think that it had not occurred to him to bring any provisions! He had thought of everything else. He had locked up the house; filed away letters and business documents; remembered his dress clothes, razors, and stiff collars; but he had nothing to eat. Robert wasn't coming back. And the house looked uninhabited. Had they all fled?

Robert appeared and said simply, "There's nobody there. No one's answering the door."

"We'll try a bit further on, as soon as we see a house."

For a long time they were forced to wait where they were. At last the line of cars began to move. Monsieur Rose tapped on the window. "Here, I can see a light."

Robert got out of the car. Monsieur Rose drummed the "March of the Little Wooden Soldiers" on his knee. The minutes passed. Robert came back empty-handed.

"There's nothing."

"What do you mean, nothing? There are people living there."

"They're packing."

"But they must have a bit of bread left, or cheese, or pâté, at least something to eat?"

"Nothing," said Robert again. "Monsieur must realize, with all the traffic there is on this road . . . we'll get nothing to eat until tomorrow . . . or next week. If Monsieur doesn't believe me, he can go and look for himself."

Monsieur Rose was already getting out of the car.

"I certainly will. You're too tactless, my boy. I'm sure you talked to them rudely and disagreeably—as you so often do. People aren't savages, for God's sake! You don't refuse to give a bit of bread to your neighbor and anyway," he finished angrily, "I'm not asking for charity!"

He made his way with difficulty through the cars trapped bumper to bumper. Their headlights were off; people's heads were tilted back, as their eyes anxiously followed a shadow flitting from one star to another. Was it a cloud or an enemy plane?

He thought he could hear the noise of an engine, but it was just the constant, muffled sound of the crowd, which was rising into the sky: footsteps, voices, bicycles being wheeled over stones on the road, the stifled, gasping breaths of thousands of people, and the occasional cries of children. Monsieur Rose walked away from this with a feeling of relief, as if waking from a nightmare. It seemed to him that he had been miraculously transported back several centuries and that he had become part of one of the great human migrations of the past; he felt horror-struck and ashamed. Rather more quickly than he would normally have done, he walked up the path to the farm. Robert had not been lying. In the main room he saw two women weeping as they threw household linen into an unfolded blanket. An old woman stood at the door, ready to flee, two children in her arms and two more clinging to her skirt. The kitchen cupboard was open and empty.

"There's nothing, monsieur, I'm sorry. We have nothing left. Look, we only have a little dry sausage left for ourselves, and some milk for the children. That's all. We're leaving now."

Monsieur Rose apologized and retraced his steps.

"I'm going to have trouble finding Robert," he

thought, as from the top of the slope, he watched the black stream winding slowly on.

All the cars looked the same with their mattresses fixed to the roof. His car had probably moved on a bit. He could no longer tell which was his. He walked on and called out, "Robert! Robert!"

At first his voice was strong and forceful, then it became anxious, then frightened, then shaky and pleading. No one replied. Robert had abandoned him; he had gone with the car, the trunks, the silver, and the clothes.

"Bastard! Thief!" howled Monsieur Rose, losing his head.

He ran, stumbling along the top of the bank, looking for he knew not what—an inspector, a local policeman, someone he could complain to, who would protect him. But there was no one. Everyone was fleeing and no one was interested in him.

Finally, out of breath, Monsieur Rose collapsed onto the grass. As he clutched his chest, his hand touched his wallet and he felt calmer. It was as if he had rediscovered solid ground: he felt anchored and strong, ready to take his place in the world again.

"This has simply been a difficult night to get through. I'll report Robert first thing in the morning and he'll be locked up. There's no question of him getting across the border. And if he stays in France, I'll be able to find him."

All he had to do now was to get to a town or a village.

But how? Everywhere he looked the road was packed with cars, trucks, three-wheelers, motor bicycles with sidecars, and carts, all inching slowly forward; the parcels, boxes, prams, and bicycles piled on top of them looked like rickety scaffolding towers. There was nowhere to sit, nothing to hold on to. No. There was no room for Monsieur Rose! And the crowd of pedestrians was already sweeping him along.

"Well then, dammit, I'll walk!" he said out loud.

"Has your car been pinched, monsieur?" asked a young man walking beside him. "It's my bike that's gone."

At first Monsieur Rose did not answer. Normally he did not talk to strangers. He looked at the young man, who must have been sixteen or seventeen but was so well-built, sturdy, and tall that Monsieur Rose thought to himself, "He could be useful."

Was this a throwback to former times, when the only things that mattered were strong muscles and hard fists? The young man could, after all, help Monsieur Rose as they walked; he could find him something to eat, or somewhere to stay.

Monsieur Rose said, eventually, "Yes, my driver thought it a good joke to abandon me. But what about you?"

"Oh, someone asked me to lend a hand repairing a flat tire. I left my bike in a ditch and when I went back it was gone. Luckily I've got a good pair of legs."

"Yes, that is lucky. Have you come a long way?"

"From my school, fifty kilometers away. We were all sent home. I was supposed to go with one of the teachers. But in the end it was such chaos that I never found him. We were bombed, so I left."

"What about your family?"

"They're in the country, near Tours."

"Are you planning to join them?"

"In theory, yes . . . I set off hoping to do so, but I have to tell you, monsieur, that I've changed my mind now. I'm seventeen. I could serve my country. As I said to my father at the beginning of the war, now people must make a choice between leading a heroic life or an easy one."

"That choice has already been made for me," muttered Monsieur Rose bitterly, as he stumbled over the stones in the road.

The young man smiled.

"Of course, at your age, monsieur, it's hard. But I thought I'd join up. I know there's a camp near Orléans. I'll enlist; every man ought to fight."

"What's your name, young man?" asked Monsieur Rose.

"Marc. Marc Beaumont."

"Do you live in Paris?"

"Yes, monsieur."

They went on in silence for a while. They walked for hour after hour. It seemed impossible for the crowd to get any bigger, but from every track and every crossroads shadows appeared, joining the first wave of refugees and walking beside them in silence. People did not talk much; no one complained, no one cried or shouted; everyone instinctively saved their breath for walking. Monsieur Rose's painful feet could hardly carry him.

"Lean on me, monsieur, don't worry, I'm strong," the boy said. "You've had enough."

"I need to rest . . ."

"If you'd like to . . ."

They tumbled into a ditch and instantly the young man fell asleep. But Monsieur Rose was at an age when exhaustion overstimulates the mind and drives sleep away. He lay quite still, occasionally covering his eyes with his hands.

"What a nightmare," he said mechanically. "What a nightmare . . ."

THE JUNE NIGHT was soon over. In the morning they set off again. There was no food to be had, and nowhere to stay. People slept in the fields, by the side of the road, or in the woods. After forty-eight hours, with his grimy shirt, crumpled suit, and dusty shoes, Monsieur Rose— who had not washed or shaved for two days—looked like a tramp.

"I suppose we'll carry on like this, on foot, until we reach Tours," Marc Beaumont said.

Monsieur Rose protested sharply, "On foot! We're

not traveling on foot! That's ridiculous! You mustn't give in to the deplorable habit of overdramatizing the situation, my boy. Later you'll be able to tell your children, 'During the great exodus of 1940 I walked from Normandy to Tours.' In fact, you will have walked for part of the way, but for some of it you will have traveled in a truck or a car, or even on a bicycle, and so on and so forth. You should realize that there's no such thing as pure tragedy; there are always varying degrees of it." As he spoke, Monsieur Rose fell and then got up again, for his swollen knees were making it increasingly difficult for him to walk.

In fact, toward evening they were picked up by a passing truck. Some women who had been evacuated from a Parisian factory were sheltering under its wet tarpaulin. It was raining; the hastily erected cover let in water, which trickled down the women's necks. They had brought folding stools with them, on which they sat motionless, hunching their backs against the rain, guarding parcels at their feet and children on their laps. Monsieur Rose and Marc Beaumont were allocated a stool between them, and an umbrella that fell open and swung about at every jolt in the road. After a few hours they had to give up their places to some children who were picked up from the edge of a field. Fortunately it had stopped raining. They carried on walking, slept again, found some eggs in an abandoned farm, which they swallowed raw, and dragged themselves on. In a village some soldiers gave them food and told them to leave at once, as there was going to be fighting. They would not allow Marc to join them. "It's not men we need, sonny, it's equipment." Monsieur Rose and Marc set off again.

Marc, at least, was able to sleep. As soon as he lay down on the ground, he was dead to the world. But Monsieur Rose found only brief moments of rest and oblivion between nightmares. He looked at his companion closely. The child had something of poor Lucie Maillard about him. He had even asked Marc about his mother's name, somehow imagining that there might be a family link between them. But there was nothing. Nothing linked the living teenager and the dead girl, other than the feeling their youth aroused in Monsieur Rose. Marc provoked an irritable and affectionate pity in him, just as Lucie once had. He was forever ready to carry a child, pick up a parcel, or give away his meager share of food whenever he found any. On the fifth day he lost his watch. Monsieur Rose jeered at him, "Well, of course, if you will run into the woods looking for some woman's bag . . . If at least she had been pretty . . . but that old hag . . . That's how you let your bicycle be stolen. You're always going to be robbed in life."

"Oh, monsieur!" said Marc. "I won't be the only one."

He laughed. He could laugh still: he was even thinner, he was pale and hungry, yet he laughed.

"What does it matter, monsieur?"

"A bicycle might have saved your life."

"Oh, I'll get out of this somehow!"

"Of course you will, of course . . . I hope I will, too. Although I can't imagine what state I'll be in!"

THINGS BECAME MORE and more nightmarish. None of the restaurants, hotels, or private houses had a single spare room left, not even a bed or a square meter of space on the floor, and none could offer even a crust of bread. When they reached Chartres, the refugees were given soup at the gate of a barracks, and Monsieur Rose wept for joy when he was given his helping.

They continued south, toward the Loire. It seemed as if they would never get there. One night there was a shout of "run for your life!" and several bombs fell. Marc and Monsieur Rose were lying on the ground, in the shelter of a little wall; Monsieur Rose was scrabbling at the earth with his nails, as if he wanted to hide underneath it. Then he felt Marc's hand on his shoulder, a firm, gentle, but still childlike hand, which patted him shyly and affectionately: it was as if he were a new boy in the playground being reassured.

The plane went away. No one had been hurt, but a house could be seen burning in the distance. In a low voice, Monsieur Rose said, "This is too much. It's too much for me. I can't face it."

"We'll be fine, though, you'll see," said Marc, trying to laugh.

"But you're seventeen! You're not afraid of death. You don't love life at seventeen! I want to save my life, don't you see? I may be poor, old, and weak, the world may be in ruins, but I still want to live."

They set off again. Monsieur Rose didn't talk anymore. They were getting nearer the Loire. They didn't know how long they had been walking. There was a second air raid. They were in a little group of refugees, huddled together: the instinct that makes a herd of animals gather together in a storm drew them close to one another. Marc sheltered Monsieur Rose with his body. He was injured but Monsieur Rose was unharmed. He bandaged his young companion as best he could and they went on walking. At last the bridges of the Loire were in sight.

Suddenly, Monsieur Rose collapsed.

"I can't walk any further. It's impossible. I'd rather die here."

"I can't carry on either," said Marc.

His wound was bleeding and he stumbled at every step. Both of them, the old man and the boy, stayed where they were, in a heap by the side of the road, watching the Loire glinting in the sunshine and the flood of refugees going past. Monsieur Rose felt calm, indifferent, detached from everything, from his possessions, from his life. Then, suddenly galvanized, he stood up. Someone was shouting. Someone was calling his name: "Monsieur Rose! Is that you, Monsieur Rose?"

He saw a face he knew at a car window. He could not put a name to it; it seemed to belong to another world. Whether it was a friend or a distant relation, a colleague or an enemy, what did it matter? It was a man with a car. Overloaded, of course, full of parcels, women, and children like all the others, but at least it was a car.

"Do you have room for me?" he called out. "My car was stolen. I've been walking since Rouen. I can't go another step. For pity's sake, take me!"

Inside the car they consulted one another. A woman cried out, "Impossible!"

Another woman said, "They're going to blow up the bridges over the Loire. They won't be able to get across."

She leaned toward Monsieur Rose, saying, "Get in. I've no idea how, but just get in."

Monsieur Rose moved toward the car and was about to climb in when he remembered Marc. "Make room for this young man, too . . ."

"Out of the question, my poor friend."

"I won't leave him," said Monsieur Rose.

He was so tired that his voice sounded faint and distant to his own ears, as if it were someone else's.

"Is he a relation of yours?"

"No. Never mind. He's injured. I can't abandon him."

"We don't have room."

At that moment someone shouted, "The bridges! The bridges are going to go up!"

The car accelerated away. Monsieur Rose closed his eyes. It was over; he had lost his life. Why? For this child who meant nothing to him? He heard the voice of a woman beside him shouting, "There are people on it! People! There are cars!"

In the frightful chaos and confusion the bridge had been blown up too soon; so, too, had the refugees' cars, including the one that Monsieur Rose had refused to get into.

Pale and trembling, he fell down next to Marc, barely realizing that his life had just been restored to him.

La confidente

[THE CONFIDANTE]

IT WAS HERE THAT SHE HAD ENJOYED THE SWEET
sleep of the living for the last time. He remembered that
she had always slept like a child, folding her bare arms
over her heart. He stood by the bed in which she had
spent the night before the accident and touched the cold
pillow and the white sheets. He forgot that he was in a
strange house and that a woman was there with him.
He went ahead of her into each room, opening windows and cupboards. He asked, "Where did she sit
at mealtimes?" Or, "Did she keep her dresses in this
wardrobe?"

He listened to the quiet, tactful replies. "She sat
here . . . Her dresses were in the blue room, her underwear in the big chest of drawers in the alcove . . ."

He looked at the stranger who stood next to him; she

had looked after Florence as she died, held her beautiful hands in hers, dressed her for burial. She was a pale, self-effacing person, dressed in plain black, with her hair up in a thick, tight bun; to Roger Dange she appeared frail and ugly, hardly like a woman at all. Why had his delicate, brilliant Florence remained so attached to this dismal creature, this poor provincial school-mistress who had been her childhood friend? It was incomprehensible. And why had he gone so far away? Why had he agreed to a concert tour in Mexico, thought the widower. Florence had decided to go with him ini-tially; then, a week before their departure, she had changed her mind and said that she would go and live with her friend until March. He was pleased about that: he had been anxious about Florence's health on such a long journey—she had barely recovered from a miscar-riage. They had been married for two years; he was much older than his wife, he was in love, and he was jealous. He was happier knowing that she was in this remote village with Mademoiselle Cousin. (This was the old spinster's name. Strange that he should think of her as old . . . He knew that she was only eighteen months older than Florence, and Florence would be, would have been, thirty this year . . .) Yes. He had been happier knowing that she was here rather than surrounded by other men.

He thought he caught a sudden glimpse of her in this darkened room, holding a mirror up in the charming

way she had when she was powdering her cleavage and
her neck. He put a hand up to rub his forehead and
when he lowered it, found that it was damp with sweat,
although the house was freezing. After a long silence, he
at last heard Mademoiselle Cousin's worried voice
through the ringing in his ears.

"You are ill, Monsieur Dange!"

He had to take her arm to return to the dining room.
The little stove was lit and he felt better. "I'll leave you
now," he murmured. "I do apologize, I think I caught a
chill on my way here."

She moved an armchair closer to the fire.

"You can't go now. It's so cold and you're white as a
sheet, Monsieur Dange."

"But I must be in your way . . ."

"No," she replied quietly. She put a few more logs on
the fire and left the room. A young maid came in to close
the shutters. Mademoiselle Cousin returned with a
steaming hot cup of tea.

It was a February evening and the countryside was
gloomy and wet. A great gale was blowing. The two
pine trees outside the front door creaked and moaned,
and a half-broken branch knocked rhythmically against
the wall, as if someone in the dark outside were
demanding shelter. Dange flinched at every thud.

"I must have them felled," said Mademoiselle Cousin.
"In any case, they shut out the light."

"Mademoiselle, I would like to hear from you again

the story of that last day and all the details of the accident."

"But I wrote and told you. Florence had said the day before that she planned to go to Paris in the morning and stay for three or four days. She got up early—well, early for her—it was nine o'clock. School had just started. I didn't see her go. But I heard the noise the car made as it turned over on the road. It had been raining. The car skidded on the main square, in front of the war memorial. It swerved horribly, hitting the little wall in front of the Simons' house. Oh, I cannot describe the noise; it was like a clap of thunder, and then the smashing of glass as the windows broke. The village is small and peaceful, as you will have seen, Monsieur Dange, and the sound of the crash brought everyone out onto the square. You could see everything from the school windows. I ran out at once to go to her. The car was destroyed. They pulled the poor woman out of the wreckage."

"Was her face disfigured?" asked Dange.

His musician's hands were expressive, delicate and strong. As he stretched them out to the warmth of the stove, the tips of his long fingers quivered. Mademoiselle Cousin hastily replied, "No, no, her face was untouched."

"But her body?"

"Her body?" She hesitated, picturing those legs, which had been literally crushed. "Her injuries were not obvious," she said finally.

"Was she still alive?"

"She was still breathing. She was brought here—someone managed to get a stretcher. They carried her very gently. She didn't appear to be suffering."

"You must give me the names of the good people who helped her. I'd like to give them something."

"Oh, there's no need for that!"

"Yes, there is . . . And tell me again . . . you called the doctor at once, didn't you? And there was nothing to be done? Ah, if only I had been here! Why did I go away? It's odd, I felt deeply worried when I left her . . . I hated everything about the journey I was about to make. Twice I put off my departure. But we had spent a lot of money and these concerts were extremely well paid. At my request the agent had demanded exorbitant fees. I think I hoped they would turn them down, or at least negotiate, which would have given me a good excuse to pull out. But no, they agreed to everything. I left and then, a fortnight later, your telegram arrived telling me of Florence's death. I feel ashamed that I've only come now to thank you for what you did for her. I didn't think I would have the courage to enter this house, to see the room where Florence died, or to see you, mademoiselle."

"I do understand. Drink your tea, Monsieur Dange. Look, I've put a teaspoon of rum in it."

He pushed away the cup she offered him.

"This journey . . . Did she say why she was going?"

"No, she said nothing."

"She was killed on the fourth of December, wasn't she?"

"Yes, it was exactly two months ago on Monday."

He looked at her as if he wanted to say something else and opened his mouth to speak, but then his thin face was convulsed in a silent grimace of pain; he did not speak.

Mademoiselle Cousin lowered her head. The only noticeable thing about her appearance was a thick streak of silvery white in her black hair. She stroked it continually and unconsciously; she was wearing an old-fashioned jet mourning ring. Roger Dange noticed it and his innate good manners made him ask distractedly, "You have lost someone?"

"A cousin, a young man of twenty-five."

"Ah, was that a long time ago?"

"It was . . ." She broke off. "It was a few months ago," she said finally. "Monsieur, I followed your instructions precisely. They arrived too late, alas, for her burial, but by a strange coincidence I had dressed Florence in the dress you asked for. Her body was taken to Paris on the sixth of December and then everything else was carried out according to your wishes."

"You knew her well, didn't you?"

"Yes, we were childhood friends. We were born in the same little village in the Jura, as you know."

"I do know . . . but now that I think about it, I know very little about her. We were married for two years. I had met her at the opera house where she wanted to make her debut. What a lovely voice she had! Perhaps not quite powerful enough for a career on the stage, but the purest soprano I had ever heard. We fell in love almost immediately. These last two years have gone by so quickly, and my concerts, my career, my performances on the radio, all of that took from us, robbed us of time together. What's left? As young newlyweds do, we had tacitly agreed to save our secrets and memories like a nest egg for old age, in order not to miss a moment of love."

She shifted in her chair and he thought he might have shocked the old maid. He fell silent. The word "love," and especially the hoarse, passionate way he had uttered it, seemed to hang between them, reverberating and then fading away like the sound of a cello. The room was very dark; a desk lamp with an angled green shade lit up a pile of exercise books open on a table.

"I am behaving unforgivably. I arrive here, tear you away from your work, and ask you absurd, sentimental questions. And all simply to hear one more time what you have already described in your letters and which neither you nor I can change . . . You must think I'm very strange, even a little mad."

"Not at all. I well understand it, Monsieur Dange. After such a terrible blow . . ."

He gestured impatiently. "Listen . . . I must tell you . . . Something happened that particularly disturbs me. Oh, it's undoubtedly a misunderstanding, but . . . so, can you confirm that Florence talked to you the day before about the journey to Paris, the journey during which she was killed?"

"But . . . yes."

"Without giving any reason for her absence?"

"But it was only for a few days. And in any case she didn't have to give me reasons. She may have talked about going to her dressmaker or to the dentist, I forget. I don't see why it's so important . . ."

"My mail didn't reach me in Mexico—it was held up at the post office and was only recently sent on to me. I got it four days ago. There were two letters from Florence."

"Yes?"

"The first was dated the fourth of December, the day of her death, and the second was dated the fifth, the next day."

"There must have been a mistake," said Mademoiselle Cousin, dropping the log she had been about to throw on the fire. "Did you check the postmarks?"

"The first one was sent on the fourth of December and the second on the fifth."

"That's . . . incomprehensible."

"Yes, isn't it? I can think of only one explanation: that my wife was so looking forward to those busy, happy few days in Paris that she had already dealt with my request that she write me a daily letter. She must have asked someone to post them while she was away so that they would all come from the same place. She could have posted the first one herself, she might have stopped at the post office just before the accident, but she must have given the second one to somebody else, possibly some child in the village, who didn't know she was dead or who wasn't bright enough to realize that now she was dead the letter shouldn't be sent. Yes, that's what must have happened."

"And was there anything in the letters?"

"Anything about her trip to Paris, do you mean? No, not a word. Those letters . . . oh, only she could have written them: they were enchanting, sad, and crazy. She talked about music, about those tall pine trees outside your door, mademoiselle, about the snow, and about what she was reading. The one dated the fifth of December started like this"—he closed his eyes and spoke in a low voice—" 'Last night it rained very hard on the snow-covered ground. The angry rain lashed down on the pure white snow; it was as if a young girl was being whipped by witches . . . I think I caught a chill. I got up very late . . .' The rest of the letter was about Mozart's *Eine kleine Nachtmusik* and about Christmas roses, which had died on All Saints' Day, in spite of tradition . . ."

He fell silent.

"I don't understand," Mademoiselle Cousin said faintly.

"That chill she mentioned was so that she could have two or three days' peace in Paris, without having to write to me. I would have learned afterwards that she had had a touch of flu and that she was better."

"But there was nothing to stop her from telling you about the trip, for goodness' sake! She could have thought up a perfectly reasonable excuse for going."

"I've spoken to the servants. She had not given any orders for her arrival. She would never show up unexpectedly. She liked everything to be ready for her: a fire lit, her bath run, flowers . . . She didn't intend to stay in the flat that night, I'm sure of it. Under those circumstances, of course, it was natural that she should want to keep her trip a secret."

"But, monsieur, I must tell you again, her intentions were entirely innocent."

"Oh, come on!" he said, looking straight at her. "You know there can't be a shadow of doubt. I only have to look at the expression on your face, mademoiselle. The facts are clear. But don't worry, I won't ask you anything," he added, forcing a smile, "not her lover's name, nor how long their affair had been going on. You wouldn't tell me. You were very attached to Florence. You did your best to help her deceive me. Now you will loyally keep her secrets, more loyally than ever, I'm sure. There can't be much you don't know. However, as I've said, I'm not going to ask you any difficult questions. I simply wanted to talk about Florence to someone who

knew her well, who loved her; to talk about her tenderly, and at length . . . for one last time. You were very
fond of my wife, weren't you?"

She did not reply.

"She was such an exceptional person, wasn't she? I
always felt humble when I was with her. I knew perfectly well that one day she would be unfaithful or she
would leave me. Everyone knows they must die some-
day. I was twenty-two years older than her."

"But what are you saying? How can you talk like
that?" she asked quickly, vehemently. "Monsieur Dange,
have you forgotten who you are? Have you never seen
the auditorium during one of your concerts, with all
those people who admire you, who are grateful to you,
who love you? Yes, monsieur, they love you. You artists,
you live in a world that is . . ." She was searching for
the words as she looked at him with wide, shining eyes.
". . . sublime. As for us, we are nothing—poor, useless
creatures. It's so rare, so wonderful for a great artist even
to look at us, to take us away from the ordinariness of
our lives, to speak for us. That's something huge, monsieur. It's almost your duty to understand that. Forgive
me for speaking to you like this. If I seem to be lecturing
you, it's only because I admire you so much. What did
it matter that you were twenty-two years older than
Flora?"

"What?"

"Than Flora," she repeated. "She was called Flora,

you must have known that. Florence was her stage name. Twenty-two years older than her! But you, you're a genius, one of the greatest musicians of our time! You did her a great honor by letting her into your world."

He looked at her sadly. "Oh, how little you know," he said gently. "I'm famous, yes, but that . . . Once I was probably someone who was worthy of your praise. But fame, you know, is a bitter fruit picked after the tree has fallen."

"I don't understand," she said. "To me, you're a man above humankind. Your humility is not admirable; it's morbid."

"The man she loved must have been more brilliant than me and have had a greater intellect. I imagine him being like me as a young man."

"Like you?" She shook her head. "Oh, no, Monsieur Dange, he certainly wasn't like you!"

She stopped, and seemed to be waiting for him to put a question to her, but he asked nothing; he reached out toward the little table, now barely visible in the shadows, looking for his cup with shaking hands.

"Is there any tea left?"

"I'll bring you some."

"No, no, please, don't move. I love cold tea and I'm dying of thirst." He greedily drank the brick-colored tea.

"You're being very sympathetic," he said hesitantly, bending his thin face toward the fire. "But you helped her to deceive me."

"I didn't help her. On the contrary, I did my best to make her see reason, but I . . ."

"Yes, I understand, one couldn't hold out against Florence. With her beauty, her grace, that aloof manner of hers . . . Yes, that's the word I was looking for. She was so aloof, in society and with men. Sometimes she could appear cold and distracted. I knew people who thought she was superficial and not very intelligent. But what does intelligence matter? That streak of sadness and craziness she possessed . . . Her letters . . . God, how I loved her letters! I can't tell you how I felt four days ago, when I saw her handwriting on those envelopes forwarded from Mexico. I was shaking. It was devastating, but sweet as well . . . It's all over for me now, isn't it? I'm not creative, all I can do is interpret. In the end that's unrewarding, it's not enough. You won't understand that. I rediscover the dead and bring them back to life. It's a medium's job. Unfortunately I, Roger Dange, am sterile. I can't create anything. I won't leave anything behind: not a child, nor a masterpiece, not even love. Nothing."

"You have a brilliant reputation."

"All this has worn me out," he said suddenly in a different tone of voice. He could hardly move his lips. "I haven't slept for four nights, even after large doses of sleeping pills. They're not enough to make me sleep, but they make me feel as if I'm in a strange state halfway between dreaming and being awake. It's very bizarre. And this room, the fire . . . I feel feverish."

"Would you like to lie down? I can make you up a nice bed, you can sleep, and . . ."

"But I've just told you I can't sleep!" he exclaimed irritably. "No, leave me alone. I'm fine here, really I am. If you want to help, don't talk to me about myself; tell me about Florence, just about Florence . . . the simplest, most trivial things. Her clothes, for instance. What was she wearing the day she died? It was very cold, so she must have been wearing her long, gray traveling coat, the one with the sealskin collar. And which hat did she have on?"

"Which hat?" the teacher muttered distractedly. "Listen, Monsieur Dange . . ."

She stopped, lost in deep thought. "I've got some old mementos," she said at last. "Some pictures of Flora . . . of Florence, and some of her letters. Would you like to see them?"

He nodded. She stood up to take a photograph from the mantelpiece and gave it to him. It showed twenty little girls in a school playground, wearing black aprons and clogs. Their hair was unkempt and they were pigeon-toed. They were uncouth little country girls of thirteen or fourteen, sturdily built and broad-chested, bulging out of their stiff smocks and coarse woolens.

"Florence was one of these?" he asked with a tense, amused smile. "She must have been a swan among ducks."

"That's her," Mademoiselle Cousin said. "She was

solid and chubby, as girls can be at that age, but her face was charming; she had delicate features and big blue eyes. I had been boarding for a term in Besançon when this picture was taken. Flora sent it to me. Look," she said, showing him the dedication. " 'To my dear Camille from her own Flora.' I could not rest until she joined me. She didn't want to carry on with her studies. She wanted to learn how to sew and then set herself up in town. She was quite happy with her vision of the future: a sewing machine in some shabby room and an outing to the cinema on a Saturday night with the assistant from the draper's shop opposite. Like mine, her family was lower middle class and had no private means. Her father had remarried. She didn't get along with her stepmother, although she actually wasn't a bad woman, just one of those bitter, apathetic people . . . if you see what I mean. Flora was always moaning, sulking and complaining.

"During the Easter holidays, when I was at home, I went to see her parents—I was fifteen then. I don't know how I did it, but after appealing to her father, as well as first begging and then terrifying her stepmother, I finally convinced them to send Flora to the boarding school I was attending in Besançon. We were there for five years and I stayed for a further year as a tutor, so I didn't have to leave her behind. I tried to make her work, to make her take her exams so that she could become something, to stop her from giving up her singing lessons; above all, I tried to make sure that none of those horrible boys would come anywhere near her, because for me Flora was . . ."

She took the photograph from the widower and put it back in its place. She walked up and down the room for a long time, her arms folded across her chest. Her footsteps were extraordinarily quiet and light.

"No, you can't imagine what Flora was to me. I was eighteen months older than she was. She had the face, the looks, and the smile that I would have liked to have had. I've never been pretty. I knew that. At first I was jealous of Flora. I remember once ripping up the sky blue coat she wore on Sundays, using my nails and teeth like a little savage. She had left it on a chair in the hall when she had come to play with me. Everyone said, 'What a pretty pale color, and how well it goes with her blonde curls!' Then, as I grew older, that feeling vanished and was replaced by something very strange . . . You asked me just now if I felt friendship for Flora. No, I felt neither friendship nor tenderness, but I was molding her in the way I wanted, do you see? It started with little things. When there was a prize-giving, I would help her to practice her reading. I would show her how to recite, how to stand, how to curtsy, and how to make the most of her pretty profile and her curly hair. When people applauded and complimented her, I felt a bitter joy that I can't describe. I thought, 'Well, that's my doing; it's thanks to me that Flora is being admired. She would be nothing without me. She's my creation.' "

She stopped in front of Dange. " 'She's my creation.' That's exactly what I thought. Like writing a book or painting a picture. Of course, it took me many years to understand that. It's probably only for the last five or six years that I've completely understood it. In fact, I sometimes used to forget Flora. I was becoming ambitious for myself, particularly when I passed an examination with excellent marks. But then I'd say to myself, 'With the ugly face God has given you, my girl, you must ask for nothing, hope for nothing. It's for the best; at least you'll spare yourself the cruelty of disappointments.' And in any case, it was in my nature to enjoy being the éminence grise. As an adolescent I admired the Jesuits more than anyone, those clever, discreet men who advised the king behind the scenes. Don't laugh at me, Monsieur Dange. No one else knows what I'm telling you, but for once in my life I'm talking honestly, and in any case, I'm the one who gave you the Flora you miss so much."

"How can that be?" asked Dange. He was listening with intense concentration, crossing and uncrossing his pale hands while he did so.

"By the time she reached thirteen or fourteen, Flora had become very ordinary. I didn't enjoy going to see her anymore. She disappointed me and she annoyed me, so that my life became meaningless. I got good marks on all my tests and examinations without making much of an effort and my end of year reports were glowing; I was an excellent pupil, but I was bored. You know, at the age I was then, only one thing mattered: my dreams, a sort of other life in which I imagined who I could be, what I wanted to become. For years, in my dreams, I had been Flora. I had drawn out her best qualities to turn her into something extraordinary, but then she became dull, almost stupid, aspiring to be nothing more than a dressmaker. A dressmaker, can you see her doing that? Flora the dressmaker, pregnant by a shop assistant or sensibly married to some petit bourgeois. Flora . . . And what about me?

"But one day I heard her sing. It was when we were by the river during the Easter holidays. The rivers are deep and fast-flowing in our part of the world. Spring had come early that year. We had gone to dip our feet in the water and pick flowers. We were a group of five or six girls. It was dark when we got back to the village. As we walked along, arm in arm, one of us began to sing. The others all joined in the chorus, and Flora's voice rose above them with such natural grace and such purity that we gradually fell silent and were carried along, uplifted by her beautiful voice. Then, as I told you, I arranged for her to come to Besançon. It was important, you see, for her to become cultivated and well brought up, a young lady, in fact. I had read somewhere that one shouldn't start singing lessons in adolescence, but I didn't want her to waste those years without any general culture, education, or reading. I think I was quite a gifted teacher. Flora was lazy. I was the only one who could make her work. How I delighted in her progress! As for me, I was no longer such a remarkable student, merely average. I had deliberately put aside all personal ambition in order to concentrate on Flora. In a way I lived through her. You can't imagine how much I used to enjoy having this secret. I felt proud and superior to everyone, especially to Flora. As soon as she turned eighteen, I made her study singing. She went to Paris where, as I'm sure you know, she almost immediately became the mistress of a very rich man, married but separated from his wife, and they lived together openly."

"Yes, I did know that," Dange said.

"I hardly ever saw her, but she didn't forget me. She was fond of her lover, but at the same time she wanted her freedom . . . do you understand?"

"I understand."

"That period of her life was a difficult one. The man was demanding and jealous. When their relationship became strained almost to the breaking point, Flora would come running to me. She would come in here and sit in that armchair where you're sitting now. She would say, 'I've done this . . . This is what I said to him . . . What do you think I should have done? What would you have done in my place?' Then I would talk to her . . . for a long time. I would make her see reason. I . . . you see, I didn't want her to leave this man. Thanks to him, she was becoming Parisian. She dressed well; in fact, she was really beginning to look the part. Her hair, her dresses, the way she held herself, everything was perfect. Meanwhile, in my head, I was building up a great future for her. Flora was my work of art. You think that's stupid? Why? You can create a work of art with crude, inanimate material, with a stone and a hammer or a canvas and some colors, so why not with flesh and blood? Imprinting your personality on someone else, breathing your spirit into theirs is intoxicating, you know."

"And Florence obeyed and listened to you, did she?"

"How often do I have to tell you, monsieur, that you didn't know her! No one knew her, least of all Flora herself. She thought she was free, would you believe it! When I used to tell her, 'You must do this or that. You must write to him like this. I'll dictate a letter to you. You must send this man away, gently, without discouraging him, but . . . ,' she would sneer and exclaim, 'Oh, my poor Camille, you have no idea! What do you know about men, love, or life, buried in your little backwater!' I would answer, 'Well, maybe you're right, but just have a little think about it and you'll see that I'm right. That's what you must do.' In the end, after she'd followed my advice, she would persuade herself it had all been her own idea. She was so typically feminine . . ."

She fell silent; the smile on her face was sad, tender, and bitter all at the same time. Dange looked at her, aghast. After a moment's silence, she continued:

"Her lover died suddenly and, as no provision had been made for Flora in his will, everything went to his lawful wife. Overnight Flora became poor. Nothing was in her name, neither the grand house where she was living nor her car. I managed to arrange leave for a few months and we lived together in Paris. Monsieur, do you understand? I wanted to make something of this woman. I was thinking about a career on the stage. With her voice, her beauty, and her charm, she could have had one, don't you think? She could have been famous! Yet, thinking about it, that still wasn't enough. You see, it had all become a sort of delusion. I would occasionally forget that I was Camille Cousin and she was Flora Leblanc. When she sang, it seemed to be my voice that I heard. Her singing freed me from myself. We led a very quiet, reclusive life, as she didn't like people seeing her in the wretched state she had been reduced to by her lover's death. She had no beautiful dresses, no jewelry, and often couldn't afford the hairdresser. If she'd been on her own, she would have taken up with the first wealthy man who came along."

Dange interrupted her. "She's not here to defend herself," he said quietly, his voice shaking.

"Monsieur, I'm speaking to you as before God. I am a believer and I know that her spirit is here, listening to us, and can see that I'm telling the truth. I was the one who looked after her for those two years, allowing her to glimpse a wonderful future, promising her glory and love if she would only listen to me. I'll say it again, it was intoxicating to watch that beautiful creature unconsciously repeating my words, quoting my thoughts, or giving my opinions on the books we read . . . And her letters! Oh, I used to laugh sometimes . . . her letters that I wrote! She gradually came to understand what I wanted to do with her. She allowed herself to be molded and would sometimes call me her 'producer,' although she attributed the lowest of motives to me; she thought that I was assuming I'd sponge off her later on, and even—she laughed as she told me—marry some discarded lover of hers, one of Flora Leblanc's rejects, me . . ."

She repeated, "Me!," shrugging her shoulders with simple pride.

"It's now a little more than two years, monsieur, since I first heard you play. I had a few of your records and I used to listen to you on the radio, but I had never been to one of your concerts. And then one day . . . I told you earlier that you belong to all those people who admire and love you. Just think, every time you play, there is at least one person in the concert hall whose voice you become, for a few moments. People are dumb, monsieur. We're like trees or plants. We suffer and die and no one hears our cries. Still, you know all that. What you must have guessed is that, ever since that day, I have . . ."

She stopped talking and leaned back a little, so that her colorless face stayed in the shadows.

"I wasn't pretty and of course I couldn't expect anything from you, but there was Flora. So . . . I spoke to her about you. I dragged her to your concerts and couldn't rest until someone introduced her to you. Yes, it was in that empty theater, a few weeks before her debut. It's strange. You were very cold to begin with, but I knew you would end up falling in love with her."

"But her, what about her?"

"She didn't love you. She didn't know how to love. You think she was 'an exceptional being'? Not at all, she was the most ordinary of women. Oh, no worse and no more stupid than any other! Just average. The Flora Leblanc of the old days, who wanted to be a dressmaker, she was the one you loved, Roger Dange. She let you love her. You were rich and famous. Then she cheated on you. I would never have believed it. I didn't see much of her at that time, and she didn't boast about her love affairs. Six months ago she came to spend a few days here. It's strange . . . She was drawn to me but she hated me as well. She would run away from me and then come back.

"I was not alone. I had a young man, a cousin of my mother's, living with me. He was ten years younger than me, and my parents had brought him up as he was an orphan. Picture a handsome lad, half-peasant, with a snub nose, ruddy cheeks, black hair, and hard, strong arms . . . The first time I think it was just for one night, because she left again almost immediately. But when you agreed to the tour in Mexico, she came back here. He couldn't follow her to Paris. He'd bought a garage in the village; he was a crafty lad, not one to lose his head easily over a woman. Anyway, the minute she got here, the two of them . . . When I think, monsieur, that you accused me of having helped her to cheat on you! Listen, I threw her out! I couldn't forgive her—what she was doing was so base, so vile. Then she said I was jealous of her. She thought I was in love with the boy, with Robert . . . Thank God she never guessed the truth! She would have sullied it! And then she told me that her whole life was an artificial creation, that she had been born for men like Robert, not you, that they were the ones who could satisfy her, and she even added something else, something horrible: 'The body is the only thing you can trust.' I threw them out, Monsieur Dange, her and her lover. I said to them, 'When I get home from school tomorrow at lunchtime, I don't want to find you here.' They laughed, then went away. They were killed after they left here. And is that what you're in mourning for?"

She repeated "that" with a harsh, strident laugh. She looked at Dange and added, "I'm prepared to bet you don't believe me. You think I'm raving, that I'm an old madwoman. Would you like me to recite the contents of the letter you carry next to your heart? The one that starts, 'Last night I dreamt about you,' the one that talks about Monteverdi, about that lovely tune, *'Mort, je crois en toi et dans ta nuit j'espère,'* the one written to you the day before she died . . . the one you mentioned earlier. She came to find me: 'Camille, you write to him, I can't be bothered.' And so I wrote. How happy I was, writing to you!"

"Why are you telling me this now?"

"To save you, to free you from her, to help you get over her death, because she is not worth even one of your tears. What you loved in her did not belong to her."

"You swear that's the truth? That you're not lying? You're certainly not mad; you seem calm and lucid. You swear that's the truth?"

"I swear."

He stood up and walked unsteadily across the room. He took his coat and hat, and opened the door without saying a word. She did not move. She was staring at the fire.

He reached the small, deserted station an hour later. It was strange how he felt. He now understood that he had loved an illusion, a shadow. He knew with absolute certainty that he had at last learned the truth. But he was more tormented than ever because he understood what Camille could not grasp: that his wife's soul, her wit and intelligence, were of no importance—all that was superfluous. What had mattered was the gentle movement of her shoulders when she turned her head toward him, the shape and warmth of her breast, the expression on her face, her tone of voice, the quick, bored way she pushed him aside when he approached her and she wanted to escape him (now he knew why). This was what he would never get over.

L'inconnu

[THE UNKNOWN SOLDIER]

IN COMPLETE TURMOIL, SOLDIERS AND CIVILIANS were crowded together in the station at N——. Some had been recalled from leave following the German invasion of Belgium, some were traveling to sort out their affairs, and some were fleeing from areas where the war was closing in. It was a mild May evening in 1940. Nurses in long blue cloaks, fresh-faced boy scouts wearing large military hats, and the local police were all helping refugees from Belgium, Luxembourg, and Holland. The soldiers who had first of all taken over the bar and the waiting rooms were now giving them up to the incoming flood of women and children; they were invading the platforms, where they settled down as best they could. There was not a single free bench; people were even sleeping on the ground, among sacks of sup-

IRÈNE NÉMIROVSKY

plies and suitcases; others were lying on porters' trolleys. The timetables were in disarray; it was so bad that on some lines they were announcing delays of several hours. While these were being written in chalk on the blackboard under the illuminated clock, people in the crowd milled about noisily. What with the shouting and the sound of soldiers' footsteps marching over the cobblestones, one could hardly hear the little bell that rang in vain every quarter of an hour. Enemy planes were approaching and the only warning siren the town possessed ineffectually shouted "Danger" to the echoing sky. No bombs had fallen here yet, and all the siren did was wake up a child asleep in his mother's arms; he opened his eyes and gazed in amazement at all the people who were rushing around shouting to one another; then he buried his face in his mother's familiar, comforting arms and went back to sleep. The glass of the windows had been painted blue and the lamps dimmed, so that the station itself was a shadowy island among a tangle of railway lines; they gleamed inextinguishably in the starlight, as did the hills and the river nearby. They were surrounded by noise and the smell of smoke.

Two men had walked as far as the end of the platform, to the point at which the last car stopped and tufts of grass grew between piles of coal and stones. It was here that the refugees' baggage was waiting to be collected. Trunks, bicycles, baby carriages, and hatboxes had been heaped on top of one another, to a height of several meters. The men sat down there. They were brothers, both soldiers, who had been given leave for their sister's wedding; the war was about to separate them. They talked about their home, the wedding the day before, and those they had just left behind. Their conversation was broken by long silences. Trains went by at great speed, spewing hot, hissing air in their faces; people could be seen at the open windows, looking anxiously up at the sky. It was crystal clear; since the tenth of May there had not been a breath of wind or a cloud in the sky. Many of the trains went through the station without stopping, gathering speed with a piercing, ear-splitting noise. After they had disappeared into the distance the metal bridge briefly continued to vibrate, with a groaning sound that was almost musical; then all went quiet again.

Occasionally one of the soldiers went off to find out how late their train would be. The delay kept getting longer and longer.

"Not before three o'clock," he said, when at last he came back to his brother. "That's a long time to wait."

"Are you in such a hurry?" Claude asked, opening his eyes and looking at the shiny identity bracelet on his wrist, the sort that identifies dead bodies after a battle. "We'll get there eventually."

"It was good we could be together for Loulou's wedding."

"Hmm, yes, it was," said his brother. He crossed and

uncrossed his legs, raising his pointed chin so that the bluish light of the stars was reflected in his tortoiseshell-rimmed glasses, and on the narrow bridge of his nose and his upper lip, which trembled slightly.

"What's wrong, Claude, old man?" his brother asked.

"Nothing."

The younger man thought, "It's worse for him than for me. He's got a wife and kids . . ." He was twenty-five and quite happy to go and fight. He'd been stationed in northern France all winter, facing only two enemies: boredom and cold. Any change was welcome. But since September his brother had been serving in the fortifications along the Maginot Line; the ten-year age gap between them made him view this fate with affectionate sympathy. "It's not fair. They should let him have a bit of peace," he said to himself, thinking of his sister-in-law's red eyes and the children's tears.

"When's it due, exactly, the new baby?"

"September."

"Is that why you're so . . ." He stopped. ". . . Is that why you're looking so fed up?" He put his hand affectionately on Claude's shoulder in what was meant to be a friendly gesture, but was more like a schoolboy thump on the back than a caress.

"No," Claude said, "that's not why." He half-turned, so that his face was hidden in the shadows; his voice sounded hesitant and strange to the younger man.

"What's wrong?" he asked anxiously. "It's not Mama's health, is it?"

"No, thank goodness, it's not! It's something that happened recently, something so odd that I can't forget it and . . . I suppose you don't remember Papa at all?"

"Papa?" the boy repeated, surprised. "Of course not, I was two when he was killed."

"But sometimes a child's memory can be amazingly precise. For instance, I can clearly remember the cook we had when we lived in Poitiers, but I wasn't even three at the time."

"Oh, but you've always had an amazing memory. You must surely remember Papa quite clearly?"

"Yes, especially on his last leave, just after Loulou was born. It was the spring of 1917, and he was reported missing less than two weeks later, in May. It's the anniversary this month," he said, after a moment's silence.

"I don't remember him at all," François admitted. "People say you look like him, don't they? I can only tell by looking at the picture in Mama's room, where he's in uniform. He looks nice, a bit of a dreamer. He's got a little pointed chin like yours."

Claude made a sharp gesture; his brother looked at him in surprise. "What's wrong? What did you want to tell me about?"

"What did I want to tell you about? Well, four months ago, when I was on reconnaissance duty, I was one of six men who had to explore an abandoned village. We'd been told there were Germans there and our job was to investigate. I'd just been posted over there . . ." He waved vaguely, with the gesture used by soldiers to indicate eastern France, where the war was then being fought.

"Over there," he repeated. "It was the first time I had taken part in an expedition like that. It has an odd effect on you, the first one. The village looked extraordinary. Its inhabitants must have been evacuated in less than five minutes, poor things. There was still the washing that hadn't been brought in; it had frozen and become stiff old rags hanging from clotheslines in the little gardens. I looked through the open doors and saw kitchens where everything was ready for a meal, a cooking pot on the cold stove, the table laid, and an open newspaper propped up against a jug of wine—full but frozen, a block of purple ice. It was a night as clear as tonight, but very cold; there was frost on the roofs and trees, the streams had turned into skating rinks; it was like a picture postcard."

"It's true, it's been cold. Where we were . . ."

"Yes," Claude replied absentmindedly.

His brother went on talking but he interrupted him. "Listen, let me finish, this isn't easy . . . So we went through the village without finding anything; it was just one long street. You can imagine how carefully we moved forward. When we set out the sky had clouded over and we counted on there being a mist, even a slight thaw, but as we advanced the stars shone more and more brightly. Like I said, that's what let me see inside those wretched houses as we went by. You can imagine how we hugged the walls. I've noticed that one doesn't have much of a paunch in situations like that; even the fattest men make themselves thin.

"Eventually we were sure the village was deserted. We were about to go back, but we had a long, hard route ahead of us, part of which was a hellish frozen little stream that we had to slither across on our hands and knees. Obviously we thought about getting some food and drink before we set off. Opposite the church there was a café. The shutters were half-open, just as they were on the other houses. We pulled them wider and looked in: there were bottles from floor to ceiling; every shelf was stacked with full bottles! Unfortunately the bistro must have been restocked the very morning of the evacuation. As one of my lads, Maillard—he was always called Mailloche—said, 'Some people get a raw deal!' Then a couple of men climbed in through the window and the rest followed. We helped ourselves. There was a huge ham over the stove: one end of it was a bit off, but the rest seemed edible. So we're eating and drinking when suddenly one of my men says, 'There've been Germans here.'—'How can you tell?'—'Simple, there are empty bottles of beer. It's quite recent because there's still froth around the edges, and the wine in the rack next to it hasn't been touched. Frenchmen would have drunk the wine and left the beer.'

"That sounded right to me. I was hurrying up the

lads who were still in there, pretending not to hear me, when all of a sudden one of them caught my eye as he silently pointed at a trapdoor in the middle of the kitchen. It was slightly open; it must have been over the cellar and something was shining in the dark, or rather, one could see something reflected. Mailloche had lit his flashlight to unhook a salami hanging from the joist, and its light was reflected on some polished surface in the gloom. It could have been a bottle or the metal bung on a cask, but it could also have been a belt buckle or a blade. It was a fleeting impression more than anything else, and my eyes had to get accustomed to the dark to see the pale bluish light, but as I looked closely I saw that it was moving backward and forward, then gradually disappearing. I gestured silently to show the men what I had seen. We left as naturally and noisily as we could, but once we were outside we crept up to the window through which we could see right into the kitchen; the trapdoor was in front of us.

"We didn't have to wait very long. It was opened without a sound . . . by a German; he was right opposite me, although he couldn't see me, as I was hidden in the shadow of the blind. But I could see him clearly by the light of the night sky. He had a small chin and rosy cheeks; he seemed very young. He looked all around him, then turned back to beckon to someone down in the cellar. He came out, followed by several men. I thought they would certainly attack us, either then and

there or on our return journey. The only reason they
hadn't already done so would have been because they
first wanted to make sure that we were the only ones
there—that they weren't in danger of being ambushed.
Their precautions showed that we were dealing with a
single detachment, just like ours. They thought we had
left, so we were able to take them by surprise and had to
make the most of it. I say, 'I thought,' but you don't
think in a situation like that—you attack or you get out.
The instinct to defend yourself is always the same, and
on this occasion it went for attack. I leapt through the
open window and the others followed. There must have
been about fifteen of us altogether, French and German;
the sides were roughly matched. We didn't exchange
fire and no one shouted; our orders were to remain
absolutely silent in these sorts of encounters, as no doubt
theirs were, too. Poor Mailloche got it first; I heard a
body falling near me and recognized his voice calling
me, poor man. He held on to my legs and pulled me
down with him.

"Each time one of us—French or German—stopped
to get his breath back, he called for the enemy to surren-
der, but no one wanted to give in. For a first skirmish I
certainly had my fair share: four men had taken a ham-
mering, and I had killed a German. Then one of the
men jumped out of the window and the others, both
pursuers and pursued, disappeared. It was incredible:
such a silent, savage fight. As for me, I'd hit my head on

the corner of a marble table and was knocked uncon-
scious. When I opened my eyes, there was an injured
comrade with me, as well as Mailloche, dead, and the
German. On top of everything else, someone had fired,
forgetting orders, so there was gunfire from every direction. It soon stopped, but was then replaced by artillery
fire, crackling on each side of the stream we had to cross.
We had to keep our heads down then—we were worried that the Germans could come back at any moment
with reinforcements.

"My comrade said it would be best for us to hide in
the cellar, as the Germans had done. We left the two
dead men where they were and staggered down below;
we lowered the trapdoor and stayed there, my comrade
cursing and groaning and me bleeding like a pig. We
hoped that the artillery fire would stop when daylight
came, but it carried on. Durand (that was my friend's
name) had made me a rough bandage. I started to feel
better but I was very cold and thirsty. Gradually I began
to feel a bit bolder; it was morning and the Germans
wouldn't come back now. I remembered the food in the
kitchen, and a hot plate I'd seen the previous evening
that still had a jug of warm wine on it. I tried to persuade Durand to come with me but he didn't want to; he
made a blanket out of some old sacking we found in the
cellar, and he went to sleep.

"It was very hard to climb up again. The kitchen was
bright; it was broad daylight and I was frozen stiff. I

walked around the two rooms where the bodies of Mailloche and the German lay among the wreckage and—you have to believe me, François—I hardly glanced at them. It was the first war scene I had ever seen, but when you're so hungry and thirsty, you're more like an animal than a man.

"Only after I'd knocked back several glasses of the sweet hot wine and felt the warmth in my body and lit my pipe did I give any thought to poor Mailloche. I knelt down beside him. Poor kid, he looked quite calm, happy to be finished with it all, with a strange little smile on his lips as if to say, 'I know what it's like now, but you . . .'

"I crossed his hands on his chest and opened his wallet to look for his family's address. He'd told me his mother was widowed—a cleaner who lived in Saint-Mandé. He had her photo in his breast pocket, along with a bit of the rope that one of his uncles had used to hang himself after drinking too much at his own wedding. Can you believe it—my friend Mailloche thought a suicide's noose would bring him luck! It didn't protect him, poor lad. He still had his membership card for the Saint-Mandé football club and a few other bits and pieces. I searched for a long time for something to cover his face, but the bedrooms were all locked and anyway it was so cold it could wait until he was buried. I decided to dig a grave in the garden before we left, once Durand had woken up. Then I turned to the other one."

"The German?"

"Yes."

He paused for so long that François touched him on the shoulder.

"Go on, I'm listening!"

"I know."

A train went by at top speed; sparks flew out of the wheels, and the shrill blasts of the engine's whistle sounded like the shrieking of frantic birds.

"That's not ours, is it?" François asked anxiously.

"Not a chance! We'll be here till morning."

"Go on, then. What about the German?"

"I hadn't seen that many Germans before. As I looked at the one I had killed I didn't feel curiosity, pity, or even hatred—it was more a sort of disbelief. It seemed incredible to see a real dead German lying there next to Mailloche; he might have been one of the men we saw passing like shadows in the dark, whom we fired at and sometimes killed, but whose bodies are never found because their comrades carried them off. We had taken a few prisoners during a raid, but that was before my time.

"The body was that of the boy whom I had seen leading the way out of the cellar. Something about him struck me; I was astonished and uneasy and I couldn't think why. I was fumbling for something, just as you are when you try to think of a forgotten name or a tune you can't quite remember . . . fumbling and irritable at the same time. Do you see what I'm saying? He was lit up by bright, golden sunshine. Lying there on the cold floor, in his green uniform and big boots, he looked as peaceful as Mailloche, but his sharp, dimpled little chin pointed upward and made him look defiant. He was very fair; his cheeks, which were pale now, were starting to look pinched. His hand had been on his knife as he fell. If I hadn't been quicker than him, there's no way he would have missed me. Maybe I shouldn't have searched his pockets, as I'd done for my comrade, but I didn't do so with any evil intention. When the war was over wouldn't his mother, his fiancée, or some other woman want to know how he had been killed, whether he suffered, and where he was buried? He hadn't suffered; he had died without making a sound. He had a fat wallet stuffed with letters. I looked for a name or an address but there was nothing. There was a photograph of him in tennis clothes with a racket in his hand, wearing white shorts, his shirt unbuttoned at the neck and his hair hanging over his eyes; he seemed extraordinarily young. You can't imagine how I felt . . . I had killed a man of my own age, a man who . . ."

"One has no choice," interrupted François with a shrug.

"No, one has no choice. But you know, when you have kids of your own, and a younger brother you've half brought up—because I did half bring you up—well . . . There were also some photographs of a very pretty girl, and the German had taken pictures of her in at least a dozen different poses, among them some of her sitting on the grass in the middle of a garden with a black dog on her lap. I didn't feel upset; I'd seen the picture of Mailloche's old mother and that put my feelings in perspective. I was about to put the wallet back, since I hadn't found what I was looking for, when I found a photograph that was larger and older than the others; it was slightly yellow and crumpled, as if it had been carried around for a long time in a pocket or bag, rubbing up against other papers . . ." He stopped. "Do you have the flashlight on you, François?"

"Yes, why?"

"Switch it on, point it at the ground so we don't get shouted at. Even though the stars are as bright as headlights. And look . . ."

"At what?"

"This photograph. D'you see? It's the one I found on the dead German's body."

"Hang on, old man, I don't . . ."

"Doesn't it remind you of something?"

François looked at the photograph. It was a picture of a young man taken on the terrace of a country house. There was a fair-haired woman standing next to him, rather stolid-looking with a kind, placid expression.

After a moment's hesitation, François made an effort to smile. "I'd say the man looked a bit like you, but . . ."

His older brother shook his head.

"It's not me he looks like, old man. Look again; look

carefully. Look at his left hand—you can see it clearly. Can you see the scar, a deep wound going from his ring finger right down to his wrist? It must," he went on, shutting his eyes to try and remember something. "It must have created a thick ridge on his flesh, for even though it was a superficial wound, only scratching the skin, it still left a scar that didn't fade. You know, don't you, that on September fourteenth, the day Papa was wounded in the thigh and groin, a shell ripped into his hand, and two years later he was wounded a second time, in the head, just above his left eyebrow, there," he said, pointing at the photograph.

François looked at it for a long time without saying anything.

"It's not possible . . ." he murmured.

"I compared this photograph with all the pictures of Papa that Mama had kept. I found the X-rays of both wounds; the one on the forehead made a wavy line and when you look at it through a magnifying glass, which I did, you can see it's identical to the one in the photograph. You may well have your doubts, you may have forgotten Papa's face and expression, but for me . . . it's so like him, so like the way he would look over the top of his glasses; it's his smile, and the small dimple on that narrow chin, a chin like mine—and like that of his third son," he added in a strange voice.

"Are you sure this German was . . . his son?"

"Listen, the photograph is dated 1925 and higher up, can you see, there's some more writing in German."

"I can't make out the gothic lettering."

Claude read it slowly, then translated it: " *'Für meinen lieben Sohn, Franz Hohmann, diese Büd seines vielgeliebten Vatersmöge er ihn aus der Himmelshöhe beschützen. Frieda Hohmann, Berlin, den 2 Dezember 1939.'* 'For my dear son François Hohmann, this portrait of his beloved father who is watching over him in heaven. Frieda Hohmann, Berlin, 2 December 1939.' "

"He was called François?" the young man exclaimed. "François, like me?"

"Like you, like our grandfather, like one of our uncles: it's a popular family name. He also gave it to the German."

François flinched.

"I'm telling you it's him," Claude said quietly. "I can assure you that if I had the slightest doubt, I'd never have breathed a word of it to you. But it's such a . . . such an important and extraordinary thing. I didn't think I had the right to keep it from you. I thought perhaps we could do some research in Germany, after the war. We could do it together, if we can. If not, whichever one of us survives can do it."

Overwhelmed, François buried his head in his hands. "I'm stunned, old man."

"Yes, I am, too," his brother said gently. "I have dreams about it every night."

"But I thought we were quite sure Papa had died in the war!"

"I'll tell you what happened. He was reported missing on May 27, 1917. Right up until the end of the war, Mama hoped he would come back. It was only after the Armistice that one of Papa's friends wrote to tell us that he had seen him killed right next to him and that his arms and head had been blown off. His remains were never found. But you can imagine that in the noise and confusion of battle—and this one happened at dawn, in the rain; I found the details in the letter Mama kept and has just given me—his comrade couldn't have been absolutely sure about what he had seen. There was a huge number of dead and wounded that day. He said so himself, and there were all those burned, crushed, unrecognizable bodies. How on earth could you put names to all those poor lads?"

He stopped and smoked his pipe silently for a moment, his head turned slightly aside.

"The Germans wear their identity tag on their chest, attached to a chain around their neck."

"Claude?"

"Yes?"

"So does that mean . . . our father was a deserter?"

"You'd have to be very clever to find out. Maybe he was a deserter. He might have been one of those men with amnesia after the last war, who were claimed by several different families right up to the beginning of this one."

"But at least we would have known if he was French."

"Not necessarily. A uniform and identity tag can be

lost or destroyed, and those wretches with no memory had forgotten their names and had to learn to talk again, like children. Some prisoners escaped from Germany by going through Russia and if they got caught up in the revolution, it would have been easy for a man to change his identity and become French or German, just as he wished."

"What about the war?"

"The war was over."

"What about us?"

"Ah, us . . . What do you want me to say? I don't know what to think. He was a good father, but . . ."

"Did he behave well to Mama?" François asked, and it was his turn to look away.

"I don't think so," said his older brother.

"Listen . . ."

"I'm telling you, I don't think so. I was ten, wasn't I? What would I have known? It's an impression that's stayed in my ears more than in my memory or my mind . . . There were long silences at mealtimes, a tension in their voices when they eventually spoke to each other, slamming doors, the echoes of a distant storm."

"Servants' gossip, perhaps?"

"Yes, that too. But I'd rather not talk about it."

They both fell silent, overcome by a sense of constraint, shame, and anxiety. In the darkness trolleys were pushed past; trunks were still being unloaded. A train had just come into the station and a panic-stricken crowd of people got off. The refugees wandered around on the platform, calling out to one another in anguish and confusion. It was such a clear night that one could distinctly see their haggard faces, their rumpled clothes, and pathetic bundles of ragged household linen, and among them the odd birdcage covered with a scrap of dark material, a basket with a mewing cat inside, and a stretcher.

"Are they wounded?" François asked.

Someone heard him and replied, "No, it's two women about to give birth."

"What an awful muddle of people," François said after the stretcher had gone past. It was being carried by four men, shouting, "Let us through! We need a nurse or a doctor. Quickly! The baby's coming any minute!"

"There's another woman who had her baby two hours ago; she's had a hemorrhage," a voice in the crowd said. "She's dying."

Neither of the women on the stretcher made a sound; a porter had switched on his flashlight and one could see long, loose blonde hair trailing on the ground.

"You don't usually think about it," François said quietly, "but after four years of the other war, the invasion, and then our troops being posted on the Rhine, there must be other brothers facing each other as enemies."

"They wouldn't know about it. But since that German died, I've had the same dream every night: I see that dark cellar again, the half-open trapdoor, and I know that the German is going to tip it wide open and cut my throat. I fight, I'm the stronger one, I kill the German; then, when he's dead, I take him in my arms, undress him, and put him on Mama's bed, the big pink bed where I put you when you had scarlet fever when you were little; then I bend over him and I don't know if I'm seeing you or him . . . Oh, what a foul dream," he muttered, turning aside with a sigh.

François twisted his hands together nervously. "You can do what you want, my dear old man, but I swear I'm never going to go and look for information in Germany. What good would it do? For a start, I still think you might have made a mistake, that the photograph is not Papa, and if, by some bad luck it is, investigating it would only disturb innocent lives. Anyway, it's all in the past. I'm not interested and I want to leave well enough alone."

"It's him who won't leave us alone," said Claude sighing, again holding up the little identity tag on his wrist so that the metal shone with a dull gleam in the starlight. "But you're right; it would be best to keep quiet about it."

Nearby, a group of refugees was gathered around a fat man brandishing a newspaper. He was in civilian clothes, but his armband showed that he held some position of responsibility in the town, probably in civil defense. Occasionally he blew harsh blasts on a whistle and yelled out some orders; then he called out in a loud, hoarse voice. He had a black mustache and a paunch; his words reached the two soldiers.

". . . And if you'd seen all the equipment going up north, like I have, you'd have no worries, believe you me! This time it's not going to be like it was in 1914. They'll find out who they're dealing with. They'll cut and run, I promise you! For a start, men who aren't fed, how can they form an army? Well, I ask you! Won't we be fighting a bunch of men with rickets and anemia, seeing as they don't even have enough vitamins to stay healthy? I'm telling you, with our vitamins and our equipment, our energy and our pluck, dammit, we'll have 'em before they can utter a word!"

Claude gently shrugged his shoulders. "There are some things it's best to keep quiet about," he observed.

The refugees and soldiers listened to the impromptu orator and laughed and cheered him.

"Our comrade's talking sense. He's quite right!"

ALSO BY IRÈNE NÉMIROVSKY

SUITE FRANÇAISE

Beginning in Paris on the eve of the Nazi occupation in 1940, *Suite Française* tells the remarkable story of men and women thrown together in circumstances beyond their control. As Parisians flee the city, human folly surfaces in every imaginable way: a wealthy mother searches for sweets in a town without food; a couple is terrified at the thought of losing their jobs, even as their world begins to fall apart. Moving on to a provincial village now occupied by German soldiers, the locals must learn to coexist with the enemy—in their town, their homes, even in their hearts.

Fiction/Literature/978-1-4000-9627-5

FIRE IN THE BLOOD

Written in 1941, *Fire in the Blood*—only now assembled in its entirety—teems with the intertwined lives of an insular French village in the years before the war, when "peace" was less important as a political state than as a coveted personal condition: the untroubled pinnacle of happiness. At the center of the novel is Silvio, who has returned to this small town after years away. As his narration unfolds, we are given an intimate picture of the loves and infidelities, the scandals, the youthful ardor and regrets of age that tie Silvio to the long-guarded secrets of the past.

Fiction/Literature/978-0-307-38800-1

Meet with Interesting People
Enjoy Stimulating Conversation
Discover Wonderful Books